PAST LIVES

When a patient wakes up after a tumour removal operation and displays a severe change in personality, the resident psychiatrist is perplexed – until Hartman's tumour is diagnosed, a rare condition that leaves its victims deranged and hospitalised in mental institutions. The patient's vindictive husband blames the neuro-surgeon responsible for the operation, John Macandrew, and seeks cruel revenge... Macandrew retreats to his native Scotland and makes further discoveries about the mysterious illness, but the sinister biblical scholar Dom Ignatius already knows the secret and is wilfully ruining lives to achieve his own selfish aims. Worse still, he's determined not to let anyone stand in his way.

PAST LIVES

PAST LIVES

by

Ken McClure

Magna Large Print Books
Long Preston, North Yorkshire,
BD23 4ND, England.

British Library Cataloguing in Publication Data.

McClure, Ken
    Past lives.

    A catalogue record of this book is
    available from the British Library

    ISBN   978-0-7505-3168-9

First published in Great Britain in 2007 by Allison & Busby Ltd.

Copyright © 2006 by Ken McClure

Cover illustration © Brighton Studios by arrangement with
Allison & Busby Ltd.

The moral right of the author has been asserted

Published in Large Print 2010 by arrangement with
Allison & Busby Ltd.

Magna Large Print is an imprint of Library Magna Books Ltd.

Printed and bound in Great Britain by
T.J. (International) Ltd., Cornwall, PL28 8RW

Better by far you should forget and smile
Than you should remember and be sad.

'Remember'
Christina Rossetti
(1830–1894)

PROLOGUE

**Jerusalem, Israel
September 2000**

Ignatius stood motionless while Stroud slowly injected the contents of the syringe into the subject who was already heavily sedated and couldn't quite keep his eyelids open for more than a few seconds at a time. Although it was quiet inside the room the muted sound of religious chant came from somewhere else inside the building. It contrasted with the distant sound of a *muezzin* calling the Muslim faithful to prayer at the end of another long, hot day – everyday sounds of Jerusalem.

'You can begin now,' said Stroud.

'Tell me your name,' said Ignatius. His voice had a calm hypnotic quality.

'Saul ... Saul Abe.'

'What do you do, Saul Abe?'

'I'm ... a builder.'

'Where?'

'In Jerusalem.'

'What are you building?'

The question seemed to cause the man distress. He started to fight for breath.

11

'What's the matter?'

'The ... stone!'

'What about the stone?'

'It's falling on my legs!' Abe let out a scream of pain.

'What's happened?' insisted the calm voice.

'The stone rolled off the cart... I couldn't get out of the way... It crushed my legs.' The painful memory seemed to put Abe into merciful white oblivion for a few moments, then he stirred.

'What's happening now?' asked the voice quietly but firmly.

'Two men... They are trying to lift the stone off my...' Abe let out another scream. He was unaware of a second needle entering his arm. The injection calmed him a little.

'My legs are broken and bloody... They say they'll have to cut them off!'

Saul Abe stopped breathing for a full thirty seconds, his eyes wide with horror as he relived the nightmare.

Stroud said, 'We can't hold him at this point. It's dangerous.'

'All right, take him back further,' said Ignatius

Another injection and Abe relaxed on the pillow in a seemingly content slumber but it wasn't long before he became agitated again.

'Leah! Leah!'

'Who is Leah?'

12

'My wife.'

'Who are you?'

'Isaac... I can't find Leah! Where is she?'

'Who are you, Isaac? What do you do?'

'I'm a soldier. I've come home but I can't find Leah!'

'Where have you been, Isaac?'

'Fighting the Romans. We set up an ambush near Bet Hakem but we were betrayed. I'm the only one left alive apart from my brother... Oh God, my brother...'

'What about your brother, Isaac? What happened to him?'

'The Romans have him.'

'Take your time.'

'I can hear his screams... The Romans are torturing him. He's calling out my name and I'm doing nothing! I'm pretending to be dead down in the gulley. I'm too frightened to move. The sun is burning my neck. He needs me and I'm ignoring him!'

'You can't help him, Isaac. There are too many of them. It's not your fault. Why are they torturing him? What do they want from him?'

'They want to know where the Nazarene is.'

'The Nazarene?' said Ignatius, his voice almost a croak as his throat dried with excitement.

'Where's Leah? Why isn't she here at home...?'

'Isaac!'

'What?'

'Tell me about the Nazarene!'

'I must find Leah.'

'Listen to me! You know him, don't you? You've met the Nazarene.'

'Why does everyone want to know about him? He's all mouth and riddles. The temple's full of talkers. It's fighters we need.'

'But you do know him?'

'Leah, where are you? Why don't you come to me?'

'Try to relax,' said the voice.

'Leah! Leah!'

'He's becoming too distressed,' said Stroud.

'We need to know more!' insisted Ignatius.

'You'll kill him!'

'Tell me about the Nazarene, Isaac.'

'Leah... Oh, Leah, you're dead.' Saul Abe started to shake all over as if he had suddenly become very cold. At first it was a gentle tremor but it gathered strength until the bed itself rattled on the tiled floor.

'He's fitting!' said Stroud. 'I warned you!'

Ignatius looked down at the tremulous figure on the bed, his expression betraying nothing but disappointment and annoyance.

Abe went into rigid spasm. Every muscle in his body locked solid. For a brief, frightened moment he opened his eyes wide then his eyeballs rolled slowly up in their sockets and he was still.

'I warned you,' said Stroud.

'But it works,' said Ignatius.

CHAPTER ONE

Kansas City, USA
October 2000

John Macandrew got out of bed and walked over to the window in bare feet. He opened the blind and blinked at the early morning sunshine. The sky was blue and the leaves on the trees across the street had finally made the transition from green to gold, something he had been monitoring for the last three weeks with growing pleasure. Summer in Kansas City could be hotter than hell and winter could freeze your eyes but the fall however, was pleasant.

This was especially true on days like this, when the sun shone down from a cloudless sky and the wind held its breath. The city, sprawling astride the Kansas/Missouri state line, could lay no great claim to beauty but when the trees turned colour and their leaves carpeted the sidewalks, a dreamer could narrow his eyes and pretend he was in New England rather than the featureless plains of the Midwest.

Macandrew decided that today he would walk to the Medical Center and leave the car in the garage. He turned away from the window and switched on the radio before padding through to the kitchen to load the coffee grinder. He smiled as he heard the announcer report the success of the Chiefs in their pre-season game; they had won by more than thirty points.

Macandrew hadn't had much interest in football before taking the job in Kansas City but now he was a regular at the Chiefs' home games out at Arrowhead Stadium. He found diversion in the game. There was something therapeutic about watching two teams of athletes face up to each other in a contest of pace and strength. It afforded him some respite from the demanding precision of his own job. Macandrew was a neurosurgeon and jobs didn't come any more demanding than that. For much of his working life he was within millimetres of disaster. Mistakes were not permitted in his line of work. Society was happy to accept that everyone had an off day except for surgeons and maybe airline pilots. Yes, definitely airline pilots.

As he poured his coffee he heard a time check say that it was a quarter after seven; he glanced his watch. He had lots of time; the operation was scheduled for ten o'clock and it would only take him thirty minutes to walk to the Med Center. Unlike most of the staff, who stayed outside the city in the pleasant avenues of suburbia, he had made a conscious decision to live inside city limits. It was an unfashionable choice but, being unmarried, he felt that he was a wife and a couple of children short of the requirements for living the American dream. Apart from that, he disliked suburbia: he saw it as society on a life-support system – comfortable but barely alive. Instead, he rented the top floor of an old colonial-style house on Cherry. It had seen better days and was in the early stages of not so genteel decay but it was less than two miles from the Med Center and the landlord and his wife, the Jacksons, didn't bother him much. They spent most of their time visiting a nationwide diaspora of grandchildren. They were up in Michigan at the moment with their youngest daughter and her family but were due back next Wednesday.

Macandrew thumbed back the catches on his briefcase and took out a clear plastic file of notes on the patient he would be operating on that morning. He took them over to a seat by the window and sipped his coffee as he flicked though them. Jane Francini was thirty-four years old, two years younger than he himself, and had been suffering from increasingly severe pain behind her eyes. She had been treated for migraine by her own

17

physician for several weeks before finally being referred to the Med Center where a battery of tests had revealed the presence of a tumour in her pineal gland. This morning Macandrew was going to remove it.

Normally, the surgical aspects of this procedure would present no special problems, but Jane Francini had a history of heart trouble and had undergone cardiac surgery less than three years before. There was a question mark over her level of general fitness to undergo major surgery but only an academic one. The operation was essential. The tumour had to go.

Jane's husband, Tony Francini, a successful businessman who sold farm machinery all over the Midwest, had been keen for her to have the operation done at one of the big teaching hospitals on the West Coast, but Saul Klinsman, chief of neurosurgery at the Med Center, had persuaded him that Kansas City could handle the job. Francini had finally agreed but only after an aggressive inquisition of Macandrew on learning that he would be the surgeon doing the operation.

Macandrew's background of Columbia Medical School and subsequent positions in several prestige-name hospitals and clinics back east seemed to satisfy Francini whose bluntness had culminated in the question, 'So what the hell are you doing here?'

Although he did not suffer from the paranoia of some of his more senior colleagues, Macandrew was irritated by Francini's attitude. He was typical of the type of man who thought financial success an acceptable excuse for a total lack of charm and manners. Macandrew was well aware of his nation's lack of esteem for the Midwest, assuming that because its people had the reputation of clinging to the values of a bygone age, science and the arts must be stuck in a similar time warp. They were not entirely mistaken but KC Med Center was good by any standards.

Macandrew's original, unashamed career plan had been to work for three years on the East Coast and then head for California in search of big bucks and the good life. He had surprised himself when a job came up in Kansas City and he had applied for it, arguing to Kelly, his girlfriend at the time, that it would be invaluable in adding to his all-round experience of American medicine.

The real reason however was somewhat different and had much to do with his family background. His great-grandfather, after emigrating from Scotland, had settled in the Midwest in a place called Weston, Missouri. For reasons, which he himself could not properly explain, he felt that he wanted to follow in his footsteps and reinforce a link with this part of the States. Kelly had made it clear that Kansas was not for her or her planned career in obstetrics. They had kept in touch through phone calls and letters for a while but even that had largely stopped. Kelly had moved on to Johns Hopkins Hospital in New York and a different world.

Macandrew saw on the duty schedule that Mike Kellerman would be the anaesthesiologist today. Despite having an off-hand manner, Macandrew knew that he was good. He had worked with him in the past and had never had a moment's worry over patient stability. He didn't ask for anything more. He finished reading through Jane Francini's notes without learning anything new. He hadn't expected to; he had just been making sure that he hadn't missed anything.

As he put them down, he became conscious of the radio again. The presenters – two of them, working in tandem – were engaged in a local news round-up. The way they fed each other lines and laughed at their own jokes irritated him – a sure sign that he was becoming edgy, but then, he always was before an operation.

His walk to the Med Center followed a route parallel to 39th Street, avoiding the main thoroughfare until it became unavoidable. The sidewalks were in bad condition but he was used to that. No one walked anywhere in Kansas City unless they were too poor to do anything else and therefore damaged sidewalks didn't matter in the great scheme of things. Home – car – office, office – car – home was the routine for the overwhelming majority. The lack of people however, made the walk more pleasant – although it was necessary to run the gauntlet of an occasional guard dog, straining at its leash as he passed. The dogs were trained to regard anyone on foot with grave suspicion.

He crossed 39th Street near the intersection with Rainbow Boulevard and entered the Med Center through the swing doors. Just before he did however, he took off his topcoat in preparation for the warmth he knew would hit him like a wall.

'Good morning, Doctor Macandrew,' smiled one of the nurses. 'Miss Givens has been paging you.'

'Thanks,' replied Macandrew mechanically, glancing at the clock on the wall. It was a few minutes after nine. He approached Reception and a woman in her early fifties, wearing ornate glasses perched on the end of her nose, smiled at him and handed him a piece of paper that she tore from the pad in front of her. 'Mr Francini would like a word, Doctor,' she said in the manner which fifty-year-old women wearing ornate glasses regarded as 'gracious'.

Macandrew looked at the paper and saw that Francini had been put in G4, one of the rooms on the ground floor used by staff to

21

give out news of progress or lack of it to friends and family of people brought into the Emergency Room. As he passed G3, Macandrew looked in through the small glass panel in the door and saw a Hispanic woman sitting there with a white handkerchief pressed to her face; he could hear sobbing. He hoped Francini couldn't.

'Good morning, Mr Francini. What can I do for you?'

Francini got up from his chair and smoothed back his shiny black hair with both hands. His suit, silk tie and Gucci shoes spoke of money but his swarthy features said Italian peasant stock.

'I know Janey's got to have this operation, Doc, but I just thought I would remind you to be careful with her. She's the only wife I got.' Francini laughed at his own joke but it was forced and his eyes remained hard.

'Of course, Mr Francini.'

'Shit, I don't know how you guys do it,' said Francini, affecting a broad grin, which showed off expensive dental work. 'You're about to take somebody's life in your hands and you're Mister Cool. I gotta hand it to you. You guys are somethin' else.'

'It's my job,' replied Macandrew. 'It's what I've been trained to do. I don't think I'd be very good at selling harvesters.'

Francini snorted and laughed. He said, 'Hell, anyone can sell harvesters in Kansas.

Now, selling harvesters in Boston? That might be different...' He laughed again.

Macandrew smiled and glanced at his watch. It had the desired effect. Francini said, 'I won't hold you back any longer. Just remember what I said, huh?'

'I will. I promise.'

Macandrew escorted Francini to the front door and then went upstairs to his own office. He phoned and checked with the head nurse that Jane Francini had been given her pre-med on time and that there were no hitches.

'She'll be ready for you, Doctor,' replied the nurse.

At nine-thirty, Macandrew drained the last of his coffee from a paper cup and went along to surgery to begin scrubbing up. He found Mike Kellerman already there.

'And how's Mac the Knife on this fine morning?' asked Kellerman with a smile.

'Fine, Mike. How are you?'

'A man barely alive,' replied Kellerman with mock solemnity. 'What that woman demanded of me last night ought not to be allowed, and they call them the gentler sex!'

Macandrew smiled as he lathered his forearms. 'Let's hear what you remember of the patient's notes?'

'Thirty-four-year-old female, undesignated pineal tumour with a cardiac history, weight one thirty-eight pounds, no known allergies,

I looked in on her yesterday afternoon.'

'What did you think?'

'Seemed strong enough to me,' replied Kellerman. 'No worries from my point of view.'

'Good.'

'She told me her husband owns Francini Farm Machinery. Think we could be in for a bonus if we do a good job?'

'It could be a horse's head on the pillow if we don't,' replied Macandrew. 'Francini, Italian? Of course. I think you've just got yourself one very alert colleague.'

'Good,' replied Macandrew, elbowing off the faucets and accepting a sterile towel from the nurse in attendance. 'I'd like to get this over as quickly as possible.'

As Kellerman did the same he asked, 'You don't really think her husband's ... "Family", do you?'

'Mr Francini sells tractors,' smiled Macandrew. 'On the other hand, I'm pretty sure he doesn't write poetry or go to the ballet much.'

'A man's man eh?' said Kellerman, putting on an exaggerated male voice. 'Boy, is he in the right place!' Kellerman was a Californian.

'The guy comes on a bit strong but I guess he's just worried about his wife,' said Macandrew.

'Who's the OR nurse?' asked Kellerman.

'Lucy Long,' replied Macandrew.

'Good. I thought it might be my *"friend".*'

Macandrew smiled. Kellerman's 'friend' was Sylvia Dorman, the other OR nurse working in neurosurgery. She and Kellerman didn't get along. Dorman was a very serious nurse with a Florence Nightingale complex. She saw her career as a Christian vocation. Kellerman's black humour offended her and he knew it. It inspired him to greater heights, or depths, depending on how you looked at it. Macandrew didn't like working with the pair of them together. An operating room was no place for personality conflicts. He and Kellerman gowned up and left their masks hanging loosely round their throats as they entered the operating room.

'How are we doing?' Macandrew asked Lucy Long.

'All ready.'

Macandrew ran his eye over the instrument trays while Kellerman connected Jane Francini to the equipment he would use to monitor her condition throughout the operation. Green pulses started to chase each other across the face of an oscilloscope and a regular bleep followed the steady beat of the patient's heart. Macandrew felt comfortable. This was his world: the sights and sounds put him at ease. He supposed it must be the same for truck drivers getting behind the wheel or office workers slipping in behind their desks to begin the day's work. Familiarity could be such a comfort.

He paid particular attention to the lighting arrangements for this operation. The normal overhead, shadowless lamp would not be sufficient; he would be working close to the patient's face so he needed angled illumination. Two small ancillary spotlights mounted on the main lighting gantry, which he eased into position, would supply this. The standard route for surgery on the pituitary and pineal glands was through the bone at the corner of nose and eye. There would be no need to shave the patient's head and very little visible scarring afterwards.

'How is she doing?' Macandrew asked Kellerman.

'More stable than I am,' came the reply.

'A comfort... She's deep enough?'

'Right on the button.'

Macandrew made a last adjustment to his mask and made a visual inspection of the point of the drill he planned to use before checking the motor function. Its angry insect whine filled the room. He put it back on its stand and asked for a scalpel. It was slapped into his palm. With a slight nod to everyone, he made the first incision. 'Showtime.'

Sixty minutes later, Jane Francini's pineal gland lay in a glass dish beside her sleeping form, its normal pine-cone shape distorted by the tumour, which had almost doubled its size.

'Nasty,' said Kellerman. 'But it looks like you got it all.'

'I think so,' replied Macandrew. 'Nice and firm, no break up.' He turned to one of the nurses and said, 'Get this to Pathology, will you.'

Gloved hands spirited the dish away and Macandrew got on with ending the operation. 'Still OK?' he asked Kellerman.

'Absolutely fine.'

'Just what I wanted,' said Macandrew. 'A smooth, clean, quick job with no complications. In, out, no messing about.'

He had scarcely left the operating suite when he heard himself being paged. He called in to be told that Mr Francini had been making the staff's life a misery by demanding constant updates on his wife's condition. He was insisting on speaking to Macandrew personally the minute the operation was over.

'I'll come down.'

Francini jumped up the moment he saw Macandrew approach and rushed over to meet him. 'How is she, Doc?' he demanded. 'She's OK, isn't she?'

Macandrew had to raise his hands to keep Francini at bay. 'The operation went well, Mr Francini. The tumour has been removed and sent to the path lab for analysis. We'll know the results in a few hours. Your wife's in recovery right now. You'll be able to see her as soon as she comes round.'

'Thank Christ!' exclaimed Francini. 'I don't mind telling you, Doc, Janey means everything to me.'

'I sort of guessed,' said Macandrew.

'You'll be staying with her?' asked Francini.

'That won't be necessary, Mr Francini. She's in good hands. The nursing staff will take excellent care of her. Now, if you'll excuse me, I'm going to get out of these clothes.'

'Of course, of course,' said Francini backing away a little. 'I can't tell you how grateful I am, Doc.'

Macandrew felt uneasy. 'Mr Francini,' he began cautiously, 'Jane's tumour has been removed but we haven't had the lab report on it yet. A lot depends on that... She's not out of the woods just yet.'

'Yeah, but you got rid of the bastard, didn't you? You got all of it out?'

'I think so but...'

'Of course you did. I feel it. Janey's gonna be fine.'

The fact that the operation on Jane Francini had gone well and that the sun was still shining brightly when he walked out through the hospital doors put Macandrew in a good mood. He was whistling as he walked up to the junction of 39th Street and Rainbow, trying to decide where to eat lunch. Eating in the Med Center itself was something he had long given up on. What large institutions did to food was something he no longer subjected himself to. He opted for a quick sandwich at Wendy's; this would give him time to have a pleasant walk in the sunshine afterwards.

As he waited in line for his sandwich, he became aware of someone smiling at him out of the corner of his eye. It was Lucy Long, the OR nurse. He smiled back and, seeing that she was on her own, took his tray over to join her.

'I didn't think neurosurgeons ate junk food,' said Lucy.

'What did you think we ate?' retorted Macandrew.

'Ambrosia,' replied Lucy with a straight face.

'What did I do?' asked Macandrew, feigning hurt.

'Not you, Mac,' replied Lucy thoughtfully. 'But some of your colleagues are a different story.'

'As long as they're good at their job,' said Macandrew, raising his hands slightly to signify he didn't want to get into this kind of conversation.

'I suppose so,' said Lucy. 'I guess people

29

forgive a surgeon anything if he's good at his job. It's just that some of these guys make it a bit hard sometimes!'

Macandrew smiled and nodded. He knew that surgeons were not the easiest of people to get along with. There was often a conflict of interests between what was professionally necessary and what was socially desirable. They had to be supremely self-confident in their own ability but, as a consequence, were often self-opinionated and egotistical or – as Lucy Long would have it – 'a pain in the ass'.

Nice guys were the exception in the profession because being nice usually went with being self-critical and sensitive to alternative points of view. Surgeons had to make instant decisions, believe them to be right, and act without fear of contradiction – great in OR, not so endearing at the dinner table. The fact that Macandrew recognised the problem made him one of the exceptions. He was just as confident as the next man in OR but knew when to keep his mouth shut outside it. As a consequence, he was generally popular at the Med Center.

'You did a good job this morning,' said Lucy. 'Everyone was impressed.'

'Thanks but it was textbook stuff.'

'What made you come to KC, Mac?'

'Not you as well!' replied Macandrew. 'This is a good Med Center!'

Lucy shrugged. 'Yeah, sure, but I mean, you were working in Boston. Coming here is not exactly an award-winning career move!'

Macandrew smiled. 'I felt claustrophobic in Boston. I went to school in Boston; I went to college in Boston; I went to med school in Boston. I could have lived and died in Boston but I didn't want to.'

'Just the gypsy in your soul,' smiled Lucy.

Macandrew smiled.

'Do you intend moving on at some point?'

'Sure, I'll head west when the time is right.'

'You sound like a pioneer!'

Macandrew nodded and said, 'I've got the genes. My great-grandfather came to the USA from Scotland and headed west. He ended up in Missouri, a place called Weston.'

'I take it you've been to see it?' asked Lucy.

'I even found his headstone.'

'Must have been a strange feeling?'

'A bit like an episode of *Star Trek*.'

Lucy smiled and looked at her watch. 'I'll have to get back.' She dabbed at her lips with a paper napkin. 'You?'

Macandrew shook his head. 'I'm going to take a walk,' he said. 'I've got nothing until four.'

When Macandrew returned to the Med Center at three-thirty he felt relaxed. He had enjoyed the walk and now felt ready to face the case study meeting called by Saul

Klinsman at four. There was just time for him to take a shower and freshen up. As he stepped into the elevator that would take him up to his office he saw the nurse at Reception look up and recognise him. She raised her arm as if to attract his attention but the doors slid shut before he could hit the button. When he stepped out into the second-level corridor, the public address system chimed and its female voice asked that Dr John Macandrew contact Dr Saul Klinsman immediately.

Macandrew picked up the phone on his desk and called Klinsman's extension. 'What's the problem?'

'Can you come up to my office please, Mac?'

'Something wrong?'

The phone went dead.

Macandrew tried to think what could have caused the abruptness in Klinsman's manner but failed to come up with anything as he headed for the elevator and took it right to the top floor. The top floor was where the heads of departments and administration chiefs had their suites and offices. The carpeting on the floor of the corridor deadened footsteps and made it seem unnaturally quiet in comparison to other areas of the hospital. It was the one place in the whole of the Med Center that did not smell of anaesthetic or antiseptic because it had its own special air conditioning system. He entered Klinsman's outer office and said, 'Hello,' to Diana French, his secretary. Once again I stand before you, spellbound by your beauty.'

Diana French let him know with a barely perceptible shake of the head that this was not the time for banter. 'Go right in, Mac, he's expecting you.'

Macandrew had hoped to get a clue from Diana what this was all about but she diverted her eyes and continued working at her keyboard. He tapped lightly on the polished mahogany door with the brass nameplate on it and entered.

'How did the operation on Jane Francini go this morning?' Klinsman asked without preamble.

'Like clockwork. Why?'

'Something's wrong, Mac. She isn't recovering well.'

'In what way?'

'The nurses say she's confused and behaving strangely. They managed to reassure her husband that this was often the case when a patient came out of deep anaesthesia and suggested he come back in a couple of hours but the truth is that she hasn't improved any. Are you absolutely sure that nothing went wrong in OR this morning?'

'Of course I'm sure!'

'All right, all right, don't get on your high horse,' said Klinsman holding up his hands.

'But I need hardly tell you that Mr Francini isn't going to take this quietly if it turns out that something unforeseen has happened to his wife.'

'I'd better get down there,' said Macandrew getting to his feet. Klinsman was about to say something when the sound of raised voices from the outer office interrupted him. The door burst open and Diana French, looking red-faced and harassed, said, 'I'm sorry, Doctors.'

Tony Francini pushed past her into the room. He came up to Macandrew, clenching his fists. 'Straightforward, huh? A routine procedure, huh? What kind of an asshole are you? What the fuck have you done to my wife?'

'Mr Francini, I've just this minute come back to the hospital. I haven't been down to see your wife yet, but let me assure you, the operation this morning went very well. There were no complications and I'm sure that whatever's alarming you is probably just some temporary reaction to the anaesthetic.'

Francini moved up even closer and poked his forefinger into Macandrew's chest. He said in menacing tones, 'Now let me tell you something, Doctor. You'd better be fucking right because I've just been down there and the woman in that bed ... is not my wife.'

CHAPTER TWO

Tel Aviv, Israel
October 2000

Benny Zur stuffed the last of his burger into his mouth and wiped his hands on his jeans. Dark stains on the denim said that it wasn't the first time he'd done this. He looked around anxiously and then stamped his feet impatiently on the ground. The last bus was about to leave for Jerusalem and Eli Aswar still hadn't turned up. If this was all a joke, he was going to be real mad, but surely Eli wouldn't do something like this to him: they had been friends since childhood.

If, for whatever reason, Eli didn't show, he was still going to have to stay out all night. He had lied to Shula about having to do an extra shift at the factory so he couldn't change his mind and go home without some good explanation. He indulged his frustration and took a kick at a pile of old cardboard boxes lying stacked up against a wall behind the bus. A rat scurried out of the heap to run for cover elsewhere. Rats liked the bus station; they grew fat there. There were always plenty of discarded *falafels* to

35

feed on. When night fell and the buses stopped running they took over from the creatures of the day.

The driver, who'd been speaking to two other drivers at a neighbouring stance, turned away and came towards his bus. He paused to stub out his cigarette on the ground and hitch up his trousers over a fat gut, tucking in his wayward shirt with both hands before looking towards Benny and enquiring with an inclination of his head whether or not he wanted to get on board. Benny scratched nervously at his stubbly beard and gave an ambivalent shrug as he looked again towards the station entrance.

Suddenly Eli came running round the corner, one hand clutching a striped fabric bag, the other holding a baseball cap on his head.

'Where the fuck have you been, man?' demanded Benny.

'Couldn't get away,' explained Eli, still badly out of breath. 'Kepes wouldn't let me leave the dishes till the morning and the place was full of tourists till late.'

'Tourists,' said Benny with an inflection that needed no further explanation.

The driver started the engine and a cloud of blue smoke drifted out the back. The whole bus shuddered and vibrated in sympathy with a diesel engine whose pistons seemed to be working in opposition rather than harmony. He looked round and counted the passengers before marking the figure down on a clipboard and pushing it into a pocket in the back of his brown plastic bucket seat. He took a swig from a bottle of water parked at his feet, wiped his mouth with the back of his hand and released the handbrake.

The bus pulled out of the station and started out slowly and laboriously on the road up to Jerusalem. It sounded so sick that both men wondered if it would manage the steep climb. Benny shouted as much to the driver but the man dismissed the suggestion with a wave of his hand.

Now that he'd calmed down and things were going according to plan again, Benny took time to look round at the other passengers. They comprised mainly Arab women – wearing shawls and carrying covered baskets – but there were two European tourists on board, a thin, round-shouldered man and a blonde woman who was wearing shorts. They were young and had rucksacks tucked in at their feet. They averted their eyes when Benny looked at them so he took comfort from the fact that the girl was due for a nasty surprise when they reached Jerusalem. It might be thirty degrees centigrade down in Tel Aviv but it would be a lot colder up in the hills. Shorts were a big mistake.

Benny turned to Eli and said, 'Tell me

again what this guy said.'

'Three hundred shekels is what he said,' replied Eli with a grin of satisfaction.

'Each?'

'Yes, each; I've told you a hundred times, man.'

'I just like hearing it,' said Benny with a grin that exposed bad teeth. 'But why us?'

'Because we are Israelis – native Israelis, not Russians or Germans or American Jews who've come here to live here but true Israelis who were born here and whose parents were born here and whose grandparents were born here.'

'I still don't get it.'

'Look, he wants to ask us things about our past, what we did, where we lived, stuff like that.'

'You said this guy's a priest? What kind of priest?'

'They all look the same to me. You know, Christian, dressed in black with a cross round his neck.'

'How'd you meet him?'

'He came to the restaurant one night last week. I was emptying the bins when he left and he came over and spoke to me. He asked lots of questions about where I was born, where my parents came from, had I always lived in Israel. I told him me and my folks had always lived here. He seemed pleased at that and told me I was just the kind of guy he was looking for. If I was interested in making some good money I should meet him when I finished at the restaurant and he'd tell me more.'

'So you did?'

'I met him in a café down in Atarim Square. He bought me a couple of beers and told me how I could help with his research.'

'Research?'

'He said it was just a case of answering questions under what he called "controlled conditions". He said it was nothing to worry about but I would have to go up to Jerusalem and it would mean staying the night. Then he told me how much. Three hundred shekels! Just for answering some questions and staying over at his expense!'

'I thought these guys were supposed to be poor.'

'They pretend that,' said Eli. 'It's crap. Miriam Cohen says they're the richest organisation in the world. I asked him if I could bring along a friend. He didn't seem that keen at first but finally he said it would be OK providing my friend and his family had always lived here in Israel. I said I knew lots of people like that but he said just the one, so I asked you, my friend.'

Benny smiled with satisfaction. 'Three hundred shekels,' he sighed.

'For one night.'

After a few moments Benny's smile faded

as worries returned. He turned to Eli, 'Shit, you know this doesn't make sense. This guy wants to know about *us* … a floor sweeper and a dish washer! And for that he's going to pay us three hundred shekels each? He must have missed out the bit about wanting our kidneys.'

'Relax,' said Eli. 'Just think about what you're going to do with the money.'

'There has to be more to it,' murmured Benny.

Eli grinned. 'Come on, we deserve a little luck in our lives, and think what Shula will say when you hand her three hundred shekels.'

Benny went quiet and Eli raised his eyebrows. 'You didn't tell her?'

'I told her I was working an extra shift at the factory,' said Benny, moving uncomfortably in his seat.

'You cunning bastard! You're going to keep the money for yourself!' chuckled Eli.

'And you're not?'

The two men lapsed into silence as the bus ground its way slowly up through the Judean hills in the darkness. The Arab women stared into space as if in a trance; the European man had put headphones on and the blonde girl rested her head on his shoulder. Occasionally, when the driver took a long time to change gear and the engine revs dropped, vague musical sounds escaped from the headphones, a thin, tinny sound.

It was just after eleven-thirty and the moon was high above the Mount of Olives when the bus ground its way into the bus station and disgorged its passengers. Benny smirked as the blonde girl reacted to the temperature by hugging herself and complaining to her friend. Benny and Eli started making their way towards the walls of the old city.

'He said to enter at the Jaffa Gate,' said Eli as the walls of the old city stretched out before them, 'and then make our way to...' He paused while he fished out a grubby piece of paper from inside his leather jerkin, 'the convent of St Saviour.'

'True Israelis, eh?' said Benny, puffing out his chest. He had been considering what Eli had said earlier. 'He's right. We belong here. This is our land and the Christians know it.' He turned to beam at Eli who smiled at his friend's ever changing moods.

'Halt!'

Both men stopped dead in their tracks as they crossed the threshold of the Jaffa Gate and heard the command barked from the shadows. It was accompanied by the sound of an automatic rifle being cocked. An Israeli soldier materialised from the darkness, his right hand curled round the trigger of an automatic weapon. He signalled with his left hand that the two men should move towards him. Both complied. Neither was nervous; it was a common enough occurrence.

'Where are you going?' asked the soldier.

Benny replied rapidly in Hebrew and the soldier relaxed as if soothed by the sound. He motioned with the barrel of the gun that they should proceed.

'Shalom,' said Benny.

'Shalom,' replied the soldier merging back into the darkness.

St Saviour's was located down a small cobbled lane leading off the Via Dolorosa. The only outward sign was a wooden plaque on the wall, which the men had to struggle to read in the dim light emanating from the one street light fixed high on a wall some twenty metres away. There was an iron bell pull below the plaque. Eli yanked it and the sonorous sound echoed out to them from somewhere deep inside. A few moments later a hatch in the door slid back and a square of yellow light appeared. 'Yes?' said a woman's voice.

'The priest said we should come,' said Eli.

The hatch closed and Benny and Eli were left standing in the lane for more than a minute before they heard a series of bolts rattle back and saw the door swing slowly open.

'Come,' said the nun who had unlocked it; she was dressed in white with a long veil.

Benny found it hard to tell how old she was; her face was scrubbed, pink and white, a complexion he was not at ease with, and her hair was hidden by a white cowl fixed beneath her veil. He noticed that her lace-up shoes seemed too big for her: they slid off her heel and scuffed the floor when she walked. She led the way along a narrow, uneven, stone-floored corridor where they were shown into a small chapel that smelled strongly of incense. They were left alone in brooding silence.

'I don't like this,' whispered Benny, hunching up his shoulders and scowling as he looked around.

'Christian places are all like this,' replied Eli. 'They like the darkness.'

Benny frowned as he examined a painting of a man in a loincloth, his side pierced by an arrow and blood spilling out from the wound while above him two angels played trumpets. Eli ran his fingers lightly along the altar cloth and started to fondle the gold cross that stood in the middle.

'Don't touch that,' said an even voice behind him. It didn't sound angry, just authoritative.

Eli span round to find the tall figure of a man dressed in priest's robes standing in the doorway.

'Here we are then, just as I promised,' said Eli, showing his teeth like a chimpanzee.

43

'And this is my friend, Benny Zur.'

Benny switched on a grin too as the priest looked at him.

'I'm Dom Ignatius. You were born here too?'

'Hebron,' replied Benny.

'Your parents?'

'Both Jerusalem.'

'What about your grandparents?'

'My mother's people came from Jaffa. My grandfather had a fishing boat. He used to take me out fishing when I was...'

'And your father's?' interrupted the priest.

'I'm not sure,' replied Benny nervously, suddenly feeling a threat to the prospect of three hundred shekels. 'I never met them. They died before I was born. A village in the north, I think.'

'But still in Palestine?'

'Israel,' replied Benny.

'Quite,' said Ignatius as if vaguely amused then he took a breath and said, 'Good, my colleague Dr Stroud and I would both be grateful for your help with our research into life here in the Holy Land. We will need to ask you questions about your family background but, for this, you must be properly relaxed.'

Benny found that there was something unsettling about the phase 'properly relaxed'. He'd felt the same about 'controlled conditions' when Eli had used it earlier. He looked first to Eli and then back at the priest. 'Properly relaxed?' he said.

'No need to be alarmed. No harm will come to you. But we would like to put you to sleep before we ask you things. It will improve your powers of recall.'

Benny's eyes opened wide. 'You mean you want to hypnotise us?' he said, clearly appalled at the prospect.

'Something like that,' said the priest.

Benny shook his head. Eli too was unsure. Benny drew him to one side and whispered urgently, 'Anything could happen to us while we are under the influence. We could be murdered!'

'But they're holy people!' protested Eli. 'Why would they want to murder us? We've got nothing worth stealing! They've no reason to kill us.'

'They've got no reason to pay us three hundred shekels either,' countered Benny, his eyes moving between Ignatius and Eli.

The priest saw that Benny was the more anxious of the two. 'There's really nothing to be afraid of,' he said to him in a calm even voice. 'Why don't you and your friend talk it over while I ask Sister Benedict to bring you something to eat and drink. If after that you don't want to go on with it we'll say no more about it. Under these circumstances of course, we would not be able to pay you the money...'

Ignatius left the room and Eli got to work on Benny. 'We can't afford to let an opportunity like this go,' he insisted. 'How often do we get the chance to get our hands on easy money?'

'I still don't like it,' said Benny. 'I'd like to know what's going on. They could do anything to us while we were asleep.'

'Like what?'

'Steal our kidneys. You hear stories of...'

Eli's look of derision stopped Benny in his tracks. 'Stop talking rubbish about kidneys, will you?'

Benny shrugged and tried an alternative. 'So what's to stop them asking us all they want to know and then murdering us so they don't have to pay the money?'

Eli held up his hands in a gesture of exasperation. 'The man is a priest. We're not dealing with robbers and thieves here,' he said. 'Besides, what are we going to do if we don't go through with it? It's too late to go back to Tel Aviv and we've no money to stay.'

A nun entered the room carrying a metal tray with sandwiches and a jug of wine on it. She put it down and left without saying anything. Eli filled a glass and handed it to Benny. 'At least have a drink,' he said. 'Maybe it will help you to see sense.'

Benny took a mouthful then drained the glass in one go.

'That's more like it,' said Eli. He took a

bite out of a sandwich and murmured approvingly. 'You said it yourself out there,' he said. 'We are important people, real Israelis. Our help is worth three hundred shekels of anybody's money.'

Eli topped up Benny's glass and watched him continue to mellow as the wine allayed his fears. He could see he was becoming much more relaxed about the whole affair. Eventually he broke into a smile and said, 'Maybe you're right about these people,' he said. 'They probably don't mean us any harm.'

'That's the spirit,' said Eli. 'We'll finish our supper and tell Ignatius that we're going to help.'

Benny began to notice what a pleasant room this was – warm, friendly, reassuring. He was glad he had come.

When Ignatius returned, he was accompanied by a second man, even taller than he himself but not nearly so well proportioned. Ignatius was slim but the other man was painfully thin and gangly; his right shoulder drooped lower than the left and he held his head at the opposite angle, as if to compensate. He was wearing a lightweight linen suit that showed off wrinkles to advantage and the collar of his shirt had been made for a much larger man.

'Well, gentlemen, what have you decided?' asked Ignatius without bothering to introduce the second man.

'We will be happy to help you, sir,' answered Eli with an exaggerated smile. 'We feel it's our duty as Israelis.'

'Good,' replied the priest. 'This is Dr Stroud. He will make sure that no harm comes to you. Come with us, please.'

The fact that Stroud carried a small leather bag registered with Eli more than it did with Benny. It seemed that, whereas Benny's reservations had been dealt with by the wine, his own had just started to arise. They passed another small chapel where a group of five or six nuns were singing. The Latin words meant nothing to him but it was a sound he had known all his life.

Ignatius led the way down a narrow flight of stone steps near the back of the building and Eli felt the walls close in on him. They entered a basement where they all had to duck to avoid contact with the vaulted stone roof.

'In here,' said Ignatius, leaning back so Benny and Eli could enter a room at the end of the corridor ahead of him. He clicked on the light with his outstretched right hand and Benny drew in his breath and looked at Eli. This room didn't seem to belong in a church at all; it was much more like a doctor's office.

'Don't be alarmed,' said Ignatius, sensing the pair's unease. 'You'll be more comfortable here and the doctor will be able to look after you properly.'

Eli looked at Stroud and wasn't at all sure that he wanted the doctor looking after him. He looked as if he could do with some looking after himself. Stroud opened his bag and took out several glass vials and a box of plastic syringes which he laid out on a tray. Eli tried to catch Benny's eye but Benny was obviously still enjoying the euphoria the wine had bestowed on him. Eli saw Stroud remove two syringes from their wrappers and fit needles to them. Ignatius noticed him staring and said something to Stroud who responded by stopping what he was doing to open a small cabinet and take out a bottle of pills. He handed it to Ignatius who opened it and gave two pills to Eli. 'Here, these will help you relax.'

Eli was shown into an adjoining room by Ignatius while Stroud indicated to Benny that he lie down on a leather-topped couch.

Benny stared up at the ceiling, wondering why it was moving. He'd only had two glasses of wine... He felt the doctor bare his arm and rub it with a swab. It felt cold, icy cold. Ignatius had come back into the room and was looking down at him. 'Just relax,' he was saying. 'Relax and listen to what I say.'

Benny felt a slight sharp sensation in his arm. The light feeling in his head became more intense. It was as if his brain had suddenly become free of his body. His body had been a prison for his real self.

'What is your name?'

'Benny Zur,' he replied slowly. The words seemed heavy; he had difficulty getting them out.

'Where do you live?'

'I told you ... Tel Aviv.'

'How old are you?'

'Thirty-fi...'

'Relax...' soothed the voice from some-where far away beyond the horizons of light. 'Just relax.'

The sun was coming up ... no, it was night. He was in a desert ... no, he was in a forest and he was afraid. He couldn't cope with the flood of images that were streaming through his consciousness, all demanding his atten-tion. His pulse rate rose sharply. He became disorientated. The pictures kept coming and he couldn't view them dispassionately because they all featured him. Each one trig-gered a different emotional reaction and he couldn't keep up. He needed more air. He felt his legs go into painful spasm and tried to sit up. But he couldn't; he was now trapped in a body that weighed too much. He broke out in a sweat: he could feel it running down his face but he couldn't wipe it away. He was filled with foreboding. Something awful was about to happen, something awful ... had happened.

'Your name?' asked the voice.

'Ishmael Hamadi.'

'Where do you live, Ishmael?'

'Beer Sheva.'

'Tell me about yourself. What do you do? Do you have family?'

'I'm a camel driver. I live with my wife Ruth. We have two sons, Saul and Eli. Ruth's mother stays with us too – she's blind. Her father used to live with us but he died two months ago. He was eighty years old.'

'Do you own your camels, Ishmael?'

'No, they belong to Zachariah. He owns more than a hundred but I am in charge of three other drivers. Zachariah trusts me.'

'Have you ever heard of someone called the Nazarene?'

'The one the Christians follow?'

'Yes.'

'He died a long time ago.'

Ignatius nodded to the Stroud who administered another injection.

Benny appeared to have some kind of convulsion. He sat bolt upright with fear etched on his face and cried out in anguish but the moment passed and he slumped back down on the bed. Stroud indicated to Ignatius that he could continue.

'Your name?'

'Ibrahim Dwek.'

Whereas Ishmael had spoken with a coarse accent, Ibrahim Dwek spoke in cultured tones and told of his life as a librarian at the Temple in Jerusalem. He wasn't married and lived with his widowed mother Nesta and his sister Shula. Ignatius made notes while keeping up a string of questions as he gradually built up a picture of Dwek's life. 'What do you know about a teacher from Galilee, the one the Christians follow?'

'Jesus of Nazareth? He's long dead but people still speak of him and he has a big following.'

'Are you or any of your family or friends, followers?'

'No.'

'A little more, please, Doctor.'

In response to the look of doubt that appeared on Stroud's face, Ignatius whispered, 'He hasn't been put under any real stress.'

Another small injection was administered and Benny's skin became pallid and his breathing laboured. There was a vague chemical smell on his breath which made Ignatius recoil slightly. 'Tell me who you are and where you live,' he asked in his even, reassuring tones.

'James. I'm from Caesarea.'

'What do you know about Jesus of Nazareth, James?'

'He died that we might live for ever.'

Ignatius exchanged glances with Stroud. 'You're a follower?' he exclaimed.

No reply.

'You do know him?'

'The Romans crucified him the year I was born.'

The disappointment in the room was almost palpable. 'Why did you say what you did about living for ever?'

'I met a man in prison.'

'You were in prison? Where?'

'The Roman prison in Caesarea.'

Ignatius suddenly became very excited. He had to work at keeping his voice calm. 'You were in prison in Caesarea where you met a man who told you about Jesus of Nazareth?'

Ignatius did not blink as he waited for a reply. He was almost too frightened to take a breath. When no reply was forthcoming he said, 'The man who told you these things, he came from Tarsus, didn't he?'

'Yes, Paul of Tarsus.'

Ignatius silently mouthed the words, 'Saint Paul.'

'Tell me about your time in prison,' he said hoarsely.

A tremor started in Benny's hands, which quickly spread to his whole body and he became very restless. His words didn't make sense any more.

'Another injection,' said Ignatius.

'Not possible,' said Stroud. 'There's none left.'

CHAPTER THREE

Kansas City, USA

Macandrew left Tony Francini with Saul Klinsman still trying to pacify him while he went to examine Jane. What the hell did Francini mean by 'not his wife'? One of the nurses saw him as he approached the recovery suite and came over. She said, 'Mr Francini was here, Mac; he was very abusive.'

'I've just seen him,' replied Macandrew. 'What's going on?'

The nurse shrugged and looked uncomfortable. 'Mrs Francini seems totally disorientated. She's conscious but doesn't recognise any of the nurses; she didn't know her husband; I don't think she even knows herself.'

'What does that mean?'

'She insists her name's not Francini,' said the nurse.

Macandrew entered the recovery room where Jane Francini lay. It was a small, quiet room with subdued lighting in line with hospital policy that patients should come round after their operation in a calm and reassuring environment. Any medical para-

54

phernalia associated with emergency resus-
citation was stowed in cupboards behind the
patient or out of their line of sight. Jane
Francini had opened her eyes to a large print
of Kansas corn fields at harvest time hung
on a wall of sky blue but, at the moment, she
was throwing her head from side to side on
the pillow in a state of great distress.

Macandrew watched her shrug off the
attentions of the nurse who was with her.
She growled angrily at the woman and
spoke what sounded to Macandrew like a
stream of gibberish. The look in her eyes,
however, suggested that she thought the
nurse should understand and respond to
what she was saying. The nurse stepped
back to allow Macandrew to take over. She
seemed relieved.

He could see that Jane did not recognise
him or anything to do with her surround-
ings. Her eyes flitted all over the room and
she mumbled almost continuously. It disturbed him that even her voice seemed different to what he remembered. He recalled a
pleasant, quietly spoken, reserved woman
who had thanked him for explaining her
condition to her and outlining the course of
her operation.

Despite the seriousness of her problem, she
had kept her sense of humour and had com-
mented on his name, saying that she felt safe
in the hands of a 'fellow Scot'. She herself

was the daughter of second generation immigrants; her maiden name was Campbell. Macandrew remembered wondering at the time why such a pleasant woman had come to marry the brash Tony Francini and had put it down to opposites attracting.

Jane now had a deep rasping voice. Her eyes had changed too; he couldn't quite put his finger on it but there was something about her expression that alarmed him. She sounded deranged but her facial expression suggested intelligence rather than madness.

'Mrs Francini, do you remember me?' asked Macandrew firmly but gently. 'I'm your surgeon. You're in hospital. You've just had a serious operation but you've come through it well.'

Jane Francini's head stopped moving and her face turned towards him. He saw that she was afraid. She started to speak again and a torrent of unintelligible words swamped Macandrew. Jane Francini's hands reached up to grab the lapels of his white coat as if imploring him to do something, but what?

'Take it easy,' he soothed. 'There's nothing to worry about. Everything's going to be all right. Just relax and get some rest. You'll feel better real soon, I promise.' Macandrew gave her a sedative.

In an almost seamless transition, the look in Jane Francini's eyes changed from fear to puzzlement; her voice also changed. She

56

now spoke in a soft young voice, as if she was a little girl, but quite coherently. She looked appealingly at Macandrew.

'I have to get back now. It's getting dark. My mother will worry if I'm not home soon.'

'Where's home, Jane?'

'Fulton Grange.'

Macandrew looked to the two nurses who shook their heads but before he could ask Jane anything further, she grew very tired as the drug took effect and her head fell back on the pillow.

'I've given her enough to keep her out for a while,' said Macandrew. 'This business isn't going to do her heart condition any favours.'

'What's wrong with her?' asked the younger of the two nurses in the room.

It was a simple question and Macandrew found himself wishing he had a simple answer other than, 'I don't know.'

With Jane sedated and sleeping peacefully, Macandrew returned to Saul Klinsman's office, albeit with some trepidation. He wasn't looking forward to another verbal assault from Tony Francini. When he entered, he found Francini sitting in Klinsman's green leather armchair nursing a drink; he could smell it on the air; it was brandy. He appeared to have calmed down although

Klinsman was still speaking to him in appeasing tones, assuring him that nothing had gone wrong at the operation. The tumour had been removed cleanly and without complications but he had to understand that his wife might still be very ill; it all depended on what the lab report said about the tumour itself.

'How is she?' Klinsman asked as Macandrew came into the room.

'Sleeping. I've sedated her.'

'What's wrong with her?' asked Francini. His earlier aggression had been replaced for the moment by vulnerability. His eyes appealed for answers.

'Quite frankly, Mr Francini,' said Macandrew softly, 'I haven't come across anything quite like this before.'

Francini slumped forward in the chair and then re-donned his tough guy mantle. 'I should have taken her to LA,' he said to no one in particular. 'Letting some hick with a knife loose on Janey wasn't the brightest thing I've ever done.'

Macandrew took the insult stoically. The man was hurting. Klinsman moved uncomfortably in his chair behind the desk as Francini went on to slate the Med Center as if no one was present. 'Fucking two-bit hick dump...'

'Mr Francini,' began Macandrew in controlled fashion.

Francini looked up from the floor and Macandrew almost recoiled at the hate he saw there in his eyes. 'Your wife is sleeping; she'll be out for some time. Why don't you go home and get some rest? We'll call you if there's any news.'

Francini got up slowly and came towards Macandrew. Macandrew held his ground and did his best to remain motionless when, in reality, his brain was warning him to take some defensive action. Francini stopped short in front of him and stabbed his finger into his chest. 'If I lose her...' he warned. 'If I lose her...' Francini turned and walked out of the room.

Klinsman let out his breath in a long sigh and Macandrew slumped down in a chair and closed his eyes. 'I thought he was going to hit me.'

'He might still,' said Klinsman. 'Just don't hit him back. We're in enough trouble.'

Klinsman's comment had not entirely been concerned with ethics. Macandrew was a surgeon but he was built like a light-heavy-weight boxer. He was at least six inches taller than Francini and probably weighed fifty pounds more. Although his features were refined and his manner gentle, he'd always felt his size was a disadvantage in his chosen profession. Joe public preferred that neuro-surgeons be slim and studious – preferably with a mid-European accent and wearing rimless glasses. To be tall and broad was fine for a lumberjack but in the operating room, people started equating size with clumsiness and wondering about dexterity. Even his name was wrong; John Macandrew sounded more like a ranch owner than a doctor. Operate on my kid? The hell yuh will...

'I really don't know what's going on,' said Macandrew wearily. 'I only hope it's some weird reaction to anaesthesia and she'll be OK when she wakes up.'

'You and me both,' said Klinsman. 'The Med Center can do without this right now.'

'What do you mean by "this"?' asked Macandrew, displaying uncharacteristic paranoia.

Klinsman looked at him dispassionately and said, 'I have to think of the Med Center's reputation, Mac. Mistakes can lead to damaging publicity, not to mention lawsuits.'

'There was no mistake,' Macandrew insisted. 'It was a textbook operation. The tumour was removed cleanly and in its entirety. There was no damage done to any other area of the brain. We haven't had a full path report yet, but there was no surgical damage. Period.'

Klinsman held up his hands as if in self-defence. 'I'm not suggesting you screwed up, Mac,' he said. 'Believe me. It's just that I'm sitting in the hot seat and we have a patient who appears to be, for the moment at least, post-operatively damaged.'

Macandrew calmed down and thought for a few moments before deciding that there was no point in continuing the conversation. He got up to leave.

'Keep me informed,' said Klinsman.

Macandrew paused for a moment outside in the corridor suddenly feeling very alone. On the way back to his office, he felt sure that people were looking at him accusingly out of the corner of their eyes. He told himself it was probably his imagination – and it was – but he was still relieved when he reached his office and closed the door behind him. After a few minutes of just sitting at his desk with his chin resting on his folded hands, he picked up the phone and called the path lab. 'Any word on the Francini case?'

'One moment, please.'

Macandrew glanced out at the reddening sky while he waited. It would be dark soon. Not exactly the perfect end to a perfect day.

'Mac, it's Carl,' said the voice of Carl Lessing, Chief of Neurological Histopathology. 'I was just about to call you. I've been looking at the Francini sections. Sorry for taking so long but it's bad news, I'm afraid. The tumour was malignant and pretty aggressive too. If you have a moment maybe you could come down. There's something I'd like you to see.'

'On my way,' said Macandrew.

Macandrew took the elevator to the basement where the Pathology Department was situated. His eyes watched the floor indicator but his mind was on other things. Jane Francini's pre-op scans had only shown up a single tumour but in view of what Lessing had just told him about the tumour's aggressive nature, maybe there had been small secondaries that hadn't shown up or, worse still, had been so small that he'd missed them. This would be one explanation for her condition.

Lessing, a thickset middle-aged man with a mane of white hair and a goatee beard sat at his microscope with his glasses pushed up on his forehead. The fingertips of his left hand adjusted the fine focus control of the instrument while he made notes on a spiral-bound pad with his right.

'What have you got?' asked Macandrew.

'Take a look at these two tissue sections. Tell me if you see a difference.'

Macandrew took Lessing's place and widened the binocular eyepieces a little before looking down. After a few minutes he said, '*Both* are malignant.' He sounded surprised. He had expected one to be normal.

'No difference?'

'Stain colour maybe.'

'Exactly,' said Lessing, pleased that Macandrew had picked up on it. 'The one on the left is Jane Francini's tumour but the haematoxylin staining is a different colour from the more normal reaction of the other one, although, as you say, both are malignant. That's what caught my attention. The colouring's unusual and it rang a bell from way back: I think the Francini tumour is a Hartman's tumour.'

'A what?'

'This is not a big gap in your knowledge,' said Lessing. 'It's only the second I've come across in twenty years. It was named after the first patient to present with it, Mona Hartman. The tumour cells produce some kind of acidic chemical that affects the staining process in the lab. That's what brought it to mind – that and the fact that some guys over in Europe did some research on it a couple of years ago and I remembered reading about it. How's the patient doing anyway?'

'Not good. I was confident I'd got it all out but the way she's behaving says there's something really wrong ... maybe there were secondaries that didn't show up on the scan – or I didn't pick up on them...'

Lessing could see that Macandrew was worried. 'Would it help if I was to have a look at the scans?' he asked.

'I'd be grateful.'

Lessing asked one of his technicians to fetch Jane Francini's brain scans. Macandrew told her where to find them.

'Coffee?'

They went next door to Lessing's small and cluttered office and he poured coffee from a large flask sitting on a hot plate on top of a filing cabinet. Lessing lit a cigarette.

'These things will kill you,' said Macandrew in a weak attempt at humour when he didn't feel in the least humorous.

'Something's going to for sure,' replied Lessing, displaying the philosophy of a long-serving pathologist.

The technician returned with the scans and Lessing clipped them up on a light box. He examined them for a good five minutes – occasionally employing a small magnifying lens – while Macandrew sipped his coffee and watched.

'Just the one, as far as I'm concerned,' announced Lessing.

Macandrew let out his breath in a long slow sigh. 'Thanks, Carl. I didn't think I'd missed anything but you never know...'

'I'll see what I can dig up on Hartman's tumours,' said Lessing. 'I'll give you a call.'

Macandrew went back upstairs and called Klinsman from his office. Diana French answered. 'I'm sorry, Mac, Saul has gone for the day.'

Macandrew called Klinsman at home but there was no reply and he decided not to leave a message on the answering machine.

He thought about contacting Tony Francini personally to tell him the bad news about the tumour but decided against it. There was still a slim chance that Jane might come out of it OK. He would wait until she surfaced from her sedated sleep before saying anything to anyone. He looked at his watch. With the schedule he had written her up for, Jane Francini would be out for another eight hours at least.

Macandrew didn't feel like cooking when he got in. Instead, he fetched a packet meal from the freezer and put it in the microwave. When it emerged, it bore little or no resemblance to the appetizing delight depicted on the pack. 'Delicious Cod Steaks in a light wine sauce, had become amorphous yellow goo. He got a Bud Light from the fridge, picked up a fork and settled himself in front of the television to watch the news while he ate. His attention span only lasted as long as the goo. He picked up the channel changer and started hopping through the stations. Nothing could hold his interest. He couldn't get Jane Francini out of his mind.

At first, he found his preoccupation hard to bear. After all, he wasn't an intern wrestling with his first brush with failure. He was a seasoned surgeon who knew and understood the score. Dealing with life and death was part of the job. He was good at his job but he wasn't a miracle worker. He didn't pretend to be. So why couldn't he come to terms with the Francini case? Maybe it was her husband who was bothering him? Listening to him hadn't been pleasant but then people said all sorts of hurtful things when they were upset and Francini had certainly been that. His wife, as he had put it, was everything to him.

It wasn't Francini's behaviour, he concluded, it was Jane herself. He had come across patients who had lost their minds before but Jane Francini was different. Something her husband had said kept coming back to him. He said that she looked like Janey ... but she wasn't.

The more he thought about it, the more convinced Macandrew became that he was right. She just wasn't Jane Francini any more...

Macandrew didn't have an operation scheduled for the following day so he permitted himself a couple of large Bourbons. He needed a good night's sleep and the alcohol would help. Normally he would sleep late when he wasn't operating, take a leisurely shower and read the morning paper over breakfast but tomorrow he wanted to get into the Med Center early. He wanted to be there when Jane Francini came round. Please God she would have recovered but somehow he feared that this was wishful thinking. He tried looking up Hartman's tumour in his text-books but failed to find any mention. If Carl Lessing didn't come up with something, he would take a trip to the Med Center library.

Jane Francini regained consciousness shortly after six-thirty a.m. For a few brief moments Macandrew thought that things were going to be fine; she appeared relaxed and sleepy and the sounds she made were soft and feminine as she moved her head on the pillow. But as he came closer to listen to what she was saying, he realised that all was not well. Jane was speaking in the little girl voice that she had lapsed into on one occasion yesterday.

'Jane!' whispered Macandrew in her ear. 'Can you hear me?'

'Why are you calling me Jane?' replied Jane, without opening her eyes.

'Because that's your name,' continued Macandrew gently.

'Don't be silly, it's Emma.'

'Emma who, Jane?'

'Emma Forsyth. Stop calling me Jane! Where's my mother? She said she would take me to town today.'

'Town?'

'To get me a new dress. Daddy's coming home soon and she wants me to look pretty for him.'

'Where has your father been, Emma?'

'Fighting the enemies of the King. He's very brave.'

'The king, Emma?' asked Macandrew. 'What king?'

'There's only one king, silly,' said Emma. 'He's...' The words froze on Jane Francini's lips and for a moment she appeared to have gone into a trance then slowly she opened her eyes and recoiled when she saw Macandrew leaning over her. She behaved as if she'd never seen him before. Her tone of voice had completely changed too as she let out a torrent of meaningless words.

Macandrew backed away from the bed and a nurse murmured, 'That lady has a problem...'

Jane Francini had now surfaced from the sedation she had been under and was clearly a seriously disturbed woman. Macandrew became aware that the nurse was waiting for him to say something. 'I'm going to have a psychiatrist take a look at her.'

'Yes Doctor,' replied the nurse.

'For the record,' said Macandrew without turning round, 'Mrs Francini's tumour was both malignant and aggressive.'

'Tough break,' said the nurse.

Macandrew returned to his office and picked up some coffee from the machine on the way. He sipped it while he waited for Tony Francini to arrive, half hoping that

Saul Klinsman might arrive first but recognising that this wasn't likely. The head of surgery usually arrived late and left early: this was written in the stars. The phone rang.

'I came up with some stuff on Hartman's tumours,' said Carl Lessing. 'Not that it's very encouraging, I'm afraid. From the few recorded cases I managed to find, the prognosis is bad. None of them ever recovered.'

'Secondary invasion?'

'Strangely enough, no. Removal of the primary tumour seemed to stop the cancer in its tracks. It was more a case of being left with residual brain dysfunction.'

'What level of dysfunction are we talking about here?'

'Euphemism level,' said Lessing. 'They were out of their trees: they were all committed.'

Macandrew closed his eyes and screwed up his face. It sounded as if the clinical picture in Jane Francini's case was matching up to Lessing's information.

Francini arrived in the Med Center a little after seven-fifteen to find that his wife had been put under sedation again – Macandrew had written her up for this before leaving her to come upstairs. The nursing staff relayed the message to Francini that he should go straight on up to Macandrew's office.

'How come she's still out?' demanded

Francini without any preamble.

'She came round a short time ago,' said Macandrew softly. 'She was very disturbed. I put her under again.'

Francini looked at Macandrew in silence for a moment. At first his expression was questioning, and then it changed to accusation. 'What are you trying to tell me?'

'Sit down, Mr Francini.'

'I don't want to fucking sit down,' retorted Francini. 'I want to know what's wrong with my wife!'

'Your wife is a very sick lady, Mr Francini. Her tumour was malignant and it's a very aggressive kind of cancer. The pathology lab made the diagnosis last night.'

'But you removed the damn thing. You said everything went well.'

'It did from a surgical point of view,' said Macandrew. 'But it so happens that this particular kind of tumour tends to leave patients brain damaged. We're not sure why. There may be hidden secondaries or damage we can't see on the scan. There hasn't been enough research done on it. It's a very rare type.'

'Damaged?' whispered Francini as if he was scared of the word. 'What the fuck do you mean, damaged?'

'The few similar cases we've been able to trace were left very severely confused with regard to cerebral function.'

70

'You mean Janey is nuts?' asked Francini, suddenly wide-eyed and vulnerable.

'I'd like one of our psychiatrists to see her before we make any kind of formal assessment.'

Francini suddenly buried his head in his hands and started to sob. 'Oh Christ,' he wept. 'What the hell am I gonna do?'

'I'm very sorry,' said Macandrew, suddenly feeling for the man. 'I assure you, we'll do our very best for her.'

Francini suddenly jerked his head up and spat out, 'No, you won't! You assholes have done enough to Janey. I'm calling in a real doctor.'

'I'm sorry you feel that way, Mr Francini,' said Macandrew. 'But I don't think you'll find any comfort in a second opinion.'

Francini stifled his reply as the door opened and Saul Klinsman came in. 'I was just telling this guy here that I don't want any of you hicks touching Janey any more. I'm calling in some brains.'

Klinsman shot Macandrew a questioning glance and Macandrew said, 'Mrs Francini's tumour was malignant and aggressive – a Hartman's tumour. I've told Mr Francini that it wouldn't be right for us to reach any firm conclusions on her condition without his wife being seen by a psychiatrist,' said Macandrew.

'That would be sensible,' agreed Klinsman.

'And I was saying, I don't want you guys touching Janey,' interrupted Francini. 'I'm calling in my own people.'

'That is your prerogative, of course,' replied Klinsman, 'but that will probably take a few days if you're going to bring in someone from out of town. Surely it would be in your wife's best interests if we were to continue caring for her?'

'No!' insisted Francini. 'I don't want you bastards causing any more damage. She's not to be given anything, especially not the knock-out drops this guy's been using to shut her up.'

Macandrew bit his tongue and said, 'It's important that your wife should not be allowed to get overexcited, because of her heart condition. That's why I sedated her.'

'I want her conscious and alert when a real doctor gets here, not acting like some spaced-out zombie!'

'I'll need you to sign something to that effect, Mr Francini,' said Klinsman. 'You could be putting your wife's life in danger.'

Francini snorted and said, 'Danger? After what you assholes did to her? That's fucking rich!'

Macandrew knew he was in danger of losing his temper. He appreciated that Francini was very upset but the man was pushing things too far. His wife's condition had been fully diagnosed. The tumour had done the damage to her, nothing else. There had been no mistakes, no overlooked secondaries, no incompetence, and he was not keeping her sedated to cover up his own blunders. He was doing his level best to keep her stress levels within reasonable bounds. He looked away so that Francini would not see the anger he felt. He was going to keep his temper if it killed him.

'When will she come round?' asked Francini.

Macandrew took a deep breath. 'Without any more sedation, she should be fully alert in four hours,' he said.

'See that she is,' said Francini, getting to his feet and leaving the room without another word.

Macandrew thumped his right fist into the open palm of his other hand. 'Christ, that guy is crossing the line!' he exclaimed.

Klinsman nodded. 'Mr Francini does lack a certain basic charm.'

'I really think that Jane might be in danger if we withdraw sedation completely,' said Macandrew.

'It's Francini's call. We can't risk him taking us to court,' replied Klinsman. 'He may not be the brightest guy in the world but he's rich and that's all you need to be to hire the legal brains who'll crucify us in court whatever the rightness of our cause.'

Macandrew sighed and said, 'Maybe just

50mg Valium? Who'd know?'

Klinsman nodded. 'OK, but no more.'

'Do you think we can rely on Francini staying away for a few hours?' asked Macandrew.

Kinsman looked surprised at the question. 'I got the impression he wouldn't be back until his wife came round. He'll probably be on the phone most of the morning, making arrangements for some fat cat from LA or Frisco to come out here and teach us to suck eggs. Why?'

'I'd really like to have someone from psychiatry take a look at Jane Francini. What do you think?'

Kinsman folded his hands in front of him on the desk and thought for a moment before saying, 'Well, I don't suppose that could be construed as administering any kind of therapy to the patient. As long as we put it through as an internal matter and don't add it to Francini's bill I guess it'll be OK. Anyone in mind?'

'I thought maybe Karen Bliss?'

Klinsman nodded. 'Good choice. Dr Bliss does seem to have brains.'

Macandrew smiled. Klinsman's lack of regard for psychiatrists was something of a legend in the Med Center. He returned to his own office and left Macandrew to call Karen Bliss. She wasn't in her office and didn't respond to her bleep. Macandrew left a message for her to call him when she got in. She called an hour later.

'So you finally got round to asking someone how the thing you cut up all the time really works?' said the female voice.

Macandrew smiled and said, 'I thought maybe between us we could come up with something.'

'What can I do for you, Mac?' asked Karen.

Macandrew told her about the Francini case. 'I keep thinking she's not deranged in the usual sense. There's more to it but I can't say what.'

'From what you say, it sounds like a gross personality change post surgery,' said Karen. 'It wouldn't be the first time. But I'm intrigued. What kind of tumour did you say she had?'

'Hartman's. It's a pineal gland tumour.'

'The third eye,' said Karen.

'What d'you think?'

'OK, I'll take a look at her,' said Karen.

'Good,' said Macandrew. 'There's just one little problem.' Macandrew told her about Jane Francini's husband.

'I'm not so sure I like the sound of this any more.'

'He'll be gone for the best part of the morning,' said Macandrew. 'I was a bit conservative about when Janey would come round. I told him four hours but the truth is she should be starting to come round by eleven. I'd particularly like you to see her at that point. If you could come down about then you should have a clear hour with the patient and map the changes in her.'

'OK, see you a little before eleven.'

'Bring some recording equipment with you. I don't think we'll get a second chance.'

CHAPTER FOUR

Jerusalem, Israel

Eli Aswar was uneasy. He'd been given pills but hadn't swallowed them: he was suspicious of everything. He'd let Benny have most of the wine to overcome his early reluctance, so he didn't even have Dutch courage to help him combat his longtime fear of all things medical. He kept the pills under his tongue until Ignatius turned his back for a moment and then spat them into his palm and pocketed them. He suspected it was some kind of drug to put him to sleep and he was having none of it. They were questioning Benny and he wanted to know why they needed needles and just what they were going to do with them. It was one thing to be hypnotised, quite another to be injected with some truth drug. He'd heard about these things. Once you'd been given one, you couldn't help but tell the truth and there had been one or two things in Eli's past life that he would rather be kept under wraps.

His blood ran cold as he heard Benny cry out in distress. Confusion and fear threatened to become panic. His mouth went dry. He forced himself to think clearly and it didn't take long to decide that he wasn't going to hang around any longer. He had to get out but how? There were no windows: they were below ground level.

There were two doors leading out of the room. One led to the place where they were holding Benny and he had just discovered that the other was locked. Slowly he released the handle so as not to make any noise. He supposed he could charge straight out through the room where they had Benny but he suspected that the upstairs door would be locked. The alternative was to try and pick the lock of the door he was still holding. The mechanism looked simple enough and he was not entirely inexperienced in such matters: he had not always been a dish washer. This was the option he'd go for.

Stroud had left some instruments lying on the table by the bed. Eli selected what experience told him would be most suitable for the job and started to probe the lock. He heard more anguished cries coming from his friend next door and felt a pang of guilt in taking comfort from the fact that the sound would cover any noise that he might be making. Ignatius was shouting. He sounded angry but not at Benny because he could hear Stroud shouting back. He couldn't make out what the argument was about but he wasn't going to hang around to find out. With a final twist of the improvised pick, the lock turned and he stepped out into a narrow stone passage.

His heart sank when he saw that it didn't seem to lead anywhere. In fact, it appeared to end about five metres to his left in a solid stone wall but he decided to check it out anyway. He edged his way along, stretching his arm out in front of him. It did end in a wall but there was a small recess to the left where a wooden ladder was propped up. It was rough to the touch and smelt old and dry.

As his eyes became accustomed to the gloom, he could see that the ladder led up to a trap door in the roof. There was no place else to go so he climbed up and started to work on freeing the rusty bolt that secured it.

It took several attempts before the bolt finally yielded and slid back in a shower of metallic dust. He blinked to clear his eyes and spat out the rust that caused his mouth to pucker. He moved up another rung and applied his shoulder to the hatch cover, only to be rewarded with another shower of dirt but at least the cover moved. He raised it a little and looked out through the gap to see a broad, stone-walled passage. It was considerably wider than the one he was currently in and had lights along it at regular intervals. There were also lit candles in small alcoves, flickering in front of religious statues. The passage seemed deserted so he opened the hatch fully and hoisted himself up through the space to sit on the edge of the opening and pausing to consider whether or not it was wise to burn his bridges.

The passage was clearly part of the convent but it didn't smell like it. No incense. It didn't have the clinical smell of the cellar he'd just left either; it had a different smell. It smelt like a prison. For Eli it had been a while but it wasn't a smell you forgot easily, if ever. He was still in two minds about continuing when he was distracted by a cry of anguish echoing up from the tunnel below. He didn't feel good about it but he let the hatch cover fall back into place and committed himself to going on.

He listened for a moment before setting off along the new passage, taking comfort from the fact that he must now be up at ground level. With any luck he could be out of here soon. He would raise the alarm and get help for Benny. He turned the first corner then froze as he heard sounds coming from up ahead. His first thought was that it was the chanting the Christians were so fond of, but, as he neared the wooden door it seemed to be coming from, it was clearly too discordant for that. It was more like the moaning of people in torment.

The door suddenly opened and a nun stepped out into the passageway. She was wearing a plastic apron over her robes and carrying a tray with crockery on it. She got as much of a surprise as Eli and dropped the tray. Plates smashed on the stone floor as she opened her mouth to cry out but Eli hit her before she could make a sound. She fell over backwards and cracked her head on the floor – a sound which paralysed Eli with fear for a few moments. He'd never meant for this to happen. He'd acted on impulse and was now filled with remorse. Whatever way he looked at it now, he was in big trouble. The nun might even be dead! She was lying very still and he couldn't find a pulse in her neck when he tried but his hands were trembling so much he couldn't be sure.

The nun had not had time to shut the door behind her: it was ajar. Eli looked through the crack and saw the figure of a man in the shadows. His eyes were rolling and saliva was running down his chin. He seemed completely unaware of Eli's presence. Eli pushed the door open a little further. His nostrils wrinkled at the smell. There were more men in the room – he reckoned about twenty. Each of them had a pallet bed but conditions seemed to be appalling. The room was totally inadequate for so many sick people and these men were more than sick. They were clearly mentally ill.

Eli walked slowly up the line, amazed that no one was taking any real notice of him or of each other for that matter. Each seemed to be absorbed in his own little world. What kind of place was this? A lunatic asylum? That's what it appeared to be but why would the Catholics be running such a place for Israelis in the heart of old Jerusalem?

The much more awful explanation that occurred to Eli was that these men had come here to earn three hundred shekels and this was the result. It was the fate that was about to befall Benny and he himself, should he be caught.

'The bastards,' he murmured.

The unconscious nun had a bunch of keys attached to the broad black leather belt that secured her plastic apron over her habit. As he knelt down beside her, Eli put the back of his hand against her cheek and was relieved to find it still warm. Please God she was still alive. Her skin was white and soft like the petals of a flower but there was a network of veins across the top of each cheek. Her glasses had been knocked off by the blow and lay broken at her side.

Eli removed the keys from her belt – all of them. There was no telling how many doors he would have to unlock before he got out of this place. He weighed them in his palm, for a moment then froze as the nun gave a low groan. He felt a mixture of relief and apprehension. If he hurried, he should still be able to lead the patients away from here before she became a problem. Besides, he had the keys. He would release the men and lock her inside; see how she liked it. He started trying keys in the door.

The men appeared not to notice the open door or perhaps didn't care. For the most part, they remained sitting on their beds, cross-legged, muttering and moaning. Eli had to cajole them into action. He practically had to push some out into the corridor and this was all taking time. Ideally, he needed the men to form an orderly line so he could lead them to freedom but this was like herding cats. The noise they made was unsettling him. Even if they were out of their minds, surely some of them should sound happy – demented perhaps, but happy. Without exception, these men seemed to be in torment. One was weeping openly; another had placed both hands on the stone wall and was scraping his fingers down it so hard that blood was oozing from his fingertips.

'Come on!' urged Eli. 'Let's go!'

The nun had recovered consciousness and

was sitting up, trying to make sense of what had happened. She blinked as she struggled to see without her glasses, searching the floor around her with the palms of her hands. When she found them, one lens was still intact. She held the broken frames to her face and saw Eli. Now she remembered, and could see what he was doing.

'No!' she cried. 'You mustn't. They are sick people!'

'They need a proper hospital,' responded Eli. 'Not a filthy prison.'

'You don't understand,' said the nun. 'We don't have the facilities: the sisters are doing their best but they have no experience of nursing such people. But it will only be temporary. The doctor says they'll recover soon and be able to go home. If you let them go now it will ruin the Father's research!'

'The police will ruin his research by putting him in jail where he belongs!' retorted Eli.

'Please try to understand,' pleaded the nun. 'The men will be none the worse for their experience. The good Father has assured us of that.'

'He's got my friend down there... I heard him cry out... They're hurting him.'

'No, the Father says it's just like going through a bad dream for a little while. He'll be fine.'

Eli looked at the men and asked, 'How

long have they been going through their bad dream?'

'Two weeks ... maybe three,' replied the nun uncertainly.

'How many have recovered?'

The nun looked away. Eli guessed none.

'The Holy Church wouldn't have approved the work if it was going to hurt anyone. Dom Ignatius brought letters from the Vatican in Rome itself.'

Eli snorted.

The nun got to her feet and tried to push past him but she was impeded by one of the men who grabbed her by the throat as she pushed past.

'Let her go!' shouted Eli as he saw the man start to apply increasing pressure to her windpipe. Eli struggled to get to her through the milling crowd and tried to prise his hands from her throat but the mans arms were like iron. The nun was going blue in the face. She had lost consciousness by the time he had finally succeeded in breaking his grip. The man simply turned away as if no longer interested, apparently oblivious to what he had done.

Things were getting out of hand. There was no time to check on the nun's condition. He pushed his way through the men to the front and ran towards the far end of the corridor, caring little whether the others would follow or not. As it happened, most of them did, following herd instinct.

He was struggling with his third choice of key when the door was suddenly opened from the other side and he was confronted by three nuns. They were wearing the same protective aprons as the dead sister and two of them were carrying buckets of water and scrubbing brushes. Shock registered on their faces when they saw Eli. Two of them tried to close the door.

There was a brief struggle before Eli forced his way out, followed by the others. The third nun had run off to raise the alarm. Eli realised that they were now nearing the entrance hall. The front door was only about twenty metres away. He glanced behind him and saw that one of the nuns who had tried to bar the door had fallen to the floor; she was being trampled on by the men who were streaming out. A plaster statue tumbled from one of the alcoves as one of the men brushed against it and broke into pieces as it hit the floor. Shards of plaster were kicked all over the place by the feet of the mob.

Eli found that he couldn't open the front door, not even after trying all the keys. The thick wood absorbed his blows like a sponge. It didn't even rattle in its hinges.

'Enough!' said a voice behind him and his blood ran cold. It was Ignatius.

Eli turned to find him standing there, accompanied by four nuns and Stroud who was now moving among the men, administering tranquilising injections.

'No!' Eli exclaimed. 'Don't let him do that to you!'

Ignatius came towards him. 'Be quiet, you moron,' he hissed. 'Haven't you caused enough trouble?'

'Look at them!' countered Eli. 'Look what you've done to them and you talk about me causing trouble! Where's Benny? What have you done to him? Some questions, you said. Look at these poor bastards! They're out of their minds!'

'It's just a temporary after-effect of the drug.'

'Temporary, my arse!'

The look Eli got in reply chilled him to the bone.

In the background he could see that some of the men had already succumbed to Stroud's medication and were docilely being led away by the nuns. 'Get away! I want out of here,' yelled Eli as Ignatius came nearer.

'Calm down,' said the priest.

'Open this door!' said Eli. He picked up a heavy piece of plaster statue that had been kicked along by the feet of the mob and raised it threateningly. 'Don't come any closer! Just open this door!'

Ignatius stopped and raised his palms. 'All right,' he said. 'Calm down.'

One of the nuns cried out and came running up to Ignatius. She had found the sister the man had tried to strangle. 'It's Sister Angelica!' she cried. 'She's been badly injured.'

Ignatius turned towards Eli. 'You?' exclaimed the priest.

'No, it was one of the men. I tried to stop him but he had the strength of ten men.'

Ignatius put his hand to his forehead in frustration. 'God, what a mess,' he exclaimed. He seemed unsure what to say or do next. The nun who had brought the news seemed to find his indecision infectious. She exchanged anxious looks with the others.

'I think you're lying,' said Ignatius, looking at Eli. He turned to the nuns. 'He's lying, sisters. He's the one who attacked Sister Angelica.'

Eli felt all eyes turn towards him. 'Nonsense. I tried to protect her! I can even point the man out to you...'

Eli's voice trailed off as Ignatius started to move towards him again. He raised the plaster he was still holding but the threat didn't work. In a desperate bid to attract outside attention, he turned and threw the plaster at a small window high up on the wall beside the door. The glass broke and he started yelling for help at the top of his voice.

Ignatius quickly overpowered him and smothered his cries for help by pushing a piece of cloth into his mouth. Stroud prepared an injection and jabbed it into his right buttock, straight through his jeans. Eli tried fighting against the feeling of tiredness that swept over him like a blanket of fog but it was a lost cause.

'We must inform the authorities, Father,' said one of the nuns, 'and call an ambulance for Sister Angelica.'

'No, Sister,' replied Ignatius firmly. 'Dr Stroud will look after her. We really must think of the consequences for our work here. We don't want the police involved.'

'But surely it's our duty...'

Ignatius held up his hand. 'No, Sister, I've decided.'

'What is to happen to him?' asked another of the nuns, clearly unhappy with the situation and looking down at Eli.

'He can help us with our work,' said the priest.

A sudden loud banging came to the front door. It was accompanied by the bell being pulled vigorously. 'Open up in there!'

Ignatius snapped out of his preoccupation and took a moment to compose himself before replying. 'We are an enclosed religious order. Please leave us in peace.'

'Open up! We heard cries for help and there's broken glass all over the place out here. I order you to open up!' There was more banging on the door. It sounded like rifle butts.

'One moment.'

Ignatius hesitated as long as he could before opening up the door to two Israeli soldiers, who entered, looking about them warily. Their automatic weapons were held on shoulder slings, barrels dipped just below the horizontal, but their fingers were on the triggers.

'We had a small disturbance,' said Ignatius, his thin lips doing their best to effect a smile. 'One of our patients became disturbed. We are a hospital and sometimes our patients do get a little excited: they are not always responsible for their actions, poor souls.'

'A hospital?' repeated one of the soldiers, taking in everything around him. 'What kind of hospital?'

Ignatius tapped his temple. 'For unfortunates,' he replied.

'It says nothing outside about this being a hospital,' said one of the other soldiers.

'It is only recently that we saw the need to take in such people,' replied Ignatius. It sounded weak and he knew it. He tried to add substance by adding, 'Our order demands that we be flexible and do what God tells us to whenever and wherever we are needed.'

The soldiers seemed less than impressed. They were more interested in Eli lying prostrate on the floor. 'What happened to him?'

'This is the patient I told you about,' said

Ignatius. 'We got his medication wrong and he went a bit wild. It took several of us to restrain him, poor man. The doctor here has given him something to calm him down. The sisters were just about to get him cleaned up and off to bed when you arrived. I apologise most sincerely for the trouble we've put you to.'

The soldier bent down to take a closer look at Eli. 'How long has he been a patient here?' he asked.

'About two months.'

The soldier nodded slowly then suddenly took a pace backwards and rattled back the bolt on his weapon. He levelled it at the priest. 'I spoke to him not more than three hours ago at the Jaffa Gate!'

'There must be some mistake,' said Ignatius calmly.

'I don't think so,' said the soldier. 'I remember him well enough. He was with another man.'

'It's a case of mistaken identity,' said Ignatius. 'If you give me a moment I will show you this man's admission papers.'

'Fetch them,' said the soldier. 'In the meantime I'm going to call my officer. Go with him,' he said to his companion.

Ignatius held up his hands and said, 'Please! Show some respect. This is a church. There's no call to defile it with guns. I'll only be a few moments. You have my word.'

'On you go,' agreed the soldier reluctantly.

'Perhaps you'll allow the doctor here to help me,' asked Ignatius. 'He knows where everything is. It will be quicker.'

The soldier nodded and waved them both away with the barrel of his gun.

Ignatius and Stroud left the room.

After five minutes the soldiers grew impatient: one went to investigate. He found an open window leading into the lane at the back of the building. There was no sign of Ignatius or Stroud. They had to wait until Eli Aswar came round, however, to find out that Benny Zur was missing too.

CHAPTER FIVE

Kansas City, USA

Macandrew looked anxiously at his watch. Karen Bliss was late and he was becoming impatient. He lifted the phone and was just about to hit the third number of her extension when a knock came to the door and he put it back down on the rest.

'Come in.'

'Sorry, I got held up,' said Karen. 'It's always the same when you're in a hurry.'

Macandrew nodded. 'All set?'

'Lead on,' said Karen, holding up the portable recorder she was carrying so that Macandrew could see that she hadn't forgotten.

They started out along the corridor.

'You're nervous,' said Karen.

'What makes you say that?'

'You checked that you had your keys twice when once would have been enough. That tells me your mind was on something else the first time.'

'God save me from psychiatrists,' said Macandrew. 'Do you analyse Jeff's behaviour like this?' he asked, referring to Karen's husband, also a doctor.

'Can't help it,' smiled Karen, 'If he's feeling guilty about anything, I'll know it before he does.'

They reached the surgical recovery suites and Macandrew checked with the head nurse about Jane Francini.

'Nurse Leiden is with her at the moment. She's showing signs of coming round.'

Macandrew and Karen entered the room and found a young black nurse trying to reason with Jane Francini and coming off second best.

'Mrs Francini, you're in hospital. You've been very ill but now you're getting better. Just take it easy, will you. Relax.'

'Stop calling me stupid names,' stormed Jane. 'I want my mother. Where is she? Why

92

isn't she here?'

Macandrew stayed in the background while Karen switched on her recorder, adjusted the levels and approached the bedside. She nodded to the nurse to step aside and took her place.

'There's obviously been some kind of mistake here,' she said soothingly.

'Yes ... a mistake. Have you seen my mother? Why isn't she here? Did she send you?'

'I'm afraid not,' said Karen. 'But maybe I could find her for you. What's your name?'

'Emma.'

'And your last name, Emma?'

'Forsyth.'

'And your address?'

'Address?'

'Where do you live, Emma?'

'Fulton Grange.

'Sorry, Emma, I'm new around here. Is that the name of a town or a house?'

'A house, of course.'

'Sounds like a big house, Emma. Is it?'

'Yes. Why are you asking me this?'

'So we can be friends. I'd like us to be friends. Wouldn't you?'

'Yes ... at least, I think so...'

'Tell me about the house. Tell me about your room.'

'Oh, it's just perfect,' said Emma, starting to relax. 'It's round, you see, and I can see just about all the garden from the windows.'

'Round?'

'It's in the tower. Father didn't want me to have it because of the stairs but I begged him so in the end he let me if I promised to be careful; the stairs are very steep. If we are friends, maybe you could go there and ask my mother to bring my doll? It's in the secret place.'

'What secret place, Emma?'

Jane paused for a moment.

'You can trust me.'

'If you promise never to tell?'

'I promise.'

'There's a big stone in the wall beneath the big window in the middle; it has a mark on it like a rose. If you push one of the petals in a special way, the stone turns and there's a secret place inside. Father showed me. He said it was to hide valuable things from robbers so I always put Lucy there when I go out so I know she'll be safe.'

Karen smiled and took hold of Jane's hand.

'Please will you go there and tell my mother to come?' asked Jane.

'Of course,' said Karen. 'But first you'll have to tell me exactly how to get there.'

'I told you. I live in Fulton Grange.'

'Yes but that's the name of your house. I need to know what town Fulton Grange is in so I can go there.'

'It's not in a town. It's in the country, silly.'

'But surely it must be near a town, Emma?'

'It's near Moscow I suppose but I don't see what that has to do with it. Everyone knows Fulton Grange.'

Karen turned and looked at Macandrew who shrugged. Up until that moment he had been worried by what he was hearing. It almost came as a relief to have something remind him that he was listening to the ramblings of a sick woman.

'So you live near Moscow, Emma,' said Karen, 'but you don't speak Russian.'

'Why should I?'

Karen smiled at the absence of logic in Jane Francini's reply. 'Tell me about Moscow, Emma. Do you go there often?'

Jane Francini opened her mouth to reply but suddenly froze as if she'd been struck dumb then she let out a loud, harsh wail of anguish.

'What is it, Emma?' asked Karen. 'What's the matter?'

Jane Francini had totally changed in demeanour. Gone was the timid little girl who wanted her mother and her doll. In her place was an angry woman who let out a stream of unintelligible words at Karen who stepped back in surprise.

Jane Francini was now completely out of sedation and obviously in great distress. She threw her head from side to side and slapped her hands angrily down on the bed.

There would be no further discussion with her.

'Aren't you going to give her something?' asked Karen who had stepped back to join Macandrew near the door.

'Her husband has forbidden us to sedate her. If I give her a shot, he'll sue the Med Center.'

Karen asked, 'Has he seen her like this?'

'No, it's only when the sedation has completely worn off that she gets like this. He's only seen the little girl character.'

'So that happens under partial sedation...' said Karen thoughtfully. 'Interesting. I've heard about this and I've read about it in the journals, but I've never actually seen it for myself,' she continued. 'Your patient seems to have developed multiple personality disorder or dissociative identity disorder as they've started calling it these days. We'll talk further when I've listened to the tape and had a think about what's going on.'

She returned to Jane's bedside and switched off her recorder. She had to move smartly out of the way to avoid a flailing arm. 'I'm sure her husband will change his mind about sedation when he sees her like this,' she said.

'What in Christ's name have you done to her?' stormed Tony Francini when he entered the room and saw the disturbed state of his

96

wife. Two nurses were trying to restrain her.

'She has been allowed to recover full consciousness on your instructions,' said Macandrew coldly. 'I strongly recommend that she be put back under sedation immediately in view of her cardiac history.'

Francini's eyes were wide and unblinking as he watched his wife rant and rave. He appeared to have been shocked into silence by the sight.

'Mr Francini, do you understand what I'm saying?'

Francini turned slowly towards Macandrew and nodded. 'I understand all right,' he said. 'You'd rather no one saw the full horror of what you've done to Janey, you butchering bastard!'

'Mr Francini, your wife's condition is the result of a brain tumour, nothing else. Now, can I sedate her?'

'Go ahead. Do what you have to to get her through the night,' said Francini with a shake of his head. His shoulders slumped forward in obvious despair. 'After that, you leave her alone. Understand? My man's flying into Kansas City in the morning.'

Macandrew nodded and told one of the nurses what he wanted given to Jane Francini. He wrote it into her treatment records.

'Oh, Janey,' murmured Francini as he stood at the foot of the bed. 'What have they done to you, honey?'

Much as he disliked the man, Macandrew felt his heart go out to him. 'I'm very sorry,' he said.

Francini's eyes hardened. 'Sorry?' he mocked. 'Oh no ... but you're gonna be, pal. Promise.' With that he left the room.

Jane's ranting subsided almost immediately the injection was given and became a murmur as she relaxed on the pillow. Her eyelids flickered briefly before she fell into a deep sleep.

Macandrew returned to his office and called Saul Klinsman. 'Did Francini say who he was bringing in?' he asked.

'Kurt Weber, from the Mayo in Rochester.'

'Jesus,' said Macandrew.

'Almost as good, I hear,' said Klinsman.

'He's going to have to sell extra harvesters for that one,' said Macandrew. 'And all for no good reason.'

'You think so?'

'I know so. She's going to have to be certified: that's what happened to all previous Hartman patients according to Carl Lessing.'

'Lessing was absolutely sure about the nature of the tumour wasn't he?' asked Klinsman. 'I have to be sure of our position. Francini is determined to apportion blame for this one and with his financial muscle he's going to be a formidable proposition.'

'Carl was certain and I don't care if Francini's got access to the Federal gold reserves. His wife had a malignant tumour and that's what caused her condition,' said Macandrew angrily. 'Bringing in the best neurosurgeon in the country isn't going to change anything apart from make the numbers in his bank account fall like leaves in October.'

'That's what I wanted to hear,' said Klinsman. 'We'll be having a meeting with Francini and Weber after he's had a chance to examine Jane tomorrow. Probably some time in the afternoon. Keep it free, will you.'

Macandrew put the phone down. He'd had more than enough for one day. He told Reception he was going home.

Macandrew's landlord was still away and the house was completely silent as he looked out of his room window and noticed for the first time what a beautiful day it had been. The sun was going down and the western sky had become a deep red. The sky directly above however, was still unbroken blue and marked only by a thin vapour trail from a jetliner heading east. It was too high to be heard.

He wished he could rid himself of the uneasy feeling that the Francini case had left him with but it persisted. The fact that someone thought he was incompetent bothered him; even if it happened to be a guy like Francini. But he could see no easy

99

way round the problem. He poured himself a large drink, put Miles Davis on the stereo and turned it up a little louder than usual.

Saul Klinsman called at four the following afternoon to say that Weber had finished his examination of Jane Francini and her medical records and case notes. Would Macandrew care to join them in his office? Macandrew was surprised to find not three men in the room but four. Klinsman introduced him to the two he didn't know.

Weber was pretty much as he expected, expensively dressed in a light grey suit, pale lavender shirt and deep purple tie which set off his tan and swept-back silver hair to advantage. His handshake was firm and his smile a tribute to the dentists' art. His voice had the practised modulation of a TV news anchorman.

The second man, Joel Kirschbaum, was introduced as Francini's attorney. He was slim and dark and avoided eye contact. It was difficult to put an age on him because of premature baldness and a naturally sallow complexion but if Francini had retained him it was odds on that he was both experienced and good. His handshake, however, was limp and wet.

'Well, Doctor, what did you conclude?' Klinsman asked Weber as they all sat down. He was doing his best to appear relaxed.

'Mrs Francini is a very disturbed lady,' replied Weber. He turned to her husband. 'Frankly, Mr Francini, I would be offering you false hope if I were to suggest to you that I could do anything about her condition. I've examined the scans and the case notes and the path lab's report and I have to agree with the conclusions of the Kansas University Medical Center that Mrs Francini is suffering brain damage brought on by an aggressive, malignant tumour, which they successfully and skilfully removed. I'm sorry.'

Macandrew felt the tension in his shoulders relax.

'But has it been confirmed beyond all doubt that Mrs Francini's current condition is due to the tumour?' asked Kirschbaum. He kept his eyes on the desk in front of him as if totally absorbed by the pencil he was turning end over end. The fact that he seemed to avoid looking at anyone directly made it difficult to know who the question was aimed at.

Weber looked uncomfortable when he concluded that it was aimed at him. He said, 'I suppose not, in the strict sense that the conclusive evidence in this case is pathological and I haven't seen it personally...'

'So, just for the sake of argument, it is conceivable that Mrs Francini's condition may have been caused by the *removal* of the tumour rather than the tumour itself? I mean, it's not beyond the bounds of possibility?'

'Now just a minute...' interrupted Klinsman.

'Well, Doctor?'

'I have seen nothing at all to suggest that,' replied Weber.

'But, as you say, you haven't actually examined the tumour yourself?'

'Well, no,' agreed Weber.

'Our chief of neuropathology made the diagnosis,' Klinsman interrupted again. 'He is a very experienced man. Just what are you suggesting, Mr Kirschbaum?'

'Collusion,' interrupted Francini, cottoning on to Kirschbaum's line of questioning. 'It's a stitch-up. They're covering each other's ass.'

There was silence in the room for a few electric moments while everyone wondered if they had heard correctly. Francini repeated it. 'Collusion,' he said. 'The bastards have fitted it up between them.'

Macandrew gripped the sides of his chair until his knuckles showed white. Klinsman shot him a warning glance. Kirschbaum tried to warn his client not to say any more. Klinsman intervened with, 'Counsellor, my colleague and I understand the anguish Mr Francini feels over his wife's condition but he is going too far. If he persists in making such scurrilous accusations we will have to consider legal action ourselves.'

'You are right, Doctor,' said Kirschbaum. 'My client is under a great deal of stress and I am sure he did not mean to suggest what he appeared to.'

Francini snorted.

'It appears to me,' said Weber, 'that this whole thing could be cleared up quickly and scientifically by an *independent* analysis of the tumour that was removed from Mrs Francini.'

'How would they know it came from Janey?' snarled Francini.

'The lab could establish that too,' said Weber. 'They could run DNA tests on both the patient and the tumour.'

There was an uneasy silence for a few moments before Klinsman took the initiative. 'Perhaps this would be the way out of our dilemma, gentlemen?' he said. 'Clear away any lingering doubts?'

'Fine by me,' said Macandrew.

Kirschbaum and finally Francini himself nodded in agreement.

'What will happen to Janey?' asked Francini, his eyes looking down at the floor.

'I suggest that we make moves to have your wife moved to Farley Ridge Sanatorium, Mr Francini,' said Klinsman quietly.

'The funny farm,' said Francini.

'Medical advances are being made every

day, Mr Francini,' said Weber kindly. 'You shouldn't give up hope.'

Francini got up and left the room. Kirschbaum said, 'Can we agree on arrangements for the tumour analysis?'

'Of course,' said Klinsman. 'I'm sure Doctor Lessing will be happy to comply with whatever you have in mind.'

Kirschbaum turned to Weber and asked, 'Perhaps the lab at the Mayo Clinic would be prepared to carry out the analysis, Doctor?'

Weber said, 'As long as these gentlemen have no objection.'

'Of course not,' said Klinsman.

Macandrew nodded his agreement.

'Would you like to speak to Dr Lessing before you go?' Klinsman asked Weber.

Weber shook his head. 'I think not. Pathology isn't exactly my field. I'll have our pathologist call yours and they can work out the details between them.'

'Then that would appear to be it,' said Klinsman.

Weber looked at his watch. 'If I get a move on, there's a chance I can get back to Rochester tonight.'

'I'll go find my client,' said Kirschbaum.

Macandrew was left alone with Klinsman. He accepted the whisky that was handed to him and said dryly, 'That was a bundle of laughs.'

'It'll all be over when the Mayo lab confirms the diagnosis,' said Klinsman. 'Put it behind you, Mac.'

'Something tells me Francini won't lie down. He's determined to blame me whatever he hears. He hates me; I can see it in his eyes.'

'Some people are like that,' said Klinsman. 'Come to think of it, a lot of people are like that. They need someone to blame. There's no such thing as fate or an accident. Someone always has to be at fault and they have to be hunted down and punished. It becomes an obsession with them. You see people screaming their joy outside the courthouse after a guilty verdict's announced. They've lost their kid or their wife and they're jumping up and down and cracking open champagne because some bastard is going down for it. Strange.'

'Maybe I'll talk some more to Karen Bliss.'

Klinsman asked, 'What did she think of Jane?'

'She was thinking along the lines of multiple personality disorder – or whatever the fancy new name is for it these days – but I haven't had a real chance to talk to her about it yet.' He looked at his watch. 'Too late now, maybe tomorrow.'

There was a message on his answering machine when Macandrew got back to his own office. Karen had called at four-thirty. If he got back before six, he should ring her; if not, he should call in the morning. It was a quarter to seven. Macandrew looked at his diary for the following day; there was no operation scheduled till the day after but he did have to see the patient and familiarise himself with the case notes. There was a clinical meeting pencilled in for two in the afternoon and a seminar he wanted to go to at four-thirty. He wondered if Karen would be free for lunch. He called her extension and left a message on her machine, just in case he should miss her in the morning. He suggested they meet at noon.

Macandrew got Karen's return message when he returned to his office next morning after examining his surgical case. Karen was free for lunch so he called an Italian restaurant down on the Plaza and made a reservation for twelve-fifteen.

'Maybe our answering machines should be having lunch,' said Karen as they drove down to the Plaza.

'I think mine is going steady with the administration people,' said Macandrew. 'I get reminders every day about forms I should have completed and returned but didn't.'

'Thank God I'm not the only one.'

The restaurant was just over half full. They

were shown to a table in a booth well away from the door and left to consider the menu beneath Italian travel posters on the walls and fishing nets suspended from the ceiling. The nets only served to remind Macandrew how depressingly far the Midwest was from the sea. The sea was what he missed most of all. Not being able to drive down to the coast was a big minus.

'Did you get permission to sedate Jane Francini?' asked Karen.

'Her husband gave it almost as soon as he saw her.' Macandrew told her about his subsequent meeting with Weber and Francini's attorney.

Karen shook her head in sympathy and said, 'Heavy stuff. Sometimes the idea of being a country doctor seems very attractive.'

'It certainly was last night,' agreed Macandrew. He took a sip of iced water and asked, 'What did you think of the Francini tapes?'

'Complicated. Little Emma threw me; she seemed so real. I started out thinking multiple personality disorder but now I'm not so sure...'

'What's the problem?'

'She never seems to be herself,' said Karen. 'That particular personality seems to have gone completely missing.'

'I suppose that's the saddest thing,' said Macandrew.

'There are lots of recorded instances of patients who've sustained head injuries in car accidents undergoing a personality change. They make what appears to be a good recovery as far as the nursing and medical staff are concerned, but once they're home, their family and people who know them start complaining about big changes in the way they behave. The words "different people" keep cropping up.'

'That's more or less what Tony Francini said,' said Macandrew. 'He said Janey was a different person. She looked like Janey but she wasn't...'

Karen nodded. 'Not too much is known about this but it's been recorded in patients who've had strokes. It's also been the basis of several lawsuits. Big insurance claims for changes of personality. Previous nice guy becomes selfish monster, that sort of thing.'

'But this is more than a change of personality *trait*,' said Macandrew. 'Jane Francini becomes an entirely different person – maybe several.'

'But it is interesting that she's always Emma when she starts to come out of sedation,' said Karen.

Macandrew nodded. 'It's only when she regains full consciousness that she becomes totally confused.'

'I tried working on the confused bits from the tapes I made but I'm really not sure what's going on. She's obviously suffering but the strange thing was that she didn't *look* deranged at any point.'

'That's exactly what I thought when I saw her like that for the first time,' said Macandrew. 'She *sounded* deranged but didn't look it. It was kind of spooky, almost as if she thought *I* was the one with the problem.'

'I suppose that might fit with multiple personality disorder. Believe it or not, Carl Jung's own cousin suffered from it. She was in reality a shy fifteen-year-old girl of only mediocre intelligence, hesitant and unsophisticated. Quite suddenly and without warning she would change into a smooth, assured, educated lady who spoke good, literary German instead of the rough Swiss dialect she normally spoke. This is often a feature in reports of this sort of case. The foreign personality is that of a much stronger character altogether than the patient.

'Jane Francini is normally a quiet, reserved lady,' said Macandrew.

'The character she becomes when she's not sedated is certainly not,' said Karen. 'But there again, when she is under partial sedation, she's a little girl from Moscow who doesn't speak Russian...'

Macandrew shook his head. 'If only one of her personalities could be Jane.'

'Mac, I know you'd like me to tell you that her condition might be treatable and, with time, she'll get better but I can't. I'd dearly like to but I can't. I think she'll have to be certified and sent out to Farley Ridge.'

CHAPTER SIX

Two days later Jane Francini was transferred to Farley Ridge Sanatorium: Macandrew was there to see her off. He knew there was a danger that his presence might be construed by some as an admission of guilt but, despite this, he wanted to be there. He'd liked her as a person in their talks before the operation and, as she had pointed out, they were 'fellow Scots'.

Jane was lightly sedated and appeared comfortable in her Emma persona. Her eyes reflected bemusement at what was going on around her but nothing like the distress she showed when sedation was completely withdrawn. She continued to ask about her mother and the staff continued to assure her that she would be along presently as they wheeled her out of the Med Center and lifted her into the back of the waiting ambulance.

'Goodbye, Emma,' said Macandrew as she passed by.

Jane turned her head towards him and

Macandrew felt a hollow in his stomach. The look in Jane Francini's eyes was perfectly in tune with her Emma character. He was looking into the clear, intelligent, innocent eyes of an eight-year-old girl who wasn't at all sure what was going on. The attendants closed up the back of the ambulance and she was gone.

Things gradually returned to normal over the course of the following week although the Francini case was never far from Macandrew's mind. He had resolved to find out as much as he could about Hartman's tumours – something which involved him spending a good deal of time in the medical library and which proved easier said than done because of a dearth of published information. There was no textbook material available on the subject: what information there was had to be gleaned from medical journals and research papers.

Starting with a short list of references from Carl Lessing, Macandrew dug out what he could in the Med Center library and made photocopies of relevant articles. There were a number of references to journals that the Med Center did not take so he asked the librarian to put out an inter-library request for them. They arrived in due course and he was able to complete a file – albeit a painfully thin one – on the subject.

Most of the published material comprised straightforward case reports on patients who had been diagnosed as suffering from the condition: these did not tell him anything new. The condition was so rare that the reports had been published for that reason alone. There was no instance of anyone ever having made a full recovery but, as Carl Lessing had pointed out, none had died from the condition either. They had survived surgical removal of the tumour, only to be left confused and facing life in a mental institution for the remainder of their days.

There were, however, a number of recent research papers which proved interesting. They originated from a laboratory in the medical school at the University of Edinburgh in Scotland. A Dr John Burnett emerged as principal investigator. He was sole author on the earlier work but appeared to have been joined later by Doctors Ashok Mukherjee and Simone Robin. Between them, these three had published several papers on the chemical changes in the brain associated with Hartman's tumours and had managed to identify an unusual acidic substance secreted by them. It was this substance that had been responsible for the colour change in the staining reaction of the tissue samples in the path lab and which had alerted Carl Lessing to the possibility of a Hartman's tumour.

As a medic rather than a scientist, Macandrew found the science hard going but the gist of the research approach seemed to be centred on finding a way to counteract the effects of the secretion on adjacent cerebral tissue. If this could be done then the damaging effects of the tumour might be limited. Using material obtained at autopsy, the researchers had identified a bank of cells in the normal brain that the Hartman's chemical appeared to affect and had subsequently gone on to describe a protein secreted by these cells that seemed to be its specific target.

By the time he had read the last of the papers, Macandrew was quite excited by their findings. If they had really identified the target protein in the normal brain then surely in this day and age it should be possible to synthesise the protein *in vitro* and replace it in brain-damaged patients?

Macandrew looked at the date on the last paper and was disappointed to find that it was over two and a half years old. He considered possible reasons for this – the most likely and most depressing being failure to synthesise the protein in the lab. But was the team still trying? Or had research on the subject stopped completely? There was also the very real possibility that funding had been withdrawn from the project. Competition for research funding was always fierce, and Hartman's tumours were such a rare condition that that might militate against support.

Macandrew considered contacting the university, but then it occurred to him that there might be a quicker way. He could use the Med Center's computer to find out if anything at all had been published by any of the three named scientists in the last three years. To survive in research, it was essential to publish. Any researcher who had failed to publish anything in three years would be in serious career trouble.

It was a system that could be terribly unfair at times and also led to the scientific journals being inundated with less than compelling work, but its best defence was that there wasn't a better way. Peer review did much to screen out the dross but, despite this, every scientific journal, with perhaps the exception of the top two or three, carried a large proportion of 'i' dotting and 't' crossing. Career fodder.

Macandrew tried entering John Burnett's name first and asked for a full list of his publications. This wasn't as straightforward as he'd hoped because there was more than one John Burnett in the database, and he had to sort though them before establishing that it was the John Burnett who worked in cell biology at Edinburgh University that he was interested in.

The publication list came up on the screen

and Macandrew read through an impressive record, finishing with the three-year-old paper in cell biology he'd just read. John Burnett had not published anything at all in the interim, not even a review – the traditional stop-gap of senior scientists when times were tough and ideas scarce.

Macandrew stared at the screen and wondered if Burnett had retired. He didn't know anything about the man. It was conceivable that he had reached retirement age and was now growing roses by the sea. If that were the case, he might be able to confirm this by judging his age from his publication list. He looked back to the beginning of the list and found two papers that were cross-referenced to Burnett's doctoral thesis. He noted the date and made a mental calculation. Assuming Burnett had had a conventional academic background, with four years for an honours degree followed by three or four more for his doctorate, he reckoned that John Burnett would be in his mid- to late thirties. A bit young for roses.

He drummed his fingers lightly on the desk while he tried to think of alternative possibilities. The librarian shot him a disapproving look and he stopped with a half-apologetic smile. Librarians could be so intimidating. He instigated a new search and entered Ashok Mukherjee's name. This produced the work he'd published jointly with John Burnett and nothing else.

The only Simone Robin in the database was listed as being on the staff of the Institut Jacques Monod at the Seventh University of Paris, France, but her publication list immediately told Macandrew that she was the lady he was looking for. He found the papers that she had published with John Burnett in Edinburgh and then four more, submitted from the French institute in the last three years but in a different area of research. He calculated that Simone Robin had left the University of Edinburgh around the time Burnett had stopped working on Hartman's tumours. She had obviously returned to France and was now working on something else entirely.

The depressing thing from Macandrew's point of view was that, as far as he could tell, Burnett's team had been the only one in the world carrying out research on Hartman's brain damage. If they had given up then no one was doing it. He copied down details of addresses and phone numbers from the on-screen information and logged off. He might not pursue things any further but then again, he just might. It would be interesting to find out why such promising work had suddenly stopped.

Two days later, Macandrew was in the scrub room after completing a long operation when a nurse relayed the information that Saul Klinsman wanted to see him. He dried himself quickly and slipped on some fresh surgical greens before hurrying up to Klinsman's office. Carl Lessing was sitting there. Neither he nor Klinsman were smiling.

'What's wrong?'

'You're not going to like this, Mac,' said Klinsman.

'Like what?'

Lessing was looking embarrassed. He said, 'Christ, Mac, I'm sorry, I don't know exactly how it happened and when I find the guy responsible I'm going to cut off his...'

'What's ... happened? What's going on?' asked Macandrew. He sensed big trouble and looked to Klinsman for answers.

Klinsman responded by looking to Lessing. Lessing said, 'The plain fact of the matter is that we can't provide the Mayo Clinic with tumour tissue taken from Jane Francini.'

'Why the hell not?'

'We no longer have it. Someone chucked it.'

Macandrew looked at Klinsman as if pleading to be told that this couldn't be true. No reassurance was forthcoming.

Macandrew found it almost impossible to speak for a few moments then he said, 'Christ, I can't believe I'm hearing this.'

'One of the technicians discarded the Francini tumour by mistake. I'm sorry, Mac.'

Macandrew rubbed his forehead nervously. 'Can't you recover it?' he asked.

Lessing shook his head and said, 'It had already gone to the incinerator before we realised what had happened.'

'Jesus!' said Macandrew, sinking down into a chair. 'So we can't prove that Jane Francini ever had a malignant tumour?'

'That's about it,' agreed Klinsman.

Macandrew sank down into a chair. 'Francini is going to be more convinced than ever that I butchered his wife.'

'Christ, I just don't know what to say,' said Lessing.

Macandrew just shook his head. 'What a fucking mess,' he whispered.

Klinsman put his elbows on his desk and leant forward. He said, 'In the final analysis, Mac, what Francini thinks, doesn't matter. It's facts that matter. We all know that Jane Francini's condition was caused by a malignant brain tumour and that's the important thing. You are a good surgeon, one of the best and you did your best for the Francini woman. Nothing that happened subsequently was your fault. It's a real bummer about the Mayo not being able to rubber stamp our pathology report but shit happens and we just have to accept that and get on with it … whatever they throw at us now.'

Macandrew felt sick. He nodded absently and got up. 'If you'll excuse me,' he said and left the room.

With every step along the corridor, Macandrew wanted to slam his fist into the wall. The pain would be a welcome relief from what was going on inside his head. Tony Francini was going to go through the rest of his life believing that he had brain-damaged his wife and then colluded with the path lab in a cover up of his mistake. The story would do the rounds. Lots of families had tales to tell about incompetent medical practitioners and how they had blighted the life of one of their own. These stories were handed down through the generations. He himself was now going to feature in that list. 'Fuck!' he raged as the elevator descended. 'Fuck, fuck, fuck.'

He was finding the thought unbearable. The theatre nurse, Lucy Long, was waiting to get in as Macandrew stepped out of the elevator.

'Hi, Mac. How's it going?' she asked.

Macandrew looked at her as if she was an alien from a different planet. He couldn't say anything.

'Excuse me,' murmured the nurse under her breath.

Macandrew sat alone in his apartment for nearly an hour without doing anything other than stare out at the sky. He could not believe that fate had been so cruel, or maybe it wasn't fate, he reasoned. What kind of half-assed operation was Lessing running down there in the path lab anyway?

It didn't help his state of mind to realise he was doing exactly what Tony Francini had been doing: looking for someone to blame. In his heart he knew well that Carl Lessing was an excellent pathologist and that his lab was extremely well run and normally one hundred per cent reliable. He also knew that Saul Klinsman had been right to point out that these things happened. It just didn't help to believe any of that right now.

A knock came to his door a little after seven-thirty and Macandrew opened it to find Mort Jackson, his landlord, standing there.

'You haven't forgotten, have you?' asked Jackson.

'Forgotten?' repeated Macandrew.

'You were coming down this evening to look at the slides Ginny and I took up in Michigan.'

Macandrew had completely forgotten but even in his current mental state, he didn't want to hurt Mort's feelings. If only he had remembered earlier he might have been able to come up with a plausible excuse for postponing it. As it was, he had to insist that he hadn't forgotten and would be down in a few minutes.

'I'll have Ginny pour a glass of her elder-

120

flower for you,' said Mort as he disappeared back down the stairs.

'Jesus,' whispered Macandrew under his breath. It was going to take a lot more than Ginny's homemade wine to take the edge off reality this evening. He poured himself a large whisky and threw it down his throat before going downstairs to be welcomed by Mort and Ginny.

Ginny was everyone's idea of what a grandmother should look like. She was plump, smiling and had a magnificent head of pure white hair. She had prepared a large plate of sandwiches and handed Macandrew a glass of wine as he sat down. Mort was about the same height as Ginny but he was thin and stooped and had a complexion the colour of leather from a lifetime spent in the open air as a lineman for the phone company. He held his left arm at an awkward angle, the legacy of an accident at work – the one which had ultimately forced him to retire.

Macandrew did his best to make light conversation while Mort set up the projector. It was easy to feed Ginny the right questions. She loved talking about her family. The lights finally went down and the slides faithfully recorded the Jacksons' visit to their daughter up in Michigan. Macandrew did his best to concentrate on what appeared on the screen rather than what was in his head

121

but he was fighting a losing battle. The Francini case was winning.

He was almost relieved when his pager went off and gave him an excuse to leave the room although this was almost immediately replaced by concern as he ran upstairs. His pager shouldn't have gone off. He wasn't on call this evening and he'd had a fair bit to drink. He wasn't drunk but he certainly wasn't fit for surgery.

'Dr Klinsman for you,' said the hospital operator.

'Mac? I've just had Kurt Weber on the phone. Carl Lessing called him about the missing tissue and he felt obliged to advise Francini's attorney of the situation.'

'And?'

'Kirschbaum asked if he would be willing to stand up in court and testify that Jane Francini's condition could have been caused by surgical malpractice.'

'And?' asked Macandrew, feeling as if he was pulling the pin from a grenade a second time.

'Weber told him that he hated the idea but, in the circumstances, he'd have to say it was theoretically possible,' said Klinsman. 'Weber just wanted us to know that it's nothing personal and he doesn't believe for a moment that that's what happened.'

'Nice of him.'

'He really doesn't have much choice in the

matter,' said Klinsman.

'Right,' said Macandrew.

'Weber says he'll point that out if he gets the chance.'

'Thanks for letting me know.'

'Least I could do,' replied Klinsman.

Macandrew put the phone down and went downstairs to rejoin the Jacksons. He would sit through the remainder of their holiday slides on autopilot.

'Everything all right, Mac?' asked Ginny as he slipped back into the room.

'Just fine, Ginny. Sorry about that.'

'This is us up at Mill Glade,' announced Mon as the next slide came up. 'That's Charlotte's friend, Sandy with us there and that's her dog, Rupert.'

'Rufus,' corrected Ginny.

'Sorry, Rufus,' conceded Mort.

'And this is us up near Jansen Creek: real pretty country up there.'

'Looks it,' agreed Macandrew, suddenly realizing that a comment was called for.

'More wine, Mac?' asked Ginny in a whisper.

'Please,' replied Macandrew.

Ginny moved across the room to the table in front of the window; she did it in a crouch to avoid the projector beam but totally without success as her shadow filled the screen.

'This was a Sasquwatch we saw while we were up there,' joked Mort, winking at

Macandrew when he saw that Ginny didn't realise she was the butt of the joke.

'And this is us with Clint, Daisy and Charlotte on the day we went down to the county fair...'

CRASH! The front window of the room exploded in a million shards of glass and Ginny reeled backwards with blood streaming down her face to fall on the floor. The glass of wine she had been pouring for Macandrew flew from her grasp and splashed across the screen.

'What the...' exclaimed Mon. 'Ginny! Ginny!'

Macandrew beat him in the race to get to Ginny and was already assessing the damage. 'Get me a clean towel, Mort,' he said. 'Quick as you can.'

'Is she gonna be all right?' asked Mort as he handed over the cloth and hovered over Macandrew and the unconscious Ginny.

Macandrew cleared the blood away from Ginny's face and stemmed the flow from the major cuts. Something had come through the window and hit Ginny on the forehead, something heavy. It had knocked her out but she would be all right. He said so to Mort.

'Thank God,' exclaimed Mort. 'What the hell was it?'

Mort started hunting round the room as the hollow in Macandrew's stomach started to grow.

'Jesus H Christ!' exclaimed Mort. He had found something and was picking it up gingerly to avoid the broken glass. 'What do you make of this?' he asked.

Macandrew saw what Mon was holding: it was a butcher's cleaver.

'It was a message, Mort,' he said in a dazed monotone, 'for me.'

'The crazy bastard,' said Saul Klinsman when Macandrew told him what had happened. 'How is Mrs Jackson?'

'She's got a real sore head and quite a few cuts, one that required stitching, but she'll be OK.'

'You called the cops?' asked Klinsman.

'No, I didn't,' confessed Macandrew. 'I persuaded the Jacksons not to either.'

Klinsman looked shocked. 'Why not?'

'I'm not absolutely sure myself,' said Macandrew. 'It was obvious that the cleaver was meant for me and we both know where it came from. I got to thinking that Francini had probably gone out and gotten hammered after what Weber had told him about the missing tumour tissue. It must have been eating away at him and he had to make his point somehow. It was probably something he did on the spur of the moment. He got my address from somewhere – not realising that I shared the place with the Jacksons – and came over to vent his anger.

125

I'm counting on this being a one-off thing.'

'That's charitable of you,' said Klinsman.

'Not entirely,' confessed Macandrew. 'If I am to be perfectly honest I worked out that if I or the Jacksons had called the police and Francini was arrested, he would have enjoyed his day in court, telling the world exactly why he did it.'

'Do you think he was bright enough to have planned it that way?'

'I wasn't betting against it.'

A week passed without further incident, then Carl Lessing phoned. 'I've been a bit of an idiot,' confessed Lessing.

'How so?'

'I still have the slides.'

'The slides?' repeated Macandrew, unaware of what Lessing was getting at.

'Mrs Francini's slides. The microscope preps that were made for diagnosis. The Mayo could use *them* for verification of a malignant tumour!'

'Are you serious?' exclaimed Macandrew. 'Would that be good enough?'

'Sure,' said Lessing. 'I just wish I had thought of it sooner. The two slides I used for the actual diagnosis were discarded but *four* were made up by the technicians from the microtome sections. I still have the unused two.'

'But surely Francini could argue that the

slides weren't prepared from Jane's tumour material?'

'I asked the guys down at forensics about that. They assure me that DNA fingerprinting will be possible from the material on the slides. We just have to get a cell sample from Jane Francini for comparison and it can be shown conclusively that the tumour tissue came from her – as indeed it did.'

'Hallelujah,' said Macandrew.

'I'm sorry, Mac, I should have thought of this earlier,' said Lessing. 'I'll get straight onto the Mayo.'

Macandrew felt better than he had done for ages – in fact, since the day of the Francini operation. The phone rang and his good humour showed in his voice. 'You sound happy,' said Karen Bliss.

Macandrew told her the good news.

'Mac, that's great,' said Karen. 'I was actually calling to ask if you'd like to come over to dinner with Jeff and me tonight but now we could make it a celebration?'

'I'll bring champagne.'

As he drove out of Cherry and turned right to head south to Mission Hills, Macandrew noticed a BMW saloon with the 'Show Me' plates of Missouri take off from the kerb and settle in behind him. He didn't think anything of it until it registered that it was still there some three miles further on. He had left home in plenty of time and had consequently not been driving fast. The BMW had had ample opportunity to pass. It had tinted glass screens but Macandrew could see that there were two men in the front. He tried persuading himself that thinking he was being followed was just too melodramatic but it didn't stop him slowing down for a while and then speeding up to see if he could lose his tail. The BMW stayed with him. It was still there when he turned off into the street where Karen lived.

As he slowed on nearing her apartment block, it suddenly speeded up and swerved in front, causing him to brake violently and mount the sidewalk. Almost before he knew it, the two men had jumped from the car in front and were running towards him. They were big and dressed in jeans and plaid shirts.

'What the hell do you think you're doing?' demanded Macandrew, getting out the car. He was unprepared for the punch that seemed to come from nowhere and dropped him to his knees. He had barely time to taste the blood in his mouth before a boot swung into his stomach and the wind was knocked out of him. Up until that point neither of his assailants had spoken, now he heard one say to the other, 'Turn him over.'

Through a haze of pain Macandrew felt himself being rolled over on to his face before he took another vicious blow to the side of the head. He was dragged forward by the hands and left face down by the open door of his car. He didn't have the strength to turn his head to see if his attackers had gone but he heard their car start up.

Slowly, he reached out and gripped the door sill of his own car with both hands to start pulling himself up. Unknown to him, he was supposed to do this. It was part of the plan. Only one of the men had returned to the BMW, the other had been standing behind him, waiting for this to happen. As Macandrew gripped the door sill, the man slammed the door shut.

Pain flooded through Macandrew's head like a nuclear explosion. The bones in his hands broke like matchsticks and through his agony he heard a man's voice rasp, 'You won't be fuckin' around with no one else's wife from now on.'

CHAPTER SEVEN

Macandrew curled up into a ball on the road and held his hands to his body. He was vaguely aware of the BMW roaring off but his mind was being overwhelmed by successive waves of pain that shot up through his arms and burst like starshells inside his head. Someone, somewhere, was asking what all the noise had been about. Another demanded that an ambulance be called. Yet someone else was telling neighbours not to get involved.

No one approached him directly. This was Kansas City suburbia where the real world never came to call. Drama was the stuff of television, always held at a comfortable distance. But now there was an injured man lying in the street, beside an empty car with its driver's door swung open.

Macandrew managed to prop himself up a little using his elbows but the pain in his hands was so bad that he feared he might pass out. His vision was being blurred by waves of red mist. 'Can somebody help me, please?' he croaked.

There was no response.

'Is anyone there?'

From a distance, a man asked cautiously, 'What's your problem, buddy?'

'My hands are bust, I need help.'

'How'd that happen then?' asked the voice.

Macandrew added despair to his agony. He took a succession of deep breaths. 'Would you please get Dr Karen Bliss for me. She lives in apartment 32, number thirty-seven.'

'Karen Bliss.'

'Yes, Dr Karen Bliss. Tell her it's John Macandrew.'

'Macandrew,' repeated the man without expression.

Macandrew could feel tears of frustration well up in his eyes. Just how far back on the evolutionary trail was this bozo stranded? A few base-pairs less and he'd be a palm tree and where the fuck were all the other people? Had they all gone back indoors? 'Jesus,' he murmured. 'Land of the free ... home of the brave...'

'Number thirty-seven. Right?'

'Jesus.'

Macandrew was losing strength fast. The terrible pain had sapped every ounce of energy from him and he felt unconsciousness beckon, promising him sleep and blessed release from the pain. His head lolled against the side of his car, and then he heard high heels clicking towards him.

'God Almighty, Mac, what happened?' asked Karen Bliss.

'Two guys ... they jumped me ... jammed my hands in the car door.'

Karen made to examine his hands but the mere thought of it made him cry out.

'OK, Mac, relax. I'll drive you to the Med Center. It'll be quicker than calling an ambulance. I'll just get Jeff.'

Macandrew passed out on the journey.

When he came round, Saul Klinsman was in the room. He was talking to a nurse but

131

stopped when he saw that he was awake. 'You're back with us,' he said.

The fuzzy feeling in Macandrew's head told him that he had been given a powerful analgesic but he had no trouble remembering what had happened. He looked down at his hands and saw that they were bandaged. 'How bad?' he asked.

Klinsman came and sat down beside him. He said, 'I'm not going to bullshit you, Mac; they're a mess. For a plumber they'd be a mess; for a mailman, they'd be a mess; for a surgeon ... they could be a serious mess.'

The comment made Macandrew attempt to flex his fingers. He was rewarded by needles shooting up through his arms. He grimaced and asked, 'A career-ending mess?'

Klinsman shrugged his shoulders. 'Frankly, I don't know. It's too soon to say. Either way you're going to need a bunch of surgery on them.'

'Thanks for levelling with me,' said Macandrew.

'Did you see the bastards who did this?'

'Sure but they were just the hired hands. We both know who was behind it.'

'That little bastard Francini; the cops have got to nail him for this.'

'Leave it be, Saul,' said Macandrew. 'It would do the Med Center nothing but harm. Francini is a powerful man. Presented as a story of good-old-boys beating up on

132

the incompetent surgeon who ruined his wife's life just might make him a hero in this man's town.'

'But it wasn't like that,' protested Klinsman.

'It's like what the papers will make it like, Saul. Francini buys a lot of advertising space.'

'Get some rest,' said Klinsman. 'We'll talk when you're feeling better.'

Extensive surgery to Macandrew's hands was carried out by the end of the week. A friend and ex-colleague of Saul Klinsman – who had called him in from St Louis – carried out the work in one long session. 'The best there is,' was how Klinsman described Paul Gonsalves. When the operation was over and Macandrew was in recovery, Gonsalves and Klinsman came to see him.

'Paul has some good news for you,' announced Klinsman.

Gonsalves, a handsome Hispanic man in his late forties with an air of calm confidence about him and a confident smile, said, 'The damage wasn't as great as we feared. The operation went well.'

Macandrew closed his eyes and savoured the moment. He almost passed out when the tide of relief in him betrayed the amount of stress he'd been under. There was nothing in the world he would rather have heard but now he feared that the next word would be 'but'.

'But ... we'll still have to wait and see,' added Gonsalves.

'Too soon for a bottom line?'

'They were all clean breaks. They should knit well with no need for splints and pins. I think there's a better than even chance of you operating again.'

Macandrew smiled. 'I think I can safely say that you have made my day, Doctor.'

'And now, Saul here is going to make mine,' said Gonsalves with a smile. 'He promised me the biggest steak in Kansas City when I'd finished.'

'I think it should be me paying,' said Macandrew.

'Maybe I'll send you the tab,' said Klinsman. 'Have you had any more thoughts about having Francini charged?'

Macandrew shook his head. It was a slight shake, designed to obscure whether he meant that he hadn't had any more thoughts or whether he did not intend to pursue the matter. Klinsman took nothing from it and said, 'You have to consider your future, Mac. If, God forbid, things don't turn out as we all hope, a lawsuit might help ... financially, I mean.'

'I hear what you're saying,' said Macandrew. 'But I still think it might be difficult.'

'Not as difficult as it was,' said Klinsman.

'How so?'

'Carl Lessing called me an hour ago. The Mayo Clinic confirmed the diagnosis of malignant tumour and that the tissue did indeed come from Jane Francini.'

Macandrew's relief felt bitter-sweet.

As the two surgeons left, he pondered on what might have been if only Lessing had thought of the slide material earlier. He looked down at his bandaged hands and screwed his eyes tight shut. Spilt milk, Macandrew. Move on.

The weeks passed and Macandrew's hands healed to the point where he could use them again – albeit for not too demanding purposes. He found himself growing restless. He had spent most of his time since coming out of hospital reading journals or walking or listening to music and now the attraction was beginning to wear thin. Time was hanging heavy on his hands and long periods of inactivity were beginning to play mind games with him.

At first, he had seen himself simply as a surgeon on sick leave and that was all right; it was an easy role to play. None of life's domestic parameters needed changing; everything was simply on hold. But lately, he had begun to question whether this was really so. He didn't know for sure how complete his recovery would be so he might not actually be a surgeon any more. He might really be unemployed and pounding the streets of Kansas City like the bums he came across while he believed he was just out walking.

Once the thought had crept into his head, nothing looked quite the same any more. The fall was over. They were into November and the weather had turned cold. The sidewalks seemed harder, the people more alien, even the smell of barbecue sauce – which was everywhere in KC – was beginning to make him feel nauseous and the thought of a long hard winter ahead was not a happy prospect.

He confided these feelings to Karen Bliss who, with her husband, had been kindness itself, having him over to dinner at least once a week and constantly checking up on him.

'What you need is a vacation, Mac,' she insisted. 'You are talking garbage. Of course you'll operate again.'

Macandrew smiled. He liked Karen's positive approach to life. It used to be his. 'If you say so.'

'I do say so,' insisted Karen. 'You are going to be as good as you ever were and even if you should turn out only to be half as good, you'll still be good enough.'

Macandrew smiled at Karen going over the top but he appreciated it.

'Karen's right,' said Jeff. 'It'll do you good

to get away from KC for a while. The snow will be here any day and the cold isn't going to help your hands any. Go get some sunshine.'

'I'm beginning to think you guys are ganging up on me! Can I have some more coffee?'

Karen refilled his cup and said, 'I don't know if you're still interested but I've been reading up on multiple personality disorder.'

Macandrew felt a shiver run through him; he clattered down his cup a little too noisily in its saucer. He hoped Karen and Jeff hadn't noticed this and put his napkin to his lips. The Francini case had been fading from his memory – or perhaps he had been successful in blotting it out – but now the mention of multiple personality disorder brought it all back. Jane's madness, her husband's hatred, the hellish trauma of the car door incident. He had relived the nightmare a hundred times in the small hours of the morning. 'Really?' he said and swallowed hard.

'It's actually very interesting,' continued Karen, apparently unaware of Macandrew's unease. 'And more than a little frightening.'

'Why frightening?'

'A lot of the stuff I came up with relates to criminal acts where the accused claims to have been another person at the time of the offence. This happens much more frequently than you'd imagine. In several instances, psychiatric reports commissioned by the court have actually concluded that two different people *were* inhabiting the same body.'

'Something tells me that's not going to help much with Jane Francini's problem,' said Macandrew.

'No, but I'm convinced it's all part of the same thing,' said Karen. 'And there's more. I came across a report in the *International Herald Tribune* about a recent scandal in Israel. I made a copy of it because I felt sure you'd be interested.' Karen looked about her as if trying to remember where she had put it. 'I'll find it later,' she said, 'Anyway it was about a mental hospital in the Holy Land being run by the Church.'

Macandrew and Jeff exchanged glances that suggested they were at the mercy of some feminine logic that was denied to them.

'It turned out the Church authorities didn't know anything about it.'

'I'm sorry but why should that be interesting?' asked a puzzled Macandrew.

'None of the patients' relatives knew anything about it either. When the police stumbled on the place and started making enquiries, it transpired that the patients were actually listed on their files as missing persons. According to their relatives, all of them were perfectly sane and healthy at the time of their disappearance and none had ever suffered from any mental illness before.'

'I'm sorry, I still don't see what...' said Macandrew.

'It appears that it was something the "hospital" did to these people that damaged their minds,' said Karen. 'According to one guy, who managed to escape, the patients were offered money to undergo some kind of chemical hypnosis and it was this that damaged them.'

'Bizarre.'

'The guy responsible – a priest, would you believe – took off when the cops turned up and now the Church authorities are disclaiming all knowledge of him. They say that the place isn't a hospital at all; it's a convent for Benedictine nuns – the Sisters of St Saviour. Now comes the really interesting bit,' said Karen. 'The patients were all taken to the Hadassah Hospital in Jerusalem,' said Karen. 'They were rambling and incoherent when admitted but ... under *sedation*...' Karen paused for effect and saw that she now had Macandrew's undivided attention. 'Under sedation they calmed down and started to make sense. The only problem was ... they weren't the same people any more.'

'You mean like Jane Francini and Emma?'

'Exactly,' said Karen. 'What's more, when the sedation completely wore off, they started raving again.'

'Good God,' said Macandrew.

'I thought you'd be interested,' said Karen.

'I'd certainly like to see the article,' said Macandrew.

'It's around here somewhere,' said Karen, starting to look. 'It's one hell of a coincidence, don't you think?'

'You said that this priest – the one running the place – made a run for it?'

'Apparently he wasn't really in charge,' said Karen. 'The convent is home to an enclosed order of Benedictine nuns who hadn't had much contact with the outside world. When this guy turned up on their doorstep, saying that he'd been sent by the Church in Rome and carrying papers stating that the sisters were to help him in his work, they accepted it without question. According to the nuns he wasn't alone. He had another guy, a doctor, working with him. But it gets weirder: when the pair of them took off they took one of the patients with them.'

'Why?'

'No one knows.'

'Crazy,' said Macandrew. 'Absolutely crazy.'

Karen again insisted that the article must be somewhere around.

Macandrew glanced at his watch and saw it was late. He got to his feet and stretched his arms in the air. 'I think I'm for home,' he said. 'But if you should come across it... Tell you what; I'm coming in to the Med Center tomorrow to see Saul. If you find it, bring it with you and I'll stop by your office.'

'Sure thing.'

Macandrew kissed Karen lightly on the cheek and nodded to Jeff. 'Thanks for everything, guys, I really appreciate it.'

Macandrew walked to the Med Center in the morning despite the fact that it was bitterly cold and there was a strong wind blowing. The trees had now lost their leaves so any East Coast allusions had gone for good. Kansas City was back to being Kansas City. The 39th Street bus passed a little too close to the kerb while he was waiting to cross at the junction of 39th and Rainbow and threw some dirt up into his face. He had to pause for a moment to remove some grit from his eye but, as he turned his back to the wind and brought out his handkerchief, he took comfort from the thought that a couple of weeks ago he wouldn't have been able to do this. He could now use his fingers well enough to manipulate a handkerchief. His hands were getting better.

'How are things?' asked Saul Klinsman, getting up from his desk when Macandrew came in.

'We're shaking hands aren't we?' replied Macandrew with a smile.

Klinsman saw the joke and put his hand to his forehead. 'I never thought,' he confessed. 'Does this mean we have an improvement?'

'A big improvement,' agreed Macandrew.

141

'I'm really glad to hear that, Mac. The sooner you're back the better.'

'You wanted to see me?' said Macandrew.

'Yes, I did,' replied Klinsman. 'I put it off for a couple of days but then I thought better of it and left a message for you with the Jacksons.'

'Very mysterious,' said Macandrew.

'It's rather delicate,' said Klinsman.

'What is?'

'I have something for you. It was addressed to me but the contents are for you.'

'What?'

Klinsman opened the top drawer of his desk and brought out an envelope. He pushed it towards Macandrew while he opened the deeper bottom drawer and brought out a bottle of good brandy.

Macandrew opened the envelope and withdrew a bundle of bank notes. 'Good God, there must be at least...'

'Twenty thousand dollars,' said Klinsman.

'But who...'

'Anonymous,' said Klinsman, 'addressed to you, care of me.'

Macandrew suddenly realised who the source must be and felt a shiver run through him. 'Francini,' he murmured.

Klinsman nodded. 'I think so. The Mayo Clinic's findings must have finally convinced him you weren't responsible for what happened to his wife.'

'And now he's saying, "Sorry I broke every bone in your hands. Let's kiss and make up."'

'Something like that.'

'Well the bastard can take his money and jam it where the sun don't shine,' said Macandrew bitterly.

Klinsman smiled wryly. 'I thought you'd see it that way. I'll see this is returned to Mr Francini.'

Macandrew shook his head and found that he had made a decision. 'I've had enough, Saul,' he said. 'I need to get away for a bit. I'm going to take a vacation.'

'Good idea,' said Klinsman. 'Where are you thinking of going?'

'Scotland,' said Macandrew, almost surprising himself.

'Scotland?' exclaimed Klinsman as if it were the last place on earth he expected to hear.

'I've often thought about it in the past but never got round to doing anything about it. I never seemed to have the time, but now I'm going off to trace my roots. I want to see where the Macandrews came from. I've seen where my great-grandfather settled in Missouri; now I'm going to take a look at the place he came from – a village in Scotland called Drumcarrick.'

Macandrew called in to Karen's office and

found her writing up case reports.

'Do you know,' she said, 'I've used at least ten ways of saying "no progress" this morning without actually saying "no progress". Does that make me some kind of literary genius?'

'Probably makes you some kind of politician,' replied Macandrew. He waited until she had finished writing before asking, 'Did you find it?'

Karen reached into her desk drawer and brought out a cardboard envelope file. 'Here you are,' she said. 'Come to think of it, you'd better have this too.' She handed Macandrew the tape she had made of her interview with Jane Francini.

Macandrew slipped it into the envelope without comment and told her of his decision to go to Scotland. She seemed pleased although surprised he hadn't picked somewhere sunny. 'Well, it'll do you good to get away, Mac. When are you thinking of going?'

'Just as soon as I can fix a flight.'

Macandrew went directly from the Med Center to a travel agent up in the Crown Shopping Center and made arrangements that would see him fly from Kansas City to Chicago and then across the Atlantic into London Heathrow. From there, he would catch a domestic flight up to Scotland's capital city, Edinburgh.

144

CHAPTER EIGHT

On the night before he was due to leave, Karen and Jeff Bliss gave a small dinner party for Macandrew. Saul Klinsman and Mike Kellerman were invited and it turned out to be the kind of evening that made Macandrew wonder why he was going anywhere at all. The food was good – it always was when Karen cooked – the wine was excellent – Saul Klinsman, who considered himself something of an expert on the subject, had insisted on choosing and bringing it – and the conversation was hilarious. Mike Kellerman was at his funniest in relating tales, either real or imagined, about his early experiences in medicine. When these were exhausted he changed to a Hollywood-Scottish accent and insisted on probing Macandrew's 'real' reasons for visiting his ancestral homeland, insisting that money must somehow be involved. Jeff suggested that Macandrew's great-grandfather was still owed five cents by someone back in the old country and Macandrew was determined to collect.

'Why do people have this thing about their roots?' Klinsman asked Karen when the

laughter subsided. 'Is it really that important?'

'Only if you don't have any,' said Karen.
'Most of us take our roots for granted. We
know where our mother and father came
from and probably our grandparents,
maybe even our great-grandparents, but not
all people have this foundation and it can be
a big miss. The people who suffer most are
orphans who know nothing at all about their
origins. Many will spend their entire lives
worrying and wondering about where they
came from and who their folks really were.'

'I guess that's why adopted kids often insist on tracing their real parents,' said Mike
Kellerman.

'Exactly that,' replied Karen. 'And it causes
such distress because it's construed by the
folks who brought them up as ingratitude.
But it's not. It's just something the kids have
to do. They can't help themselves.'

'So what's Mac's problem?' asked Kellerman.

'I suspect he's just mildly curious,' smiled
Karen.

'That's true, of course,' said Macandrew,
'but I recognise elements of what you've
been saying in my motivation. It was the
strangest feeling out in Weston when I found
the graves of my relatives. It was just as if...'

'You'd just put an important piece in the
jigsaw puzzle and seen the picture take

shape?' said Karen. 'It made you feel secure. You were part of the great scheme of things. You fitted in.'

'That's right,' said Macandrew.

It was well after midnight before anyone left, despite Macandrew's earlier insistence that he was going to have an early night because he had such a long day ahead of him. Saul Klinsman said he'd drive him home. Macandrew suspected he wanted to talk.

'Any idea how long you're going to be away, Mac?'

'Two weeks, maybe three, depending on how things go.'

'I watched you at dinner. Your hands seemed OK.'

'I can use a knife and fork if that's what you mean,' said Macandrew feeling ever so slightly irritated. 'What's on your mind, Saul?'

'I'll level with you. We're feeling the strain in Neuro. I'm going to have to take someone on.'

'Makes sense,' agreed Macandrew although he felt a definite hollow arrive in his stomach. That *someone* was going to fill *his* job.

'I wanted you to hear it from me rather than have you come back and find a stranger working your lists. This has nothing to do with the way I think things will turn out. I'm talking about a locum appointment. Gonsalves thinks you have a better than even chance of being as good as ever and that's good enough for me. I just don't want the unit building up a big backlist in the meantime.'

'Understood.'

The car drew to a halt outside Macandrew's place and Macandrew got out. He shivered in the cold night air and drew up his collar before bending down to thank Klinsman through the driver's window for the ride.

'Safe journey,' said Klinsman.

Macandrew paused for a moment to watch the Buick drive off and then looked up at the night sky as a police helicopter flew overhead on routine night patrol, its searchlight probing the ground at the back of nearby houses. He went inside and tiptoed up the back stairs so as not to wake the Jacksons. He poured himself a nightcap before slumping down in a comfortable chair to reflect on the evening.

There had been moments when he'd wondered if he was doing the right thing in going away at this time but Klinsman's talk of bringing in a new surgeon to the unit had convinced him that he was. Despite his assurance that the arrangement would be temporary, he knew that there was no real way of knowing that just yet. Things were still very much in the balance. If he hung around Kansas City he would only brood about it. He

148

was sure he'd find plenty to distract him in Scotland. Apart from that, he needed to look back at the Francini affair from a distance and maybe see things more dispassionately. He had made good physical progress but he still had to come to terms with the psychological trauma. People often overlooked this aspect of violent crime. In many ways it could be worse than the actual physical pain and discomfort involved. Constantly reliving the nightmare was only part of it.

Just before setting out for the airport in the morning, Macandrew noticed the file containing the strange Israeli news report that Karen had given him: he hadn't had time to read it yet. It was sitting on the window ledge next to the slim folder he'd compiled on Hartman's tumours. Remembering that what little work there had been done on them had in fact, been done in Edinburgh – where he just happened to be going – he slid both files into the wide front zip pocket of his leather travel bag along with Karen's taped interview with Jane Francini and looked out of the window to see that the cab had arrived.

Macandrew already felt that it had been a long day. He'd had a five-hour wait at O'Hare airport between the domestic flight's arrival in Chicago and the transatlantic take-off, but now the Atlantic Ocean was thirty-five thousand feet below and they were into the comfortable phase of the journey. The passengers had been airborne long enough for them to relax. Jackets had been removed, ties loosened and the cabin lights dimmed in deference to those watching the movie. The flight was only three-quarters full and the seat next to Macandrew was free so he kept his travel bag on it.

Having no interest in the movie, he brought out the Hartman's tumour file and switched on his overhead reading lamp to give him an island of light. He cut out background noise by putting on his headphones but without plugging them into the seat socket.

After an hour and a half without interruption, he understood quite a bit more about the work of John Burnett and his co-workers but was no nearer to figuring out why a line of research, which had seemed so promising, had come to an abrupt halt. But thinking about it wasn't going to help, he concluded, as he recognised he was going round in circles and it had been a long day. He asked the flight attendant for a whisky. The alcohol put him in the mood to catch a few hours' sleep.

It was eight-thirty local time on Monday morning when the Boeing 747 touched down at London Heathrow: it was raining heavily. Macandrew made his way through throngs of unsmiling people to find the British Airways shuttle desk and barely had time to down a cup of coffee before he was airborne again and on his way to Edinburgh. In a little over an hour, he felt the aircraft bank steeply to the left as they made a turn over water.

'First time here?' asked the man beside him. It was the first time he had spoken on the flight.

'It is, yes,' replied Macandrew.

'You're an American?'

'Yes.'

'These are the Forth bridges down there. The red one's the old Victorian rail bridge, the other's the road bridge, built in the Sixties.'

'I must have seen the old one at least a hundred times in photographs,' said Macandrew. 'And I remember it featured in a famous film...'

'*The Thirty-nine Steps*,' said the man. 'A John Buchan classic. I take it you're not here on holiday?'

'Actually I am.'

'In November?'

Within seconds of stepping outside the terminal building to join the queue for taxis, Macandrew understood the man on the plane's surprise. An icy wind was driving rain

151

almost horizontally across the tarmac and gusting so strongly that his suitcase was almost snatched from his grasp. He turned quickly to keep hold of it but, as he did so, his travel bag slipped from his shoulder and splashed down in a puddle at his feet. A leaden sky suggested there was more of this to come.

'Where to?' asked the taxi driver.

'City centre, I guess,' said Macandrew. On the way, he asked the driver about accommodation. 'I just need some place to stay until I can get my bearings and decide what I'm going to do.'

The driver nodded without saying anything and Macandrew sat back in his seat to look out of the window as they sped towards the city. Thirty minutes later he was standing outside a hotel in the Bruntsfield area of the city with the driver's assurance that he was only a mile or so from the city centre. The man smiled for the first time when Macandrew tipped him well.

Macandrew woke at seven-thirty. He knew this because he'd looked at his watch. What he wasn't quite sure of for a few moments was whether it was morning or evening. He could hear traffic sounds but it was dark outside so that wasn't much help. It was evening, he decided after a little think. Jet lag was always worse travelling west to east but at least on this occasion he was on vacation. He wasn't attending some conference or medical meeting with a tight schedule and possibly a paper to present. He could relax and take account of what his body told him instead of his diary. Right now it was telling him that he was hungry. He got up, showered, dressed and went off in search of food.

With a meal of pasta and ice cream inside him and feeling refreshed from a long unbroken sleep, Macandrew acknowledged that he felt a lot better. As a bonus, the wind had dropped, the rain had stopped and he could see that Edinburgh was a place he was going to like. He walked the entire length of Princes Street, admiring the huge rock to the south with its floodlit castle on top.

At nine-thirty in the evening, most of the shops were closed but a couple of large bookshops were still open so he went into one and looked through the tourist guide and maps section. He hadn't actually planned on doing this until the following day but if he could get what he wanted right now, so much the better. Once he had the maps, he could spend the remainder of the evening making plans. He picked up a couple of road maps and also 1:25,000 Ordnance Survey sheets for three areas in south-west Scotland. There wasn't much in the way of tourist guides for the area he was interested in but he felt sure he would be able to get these locally.

Unlike many Americans who came to Scotland armed with little real knowledge of where their forebears had originated, Macandrew knew exactly where his great-grandfather, Neil Morrison Macandrew, had come from. He had been born in the village of Drumcarrick on the Ayrshire coast in south-west Scotland, one of three sons of a farm labourer who himself had worked as a farm labourer in the area before setting out for the New World. His father had been James Alexander Macandrew and his mother, Matilda Leadbetter.

His plan was to rent a car, drive down to the Ayrshire coast and take a look at Drumcarrick. He would hunt through local graveyards and parish records if he could find them, hoping to find mention of his family. As he spread out the map in front of him, he hit his first problem. He couldn't find Drumcarrick on it. This was annoying but he refused to see it as a major setback. Drumcarrick might well be too small to be recorded on the map. He felt sure that once he was in Ayrshire he would have no trouble finding it. In the meantime, he wanted to see more of Edinburgh and to do it in daylight. He arranged for car rental through hotel reception but said that he wouldn't need it until Wednesday – the day after tomorrow.

The weather was cold and clear on Tuesday

so Macandrew dressed warmly in cord trousers, a thick sweater and a tan leather jacket. Round his neck he wore a navy blue scarf and on his head, a waterproof cap. He chose shoes that would be comfortable for walking in and checked his wallet to see that he had enough British money.

He spent the morning exploring the Royal Mile, the famous old street that ran down from the castle at its head though the old town of Edinburgh with its high tenements and ancient buildings, to the royal palace of Holyrood at the foot. Here he found exactly the kind of escapism he was looking for. Edinburgh was as different from Kansas City as Mars was from Earth.

Being the only tourist around – or so it seemed – marked him out for special attention. People were friendly and seemed anxious to tell him things. He had lunch at a pub near the palace and sampled British beer for the first time. He wasn't overly impressed, nor was he with the food but it didn't matter. The landlord was friendly and talkative – if only about American football, which he followed on television. Macandrew was enjoying himself.

There was still no sign of rain when he had finished eating so he continued exploring the myriad streets and lanes leading away from the main thoroughfare and the small shops he found there with their treasure troves of times past. He was beginning to feel a little tired – but not unpleasantly so – when he happened upon a large dark-stone building and a notice outside telling him that it was the medical school of the University of Edinburgh. He realised that this must be where Burnett and his team had carried out their work on Hartman's tumours.

The huge, arched entrance spoke of an age when doctors wore frock coats and stolen corpses were trundled through the streets by body snatchers under cover of darkness to supply the needs of the infamous Dr Knox's anatomy classes, an age when anaesthetics had yet to be discovered. Come to think of it, anaesthetics *were* discovered here. Simpson had carried out his early experiments with chloroform in this very city. And antiseptics too! Joseph Lister had introduced carbolic acid to the world of surgery in the hospital adjoining this very medical school.

Macandrew felt suitably awed to be standing outside a building that had played such an important role in the history of medicine, but its more modern link to the Francini affair through the work of the Burnett group was making him feel uncomfortable. He flexed his fingers subconsciously as he looked up at the windows surrounding the quadrangle, wondering if John Burnett was sitting behind any of them. He even considered going in and asking but stopped short of doing that. For the moment, the events in Kansas City were a long way away and that's how he wanted to keep it. Maybe he'd call in before he went home but, for now, he was here on vacation. He turned his back on the med school and walked off. He had a trip to the Ayrshire coast to plan.

Hertz delivered the hire car to the hotel just before nine on Wednesday but Macandrew decided to let the morning rush hour pass before setting out, although he did want to be in Ayr – some seventy miles away – by lunch-time. It was his intention to spend the afternoon visiting the local tourist agencies – hoping that they would be open at this time of the year – to ask about Drumcarrick. If not, he'd try local museums or historical societies.

'Your luck's still holding,' said the break-fast waitress as she cleared the table and nodded to the sunshine outside the window. It was another cold clear day.

'I think you were kidding about the weather here,' said Macandrew. 'It's beautiful.'

The waitress – who had told him earlier that the weather could change every ten minutes – gave him a pitying look.

CHAPTER NINE

Macandrew decided against using the motorway and opted instead for a meandering route across the central belt. He wanted to see as much of the countryside as possible.

'There's no' much tae see either way, mind you,' warned Willie Donaldson, the hall porter. 'If it's scenery yer after, you should be headin' north.'

After thirty minutes of driving through a bleak landscape that even sheep seemed vaguely unhappy with, Macandrew was ready to concede that Willie had a point. The countryside he'd passed through had been mainly barren, windswept moor land. His spirits began to pick up, however, when the road started to wind down the slopes of the Clyde valley with its more fertile soil and fruit farms – although it was entirely the wrong time of year to visit. Two hours had gone by when he finally joined the dual carriageway that led south from Glasgow to the Ayrshire coast. Another twenty minutes and he was entering the outskirts of Ayr.

It struck him almost immediately that the town had a feeling of small-town prosperity about it as he headed slowly towards its centre between rows of neat bungalows sitting smugly behind well-manicured gardens. The roads were pleasantly wide, giving the place an air of space and openness and the traffic seemed light. He eventually picked up a sign pointing to Beach Car Park and couldn't resist following it. This would be his first glimpse of the western shores of Scotland from where his great-grandfather had set out for the New World and a new life.

On a November day, Macandrew found himself the only person in the car park by the sea. He brought the car to a halt, facing the water, and leant forward to rest his arms on the wheel and take in the view. The beach was windswept and utterly deserted but the sand seemed white and clean and the wind was whipping it up in small clouds making the surface seem liquid. Gulls wheeled and screamed above white-crested waves which, with the tide out, were a good hundred yards away. He buttoned up the front of his jerkin, pulled his cap firmly on to his head in deference to the wind and got out of the car to jump over the low wall and start making for the water's edge.

After only a few minutes standing there, he was forced to turn his back to gain respite from the biting wind and also to get his bearings. There was a wide expanse of parkland between the shore and the first houses, which were large, stone-built villas, but he could see the spires and towers of the town to his left. He found it slightly unnerving that he seemed to be the only living thing in the whole wide, flat landscape and felt relieved when he saw a woman step on to the beach about three hundred yards away with her dog. He walked by the water's edge for another ten minutes before returning to the car and rejoicing in its calm stillness while he thought what to do next.

A first priority was a whisky to warm himself up and then he'd have some lunch. With this in mind, he headed back along the route he had come in on – remembering that he had passed a few likely hotels – and pulled into the car park of one of them. A large whisky was followed by hot soup, smoked trout and apple crumble and several cups of coffee – the waitress insisted on refilling his cup while she sought his advice about a Florida holiday.

By four in the afternoon Macandrew had visited all the tourist offices in Ayr that were open and also two local museums. No one had ever heard of Drumcarrick. It wasn't marked on any of the many maps that were consulted for his benefit and he was beginning to feel thoroughly depressed.

'You could try George Tranter,' suggested the curator of the last museum when she finally had to admit defeat. The woman was small and stooped and carried her spectacles in her hand. She would put them on and take them off again at thirty-second intervals while she spoke, as if uncertain of the effect they had on her appearance.

'He's a local historian and an amateur, but he knows more than many of the professionals round here,' said the woman.

'How do I find him?' asked Macandrew.

'He works down the coast at Culzean Castle.'

'A castle?'

'It's a National Trust property a few miles south of here. George works on the estate. He lives in one of the cottages. Just ask any of the staff there and they'll direct you.'

Macandrew glanced out of the window and saw that the light was fading. 'Too late tonight, I suppose,' he said.

'Mm,' agreed the woman. 'It'll be dark soon.'

Macandrew booked himself into the nearest, reasonable-looking hotel for the night and telephoned the hotel in Edinburgh to tell them that he wouldn't be back until the following day. He spent the remainder of the evening in a pub that boasted live music, listening to a slightly out-of-tune folk group called The McCreadys and an accordionist who played Scottish country dance music. The more he drank, the better they sounded.

After a good night's sleep, Macandrew

could hardly believe his luck when he looked out of the window and saw once more that the sun was shining out of a clear blue sky. It was bitterly cold and there was a frost on the grass where it was shaded from the sun but everything looked wonderful, especially the sea which sparkled in the distance. It looked even better close up when he saw it crash on to the rocks below the high ramparts of Culzean Castle.

'Nice day,' he said to a man repairing a section of stone wall.

'Aye,' said the man.

'I wonder if you can help me, I'm looking for George Tranter.'

'Oh aye,' said the man, continuing with his work.

'Would you happen to know him?'

'Aye.'

Macandrew felt as though he were drawing teeth. 'Maybe you can tell me where I can find him?'

'Aye,' replied the man, taking a break to consult his work plan before continuing.

There was another pause before Macandrew, misinterpreting the silence, reached into his pocket for money.

'You'll no' be needing that,' said the man with a look of disdain.

Macandrew felt uncomfortable. 'I'm sorry,' he said, 'I thought...' His voice trailed off. 'Can you help me find George Tranter?'

he asked.

'I'm George Tranter.'

Macandrew felt foolish and more than a little annoyed. He resented being made to jump through hoops and could only guess that this was because of his accent. Not everyone liked Americans; this was a fact of life. He bit the bullet and said, 'It's a pleasure to meet you, Mr Tranter. I'm told you are the man to speak to when it comes to Ayrshire folklore. The lady at the museum in Ayr told me that if you didn't know where Drumcarrick was, nobody would.'

'Did she now,' said Tranter softly.

Macandrew sensed that Tranter was pleased to hear this despite the dour front he was keeping up.

'I've come nearly five thousand miles to find Drumcarrick and you are my last hope,' said Macandrew.

'Well, you've had a wasted journey,' said Tranter in a manner that suggested he wasn't entirely heartbroken about this.

Macandrew felt utterly deflated. 'You don't know it either, huh?'

Tranter didn't reply. He returned to reading his work plan.

'Well, I guess that's that,' said Macandrew with an air of resignation. 'Maybe I'll drive on down the coast and have a root around. Thanks for your time.' He started to leave.

'You'll no' find it,' Tranter called out

behind him.

'You sound very sure,' said Macandrew, half turning.

'It disnae exist,' said Tranter.

'My great-grandfather was born there,' said Macandrew. 'It must exist.'

Tranter smiled for the first time and said, 'Oh, it did once, but it was swept into the sea more than a hundred years ago. That's why you'll no find it.'

Macandrew walked slowly back towards him. 'Are you absolutely sure about that?' he asked.

'I'm certain,' said Tranter. 'Drumcarrick stood about thirty miles south of here, on a cliff top, just like Culzean here. One night the cliff gave way in a huge storm and the whole village went into the sea, lock, stock and barrel.'

'How awful,' said Macandrew. 'Were many people killed?'

Tranter shook his head. 'No. The village had been dying for some years before that. There weren't many people left living there at the time of the storm; about eight, they reckon; all old folk. Most of the houses in the village were derelict.'

'And there's nothing left of it at all?' asked Macandrew.

Tranter shook his head. 'Not a single stone,' he said. 'The whole lot went into the sea.'

Macandrew felt even worse than he had before. He thanked Tranter and said, 'I think I'd still like to stand on the spot. About thirty miles, you say?'

'Give or take,' replied Tranter. He gave Macandrew some details about local landmarks to look out for.

'I'm obliged,' said Macandrew.

'Mind you ... the village graveyard is still there,' said Tranter, tongue in cheek.

Macandrew could hardly believe his ears.

'The cemetery didn't go over the cliff. It was set back about three hundred yards from the village. You'll have a bit of a job finding it. It'll be overgrown and pretty well hidden from the road but it's still there. I reckon about a hundred and fifty yards back from where the cliff edge is now.

'The cemetery would be just fine,' said Macandrew. 'Perhaps you'll let me buy you a drink?'

Tranter moved his head as if uncomfortable with the idea of agreeing openly but didn't overly object when Macandrew pressed a ten-pound note into his hand saying, 'Thanks again.'

Macandrew felt a growing sense of excitement as he headed south. He had reset the car's trip meter when he'd left Culzean so, when twenty-seven miles came up, he started to pay close attention to the local geography. He was looking out for Tranter's first landmark – a round stone tower with its roof missing. He felt his throat tighten as it came into view. The road should now turn inland for a mile or so before rejoining the coast after a steep downhill section. He slipped the car down into third gear as he came to it. It was very steep. He drove on until he realised he was coming to the promised long climb with a cluster of oak trees at the summit. He was now very close to the spot where Drumcarrick had once stood.

The road was narrow on the far side of the summit but Macandrew found a place where he could pull off safely – although he had to park at a bit of an angle. His unspoken prayer that there was no hidden ditch waiting for his front wheels was answered and he relaxed when the ground seemed firm enough. He got out and made his way carefully to the cliff edge to look down at the rocks below.

He supposed he still hoped that he might be able to spot some relic of the village but wasn't really disappointed when all he could see was foaming sea clambering over black rock. A hundred years was a long time to be exposed to the elements and the ocean. He took in the view for a few minutes, thinking that it was one his great-grandfather must have known well, a view he must've thought about perhaps as he journeyed across the dusty plains of the Midwest. He may even have remembered it on his deathbed.

He turned and looked to the land on the other side of the road to see if he could spot any sign of the graveyard but dense undergrowth prevented him from seeing anything at all. He would have to search blind. He crossed the road and climbed over a fence to start forcing a way through. Almost ten minutes had passed before he almost tripped over the first gravestone. It was lying flat in tangled undergrowth and there was a covering of green moss on its surface.

He used a succession of twigs to scrape the moss from the stone but the fact that it was made out of soft sandstone rather than hard granite meant that it had not weathered well. He had difficulty in making out the inscription.

There was a clear outline of a skull and crossbones near the top but the deceased's name had practically been obliterated. He guessed at James Thomson but it could equally well have been Jane Thomas. He was pretty sure however, that it was not Macandrew.

He was breathing hard by the time he had worked his way though all the flattened stones. He had not, however, found what he was looking for. Had his great-great-grandfather's stone been one of those too damaged to read or could it be the one remaining stone, which had fallen face down and which was too heavy to move? This one was made out of granite so there was a good chance that the inscription would be legible if he could only find some way of turning it over.

There was plenty of wood lying around that he could use for leverage but the stumbling block was going to be getting an end under the stone to start off with. Scraping away the earth at one corner would allow him to get the point of a stake below the stone, but it would leave him with too steep an angle to be of any use. He came up with a better idea. He would use the wheeljack in the car's tool kit. That could give him the height he needed. He made his way back to the car and fetched the whole tool kit.

He was pretty much out of breath by the time he had lugged it back though the undergrowth so he gave himself a moment to recover. Although it was bitterly cold and there was a biting wind coming in off the sea there was sweat running down his face by the time he had raised the stone to the limit of the jack and inserted the end of a thick branch beneath it. He collected two more branches and pushed them under the stone to ensure that it would stay clear of the ground when he withdrew the jack. It was now a case of building a new, higher platform for the jack and raising the stone a bit more.

After three such manoeuvres Macandrew reckoned that he now had enough height to turn the stone over, so he selected the thickest branch he could find, slid it in under the edge and started to apply leverage.

The veins were bulging on his forehead when he finally felt the stone start to move. It moved slowly upwards until it was very close to its point of balance and pressure was suddenly taken off his arms as the weight was transferred to the fulcrum. One final push and the stone tumbled over on to its back. Macandrew supported himself for a moment on the lever he had been using and looked down at the patch of bare ground that the stone had been covering. A myriad of crawling things were hitting the refugee trail in search of a new home. He started deciphering the inscription on the stone and almost immediately made out the name Macandrew. It was such a good feeling to know that he had found what he'd come for.

Feeling both pleased and relieved, he painstakingly cleaned up the writing – which had been well preserved – with twigs and read that the stone marked the spot where James Macandrew and his wife, Matilda, were buried. He searched his pockets for a pen and something to write details down on. James had died at the age of fifty-seven, five years before his wife who had been fifty-eight at the time of her death.

Macandrew returned to the car to fetch his camera. He didn't feel sad or maudlin, just … comfortable. It made him think of what Karen Bliss had said about roots.

He couldn't be sure how, or indeed if, the photographs would turn out so he was careful to look after the piece of paper on which he'd written down details of the inscription. It was the back of the bill from the hotel he'd stayed at the previous night. He put it in the zipped back part of his wallet, noticing as he did so how dirty his hands were … and how dishevelled his clothes had become. Should he drive back to Edinburgh like this or should he check into the hotel in Ayr again in order to have a bath and clean up? He opted for the latter. Apart from anything else, it would be a shame to leave Ayrshire without doing the tourist things. He should at least visit the village of Alloway and Robert Burns country. Whatever happened now, his trip to Scotland had been a success.

He had a bath and changed clothes before spending the remainder of the day driving round the Rabbie Burns trail and generally getting a feel for the area. The accents wouldn't have changed that much in the last hundred years or so and he reckoned that the same fields were being ploughed, albeit with different machinery. He felt well satisfied when he came to the end of the tour of his roots and it was time to set off back to Edinburgh. It was already dark and most of the commercial traffic would be finished for the day. With a bit of luck he should be back by ten o'clock.

Fifteen minutes into the journey, the heavens opened and it rained so hard that the wipers had difficulty clearing the windshield. From Macandrew's point of view, it couldn't have happened at a worse time. He was heading back up the dual carriageway towards Glasgow, keeping a lookout for the slip road that would take him off on to the road to Edinburgh. In the event, he overshot it and was becoming resigned to having to go through Glasgow when he picked up another sign for Edinburgh via a road he had overlooked when planning the journey – the A71. He turned off onto that, switched on the car radio and flicked through the stations until he found some music he liked – Ella Fitzgerald singing 'Summertime'.

The rain eased and visibility got better: traffic was lighter away from the main route and the car's heater was working well. He was beginning to feel more relaxed when, in negotiating a roundabout, his headlights picked out a road sign that almost transfixed him. It said Moscow.

Macandrew tightened his hands on the wheel as his head filled with thoughts of Jane Francini and the little girl she became when mildly sedated, the girl who lived in Moscow but didn't speak Russian... Emma Forsyth.

CHAPTER TEN

Macandrew now realised that neither he nor Karen Bliss had even considered a place other than the Russian capital when Emma had said her home was near Moscow. He even recalled feeling vaguely relieved when she had come out with it because she had been making them feel uncomfortable by sounding so perfectly sane and rational. There had been such a ring of truth about everything she'd said that anything to remind them that they were dealing with a deranged woman had seemed strangely welcome.

As he thought back to the events of that morning, he remembered Karen asking her why she didn't speak Russian and Emma's bemusement at the question. They had been happy to take that as a sign that everyday logic was absent from her thinking – a clear indication of mental dysfunction. But if Emma's Moscow had *not* been in Russia then her reaction had been perfectly understandable. But surely this was all some kind of weird coincidence. 'Emma' couldn't possibly have meant the Moscow he had just seen on the traffic sign. Common sense rebelled at the idea. There were probably lots of Moscows in the world. Hell, there was even one in Idaho, now he came to think about it. This niggling train of thought, however, occupied him all the way back to Edinburgh and was still on his mind when he picked up his room key at the front desk.

'Did you have a good trip, Doctor?' asked the girl on duty.

'I found exactly what I was looking for.'

'Not many people can say that in life,' said the girl.

Macandrew smiled at the philosophy and asked – almost on a whim – 'Tell me, is Forsyth a Scottish name?'

'It certainly is,' said the girl

'I was afraid of that.'

Macandrew lay down on the bed for a few moments, looking blankly up at the ceiling while he tried to think things through in a calm and rational manner. A Scottish Moscow *and* a Scottish name: it could still be coincidence but he could no longer dismiss it out of hand. He would have to go back and take a look at the place. Something told him that he wouldn't have peace of mind unless he did. He remembered that the tape of Karen's interview with Jane Francini was in his travel bag and came to a decision. He would drive out to the Scottish Moscow in the morning and listen to the tape on the way.

Macandrew slowed as he neared the roundabout just north of Galston where he had seen the sign the night before. Seeing it made him just as uneasy again. Perhaps even more so this time because the Francini tape was playing and the sound of Jane's Emma Forsyth voice was bringing back things he'd been trying to forget. He had played it through twice with an extra play-back of the section containing the description of the house where the Forsyth family lived – Fulton Grange.

On a cold November morning, Moscow did not seem any different to many of the other small villages he had passed through on the way. It was grey and nondescript. There were certainly no big houses to be seen and very few signs of life outside the small ones. There didn't even appear to be a shop in the village. Two elderly women, shapeless in heavy winter coats and head-scarves, were talking on a corner. One of them had to rein back her dog to stop it making a run at Macandrew's car. The women regarded him suspiciously as he passed slowly by, a half smile on his face by way of apology for invading their space.

Macandrew was almost relieved that the place seemed so ordinary but Emma had not said that her home was *in* Moscow, only that it was near it. But in which direction?

An added problem might be that large houses were often hidden from the road. People with money could afford privacy.

The main road out of Moscow led north but there was a minor road crossing from east to west. At the mental toss of a coin, he headed slowly east with frequent checks in his rear-view mirror for any traffic coming up behind. The road was little better than a farm-track and wound steeply uphill through a forest of Scots pine trees.

He had travelled less than half a mile when he saw what looked like evidence of a broad path leading off to the left. It didn't seem like a farm track because it was almost overgrown but it did look as if it might have been the entrance to a property at some time in the past. He parked the car on the verge to take a closer look and found clear evidence of what had once been a stone-built perimeter wall and two gate posts, although the gates themselves were no longer there. The position of the rusting hinge-bolts embedded in the stone posts suggested that the gates must have been well over eight feet high.

Macandrew cleared a path through the tangled undergrowth that had largely reclaimed the junction with the road and started to make his way up what would have been the drive. The sound of the wind in the tall trees and the darkening of the sky made him shiver and pull up his collar as he made his way to the far end of the drive where he had to stop and fight his way again through tangled shrubbery and a dense cluster of wild rhododendron bushes. This he did holding his hands up in front of his face for protection, but when he finally succeeded and stepped out into a clearing, he saw what he had almost been afraid of finding. There was a big house standing there.

The building was clearly very old and in a poor state of repair. The windows had been boarded up, and not recently for the wood had started to rot, leaving ugly jagged gaps, and weeds had gained a foothold on nearly all of the crumbling stone ledges. What caught his attention more than anything else however, was the fact that the house had a round tower. Emma's room was round because it was in a tower.

He moved slowly towards the house, fighting the fear of finding out more. There was a struggle going on in his head between his firm belief in scientific values and what was unfolding before him. He came to the steps leading up to the front door and paused to run his fingers through letters etched into a decaying stone pillar. They spelt out – as he was dreadfully afraid they must – Fulton Grange.

Macandrew rubbed his forehead gently and sought a rational explanation. How could Jane Francini have known about this place? She had never been to Scotland in her life. She had told him this in their early conversations when they had talked about their common heritage. Even if she had, it seemed unlikely that she would ever have found her way here by accident. So what was the connection between Jane Francini, Emma Forsyth and Fulton Grange?

He looked up at the brooding walls and clutched at straws. He supposed that the house might have appeared as an illustration in some story that Jane had read as a child. Emma might even have been one of the characters in it – a particular favourite of Jane's and one that had stuck in her mind. He knew nothing at all about the history of this place but he did remember 'Emma' telling Karen Bliss about the secret compartment in her bedroom where she kept her doll. Now, if he were to find that... It didn't bear thinking about.

He walked around the outside of the house until he found the window that seemed most susceptible to forced entry and started pulling away the boards. They were in such poor condition that it did not require much effort but the glass behind them was still intact. He found it harder to free the sash window in its frame than remove the wood shuttering but, in less than ten minutes, he was standing inside Fulton Grange with the smell of wood rot and fungus in his nostrils.

There was no furniture in the room and the wind moaned in the chimney of a huge stone fireplace – a sad, lonely sound. He closed the window and the air became still again. The moaning stopped and a deathly silence took its place, only to be broken by his footsteps as he walked slowly through empty apartments and finally across the main hall with its stone coat of arms above the door.

He paused as he came to the passage leading to the steps that gave access to the tower. He would have to be careful; if any of the floorboards should give way and he should injure himself, the chances of ever being found were remote.

The steps in the tower were dangerously steep – as Emma had suggested – but had the advantage of being solid stone. He climbed up, using the broad edges of the spiral steps because there was no hand rail, although he could see that there had once been a rope threaded through iron rings on the wall to serve that purpose – there was still threadbare evidence of it. He came to a heavy wooden door and paused. The house had been uninhabited for a very long time but he still felt like an intruder when he turned the ring handle and put his shoulder to it. The door swung back to reveal the panoramic windows that Emma had described. A pulse was beating palpably in his neck as he tested the floorboards in advance with his toe and then moved gingerly across to look down at the wilderness that had once been the garden. Emma's voice was in his ears, 'Please bring me my doll...'

Macandrew saw the rose carving in the stone below the large window and applied fingertip pressure to each of the petals in turn. Nothing happened. He tried again but still without success. One final attempt and, as he touched the centre of the rose with one hand and the petal below with the other, the stone turned against a hidden counterweight to reveal a dark space. He reached in ... and brought out Emma's doll.

The clothing on the little doll turned to dust in his hands and he was overwhelmed by a sudden sense of sadness and bewilderment. He didn't understand what was going on but the one thing he felt sure of was that Jane Francini was not mad. She was trapped in the mind of some long-dead character, the little girl who had owned and cherished this doll. He looked out of the window at the wild garden below and absently brought the doll up to his cheek to hold it there for a moment.

This changed everything. He had been trying to put the Francini affair behind him but this was no longer possible. He felt an obligation to Jane to talk to John Burnett at the University of Edinburgh and ask him why he had stopped such promising research.

Macandrew hurried back to the car for it had started to rain. He had done his best to replace the boards over the window and leave things as he'd found them but he had brought the doll with him, cradling it gently inside his jacket to protect it until he was inside the car.

It was three in the afternoon when he got back to Edinburgh and it was – he reminded himself – Friday afternoon. He would have to get a move on if he was to talk to Burnett before the weekend intervened. He found a safe place in his room for Emma's doll – an otherwise empty drawer – and left immediately for the medical school.

He couldn't find a place to park near the school so he took a chance and drove straight into the quadrangle, ignoring the warning signs about the need for permits. He was aware of a man in uniform starting out towards him as he got out of the car but pretended not to see him and hurried into the building.

Macandrew knew from the address given in his published work that Burnett was attached to the Pathology Department at the university. He followed the signs and called in at the departmental office.

'I'm afraid Dr Burnett is no longer with us,' said the woman. 'He left some time ago.'

Macandrew felt deflated. He had been

psyching himself up for the meeting. He said, 'I've come such a long way. I'd really like to get in touch with him if at all possible. Perhaps you have an address?'

The secretary appeared hesitant. 'I'm not sure I can give out that sort of information.'

Macandrew felt that he was making a perfectly reasonable request and tried reassuring her by introducing himself, adding, 'I'm a neurosurgeon at the University of Kansas Medical Center.'

'Would you wait here for a moment,' said the woman. She eased herself out from behind her desk, keeping her knees together in an obviously well-practised move and disappeared through the door behind her. She returned a few moments later to say, 'Perhaps you'd care to have a word with Professor Roberts?'

Macandrew was shown into a small, cluttered, gloomy office. The only view from the single, tall window behind the desk was of a stone wall less than four feet away with a drainpipe running down it. Lichen grew on the wall in the dampness on either side of it. Roberts, an elderly man with wayward tufts of white hair above his ears, held out his hand and invited Macandrew to sit. He himself leant back in his swivel chair and let his intertwined fingers rest on his ample stomach. 'Mona tells me you were asking after John Burnett?'

'I was hoping to speak to him about his work on Hartman's tumours,' said Macandrew. 'Your secretary tells me that he doesn't work here any more.'

'Very sad,' said Roberts.

Macandrew was alarmed by the word. 'Sad?'

'John has given up science. He had what people like to call a complete nervous breakdown: he decided on a complete change of direction in his life.'

'What sort of a change?' asked Macandrew.

'Religion got to him – as it does to so many at their most vulnerable. John sought retreat in a monastery. I think he has decided on making that his future.'

'He's becoming a monk?' exclaimed Macandrew as if it were the most ridiculous thing he'd ever heard.

Roberts shrugged almost apologetically at Macandrew's reaction. 'A brilliant career thrown away,' he said. 'And for what?' Roberts shook his head and lapsed into silence.

'Is anyone carrying on his research?' asked Macandrew. 'It seemed far too important just to abandon.'

'I agree,' said Roberts. 'The trouble is that John took it into his head to remove all his research notes when he left. No one could pick up where he left off, even if they wanted to.'

'But his colleagues, Dr Mukherjee, Dr

Robin. Surely they could have carried on?'

'To be quite frank,' said Roberts, 'I never quite understood their behaviour at the time. Suffice to say that neither decided to complete their contract with us. I don't know what happened to Mukherjee but Simone returned to France and has been working on a new line of research. I understand she's doing quite well: she had a paper in the *Journal of Molecular Biology* quite recently.'

'But why change when things were going so well?'

'I really don't know,' said Roberts. 'Do you have some personal interest in John's research?'

'At home, I operated on a patient with a Hartman's brain tumour. The surgery went well but she's now in a mental institution. According to the literature, this is what happens to all Hartman cases: the cancer is stopped but the patient is left brain damaged and hopelessly confused. Burnett's published work suggested that he was on the verge of finding a treatment for the after-effects of this type of tumour.'

'I see,' said Roberts quietly. 'In that case, I'm sorry. I only wish I could be of more help.'

Macandrew got up to leave but before he did he asked about Burnett's whereabouts.

'He's with the Benedictines at Cauldstane Abbey,' said Roberts. 'It's near Elgin in the north of Scotland.'

Macandrew pulled the parking ticket from below his wiper blade and stuffed it into his jacket pocket. His frustration at what he'd learnt turned to annoyance when he thought about the missing notes. Things hadn't improved by the time he was back at the hotel. Being a medical researcher wasn't just an ordinary job: Burnett had a responsibility to carry on a promising line of work or at least should have taken steps to make sure that someone else could. What kind of Christian behaviour was it to do the opposite and make sure they couldn't?

At around half past eleven that evening – his resolve strengthened by several malt whiskies – he decided that he would go visit Burnett and tell him to his face exactly what he thought.

Next morning, Macandrew wasn't quite so comfortable with his decision. The wind had risen to gale force and he was sitting in a queue of traffic waiting to cross the Forth Road Bridge at South Queensferry. High-sided vehicles and motorcycles were being turned back on the grounds that it was too dangerous for them to cross. As it was, his heart was in his mouth more than once as he negotiated the mile and a half crossing with the wind threatening to snatch the steering from him. But, after that, it was a more or less straightforward four-hour drive north to reach Elgin. He took a couple of wrong turnings in the city itself but finally found the road leading out to Cauldstane Abbey. The rain had stopped but it was still overcast. He was beginning to think in terms of an overnight stay rather than return to Edinburgh in the dark if weather conditions should worsen.

The road leading to the abbey itself was narrow, winding as it did through the vale of St Andrew and, on more than one occasion, Macandrew found himself having to slow right down and mount the grass verge in order to ease past traffic coming the other way. He let out a sigh of relief as he turned down the lane leading to where the abbey stood at the foot of a pine-clad hill.

He left the car in the small visitors' car park outside the main gate and walked up the tree-lined drive towards the abbey. He tried to picture how it would look in spring, lit by pale yellow sunshine instead of grey November light. There was no doubt about the peace and tranquillity of its setting but today there was a raw coldness about everything.

He noticed a small graveyard where the main drive curved round to the left and detoured briefly to take a look. It proved to be the burial ground of the monks.

The abbey itself was impressive; a thirteenth-century building with pointed gothic windows and arches. Sections of scaffolding and masons' tools lying near blocks of stone suggested that it was currently under restoration. He entered by the abbey's main door but found no one inside. There was a small exhibition with model buildings and photographs recording the abbey's history and current restoration programme, which he looked at before spending a few more solitary minutes walking around, gazing up at the high vaulted ceiling and admiring the stained-glass windows. He came to a door which had a sign on it saying that visitors were not permitted to enter and decided that this might be the best way to attract attention.

After knocking three times without response, he entered. Within seconds, the white-robed figure of a monk materialised to ask who he was and what he wanted.

'I'm Dr John Macandrew from the University of Kansas Medical Center. I was hoping I might be able to talk to Dr John Burnett.'

'I see,' said the monk. He was a short man, completely bald and with a dark beard shadow that made him look unshaven, although Macandrew was close enough to see that his skin was perfectly smooth – if slightly moist. He had a particularly large Adam's apple that brushed against the stole of his robe when he spoke.

'We are a contemplative order here,' said the monk. 'It is not permitted for John to see anyone without good reason.'

'I have good reason,' said Macandrew, without elaborating.

'I'd best tell Father Abbot you're here,' said the monk, deciding to pass the buck.

Macandrew was left standing in a long, covered cloister. There were several doors leading off into what he presumed would be the monks' sleeping and living quarters. He looked out at the wet grass and noticed there was a fairy ring in it. He was wondering what the inmates would make of that when the shadow-faced monk returned, accompanied by a tall, thin man whom he introduced as Father Abbot.

'You wish to see Brother John, I understand,' he said in a voice that suggested Irish rather than Scottish origins.

'I do,' agreed Macandrew. 'I've come a long way.'

The abbot held Macandrew's gaze for a moment – long enough for Macandrew to wonder what was going on inside his head because his eyes gave no clue. Finally, he said, 'John has been ill. He's recovering well but what he needs most at the moment is peace and tranquillity. He has renounced his past life and I am reluctant to let anyone from it intrude on his recovery. If this were

187

a matter of family crisis or bereavement it would, of course, be different, but I suspect that this is not the case?'

Macandrew had to agree that it wasn't.

'You're from the medical world. You want to ask him about his research, don't you?'

Macandrew was taken aback. 'I do.'

'I'm going to have to deny your request,' said the abbot.

'Doesn't Dr Burnett have any say in the matter?' Macandrew asked.

'No,' replied the abbot evenly. 'I decide.'

'John Burnett's research could make the difference between a possible cure for one of my patients and spending the rest of her life in a mental institution. There is no one else doing the work.'

'I know about Brother John's research. He told me about it when he first came here.'

'And the answer is still no?'

'Still no,' said the abbot.

CHAPTER ELEVEN

Macandrew started back down the drive, reflecting on how much he disliked organised religion and its professional proponents. There was something about the look in their eyes which irritated him, a smug self-satisfaction in their self-delusional belief that they were in possession of all the answers. As he neared the gates of the abbey grounds he caught sight of a monk approaching from a path to the left of the car park. He was carrying two metal milk churns. He had his cowl pulled up and was looking down at the ground so that he didn't see Macandrew standing there. On impulse, Macandrew called out to the white-clad figure. 'Dr Burnett?'

The monk stopped and turned. Macandrew had anticipated him being startled but the look in his eyes was quite different. It spoke more of anguish than surprise. In that instant he knew he'd stuck lucky. This man did not have the calm assuredness of Brother Francis or the abbot. He'd found John Burnett by accident.

'Yes?' said the man uncertainly.

'I've come a very long way to see you, Dr Burnett. Would you at least spare me a few minutes of your time?'

'I'm no longer a doctor. That was all in the past. Now, if you'll excuse me, I have work...'

'At least hear me out, Doctor. My name is Macandrew; I'm a neurosurgeon at Kansas University Medical Center. A few weeks ago I removed a malignant tumour from one of my patients; a Hartman's tumour. I don't think I need tell you what sort of state she's in now.'

'There's nothing I can do,' replied Burnett, avoiding Macandrew's eyes, 'nothing at all.'

'These tumours were your special interest, Doctor. You know more about them than anyone else in the world; I've read your papers. Your work was going well. You were on the verge of being able to treat these patients and then, suddenly, you give it all up ... for this? That's why I'm here. I had to find out why.'

'I was called to do other things,' replied Burnett.

'Called? Other things?' questioned Macandrew. 'What other things?'

'I've been called to serve God.'

Macandrew said nothing but his eyes never left Burnett. Burnett briefly met his gaze but then looked away, aware of the silent accusation.

'You don't think you can serve God by doing what you're best at?' said Macandrew. 'You don't think you can serve God by saving a group of people from the mental institutions where they'll undoubtedly spend the rest of their lives if you don't?'

'That is conjecture. There was never any certainty of success,' countered Burnett.

'But there was a chance,' insisted Macandrew, 'and a very good one by all accounts. Now there's none at all because you've decided to "serve God" and, just for good measure, you took all your research notes with you so no one else could move things along. What the hell was that all about?'

'You don't understand!' protested Burnett through gritted teeth and then with more control, 'You just don't understand.'

'So help me. Talk me through it. Make me understand. Convince me it's a better idea to spend your time chanting Latin on your knees six times a day than working in your lab doing some real good.'

'You're deliberately twisting things,' accused Burnett. 'It's a rare condition. We're not talking about thousands of people.'

'No,' agreed Macandrew. 'But there are a number and one of them just happens to be my patient. Her name's Jane by the way.'

Burnett did not respond but Macandrew thought he detected a flicker of doubt in his eyes when he glanced up at him briefly. He continued, 'There's something special about these patients, isn't there, Doctor? They aren't really brain damaged at all in the conventional sense. There's more to it. They become ... other people?'

For the first time, Burnett looked Macandrew straight in the eye as if conceding the conversation had moved to another level. 'So you know that much...'

'One of our psychiatrists thought it might be a form of multiple personality disorder or whatever they call it these days but that

191

didn't quite fit what we were seeing...'

Burnett appeared to consider for a few moments before picking up the two milk churns. 'I'm sorry, I really must be getting back,' he said.

'There's one other thing that bothers me,' continued Macandrew as Burnett started to move away, 'Why did Ashok Mukherjee and Simone Robin give up too?'

No reply.

'Were they called by God too?' asked Macandrew, determined to sting Burnett into responding.

'You really don't understand any of this,' said Burnett, without turning round, his voice full of exasperation. 'You don't understand and I can't tell you.'

'Why not, for Christ's sake?'

'That's about right,' said Burnett quietly. 'For his sake.'

'Fine,' stormed Macandrew, 'and a couple of *mea culpas* on your part will make the whole thing right. I'll just tell my patient that,' he said angrily. 'Not that she'll understand of course ... she's a thirty-eight-year-old woman who thinks she's an eight-year-old girl. Still, don't you worry about that; you've got hymns to sing ... prayers to chant... Maybe you could put in a good word for her? Like I said, her name's Jane, Jane Francini.'

Burnett stopped in his tracks and Macandrew felt that he might be on the edge of success. He said more calmly, 'Think about it; that's all I ask. If you change your mind about telling me what's been going on I'll be staying at the Bruntsfield Hotel in Edinburgh for another week.'

Burnett turned round and Macandrew sensed that he was wavering. He walked slowly towards him and, despite the failing light, could see the tortured look in his eyes.

'All right,' said Burnett. 'I know you want to do your best for your patient. You're a surgeon and it's just possible that something might be done to help her. But you have to agree to certain conditions.'

'I'm listening,' said Macandrew.

'I will give you a letter and a token of proof. You must take them to Dr Simone Robin at the Seventh University of Paris. The token will ensure that she will at least listen to what you have to say.'

'And the conditions?'

'If Simone says no, you must leave it at that and agree not to pester her any more.'

Macandrew was bursting with questions but he managed to hold his tongue in the interests of the greater prize. Burnett was no longer working on tumours but it seemed that Simone Robin just might be.

'When will you give me these things?'

'Come up to the abbey with me now,' said Burnett.

'I don't think that's a very good idea,' said Macandrew. He told Burnett about the abbot having refused him permission to speak to him.

'I'm sure Father Abbot was just thinking of my welfare,' said Burnett. 'But you're right. Maybe it's not such a good idea. Give me a note of your full name and your affiliations and I will write you the letter after supper. Be at the gate in the morning at eight and I'll give it to you along with the token when I go down to the guest house.'

Macandrew wrote down the details for Burnett on a page in his diary and tore it out. He handed it to him and said, 'You're a Benedictine monk, aren't you?'

'I'm a postulant,' corrected Burnett.

'But Benedictine?'

'Yes.'

'Then perhaps you'll know what happened at the Benedictine convent in Israel, the one being used as a hospital?'

'What are you talking about?'

'The Israeli police raided a Benedictine convent in Jerusalem and came across a number of people who were on their missing persons list. Although they'd been perfectly healthy at the time of their disappearance, they were now deranged and seemed to imagine that they were other people. The sisters told the police they had been the subject of experiments carried out by some priest sent from Rome.'

Macandrew faltered when he saw the look on Burnett's face. He had never seen a human being go so white before. 'Are you all right?' he asked.

'He used it!' Burnett whispered. 'He used it!'

'Used what?' asked Macandrew, but in the circumstances he really didn't expect an answer. He doubted if Burnett could hear anything he said; he seemed to be in a state of shock. 'Perhaps you should sit down for a moment...' He started towards Burnett but the monk held up his hand and shook his head. He picked up the milk churns and hurried off, leaving Macandrew standing there feeling bemused. 'Until tomorrow morning then!' he called after him but the hooded figure did not respond.

Macandrew drove slowly back into Elgin and booked into a hotel for the night. He felt confused and troubled and the cheerless room he was given did little to improve things. He ran a bath but the water was lukewarm so he couldn't indulge himself in the long, relaxing soak he'd planned. He had to towel himself down vigorously to get warm. There was a radiator in his room but it seemed decorative rather than functional and gave out more noise than heat, relaying the irregular timpani of multiple air locks in an antiquated system. The phone rang and a female voice asked him if he would be eating in this evening.

Macandrew said not. He wasn't sure where he would be eating but it would be somewhere else – somewhere warm, assuming that such an establishment existed in this city. He looked out the window into the gloomy streets and saw the shimmer of frost on the sidewalks. The temperature was falling with the arrival of darkness.

An average meal in a grubby but warm Indian restaurant was followed by a couple of beers in a smoke-filled pub with the television on. He didn't feel like a third so he drank up and plumped for an early night.

The temperature in his room and his state of mind conspired to make sure he didn't get the good night's rest he was hoping for. When he was awake, he was shivering with cold. When he was asleep, he was pursued in dreams by monks from another age, each hideously deformed and carrying an Emma Forsyth doll. He was glad when the dawn light came and chased the night away; he felt exhausted.

Being Sunday morning and 'against management policy' – as he learnt when he asked – an early cooked breakfast was out of the question. He settled for coffee and toast before checking out at seven. He comforted himself with the thought that if everything went according to plan he would be back in

Edinburgh by nightfall. He would have a hot bath, a good meal and start making plans for a trip to Paris. He drove out to the monastery and arrived in plenty of time for his meeting with Burnett: he sat in the car watching the gates.

Just after eight, a white hooded figure came round the bend in the drive and Macandrew got out of the car. He frowned. There was something about the man's gait that was wrong. The angle of the feet and the manner in which the sandals slapped down on the ground suggested a fat man. Burnett was small and thin.

The figure was now close enough for him to see that it was definitely not John Burnett. This man was middle-aged, stout, and had a florid complexion which was becoming more so through the exertion of carrying the milk churns. The bridge of his nose was depressed and his bottom lip protruded beyond his top, exposing a row of notched teeth, which suggested to Macandrew's medical eye the legacy of congenital syphilis.

'Good morning,' said Macandrew, trying to mask his disappointment. 'I thought it would be Brother John.'

The monk looked puzzled, as if not knowing what to make of Macandrew then he glanced at the guest house and asked, 'You're here on retreat?'

'Yes,' lied Macandrew.

'Brother John has been called to Edinburgh.'

'Really? I thought this was an enclosed
community,' said Macandrew. 'I thought the
brothers didn't leave here. Some emergency
perhaps?'

'Father Abbot doesn't confide in me,' said
the fat monk testily. 'He just told me to take
over Brother John's duties ... in addition to
my own.'

'Do you know if John'll be back soon?'

'No idea.'

The monk carried on towards the guest
house and Macandrew was left looking back
up the drive. 'Shit,' he murmured. *Pax* to
you too, Brother.'

He sat in the car for a few minutes wondering what to do next. He couldn't turn up
at the abbey gates every morning hoping
that Burnett would reappear at some point.
He wondered if being 'called to Edinburgh'
had anything to do with the Israeli story that
seemed to disturb him so much. He concluded there was no alternative. He would
have to tackle the abbot about it.

A flurry of snow bestowed a medieval air
on the scene as Macandrew walked up to
the abbey. As if to complete the picture, a
single file of six monks crossed from their
living quarters to the abbey, each with hood
up and head bowed, hands tucked inside the
sleeves of the robes. They had already

entered by the time Macandrew reached the door. Another monk, however, wearing a leather apron over his robe was hurrying across the courtyard and saw Macandrew standing there. He didn't say anything but looked quizzically at him.

'I must speak with the abbot,' said Macandrew.

The monk inclined his head to one side and gave a slight nod before disappearing back inside the living quarters. Macandrew looked up at the sky. The grey November light seemed strangely white despite the thick cloud cover. There was more snow to come.

The monk reappeared at the door and beckoned Macandrew.

He was shown into a room with bare stone walls where the abbot sat behind a dark oak desk. There was a spartan simplicity about the room, its only focal point being a large crucifix hanging on the wall behind the desk. It seemed to Macandrew that particular attention had been paid to highlighting the agony of the figure hanging on it. Blood ran from wounds inflicted by the crown of thorns.

'I've been expecting you,' said the abbot.

'I arranged to meet John Burnett this morning,' replied Macandrew. 'I'm told he's no longer here.'

'Brother John told me about your arranged meeting.' The abbot paused to see if this would elicit any sign of guilt from Macandrew. He continued when Macandrew held his gaze without flinching. 'He told me of your concern for your patient and asked that I give you this letter and also this.' He handed Macandrew a silver St Christopher medallion along with a sealed envelope.

'Can I ask why Dr Burnett was called away so suddenly?' asked Macandrew.

'I can't say,' replied the abbot.

'Can't or won't?'

The abbot shrugged his shoulders.

'He was very upset when I told him about a newspaper article concerning a Benedictine convent in the Holy Land,' said Macandrew. 'Did that have anything to do with it?'

'You are a persistent man, Doctor,' said the abbot. 'But I will not be cross-examined. Suffice to say, the life of the monastery has been upset more than I care for by John's coming here and now by your presence. I don't think we have anything more to say to each other.'

Macandrew got up to leave. 'Please relay my thanks to Dr Burnett when he returns.'

'God be with you.'

Macandrew thought the valediction colder than charity.

He started back towards Elgin to join the main road south, relieved that he had the all important letter and token for Simone Robin. The prospect of being able to help Jane Francini was something he couldn't have hoped for at the outset of his trip and it excited him. Perhaps the French researcher would be more forthcoming than Burnett, for it still seemed odd that anyone would want to cover up a success story. He hadn't reckoned on a visit to Paris but it was something he was now looking forward to. In the meantime, he faced the drive back to Edinburgh through snow and sleet.

A large malt whisky arrived from room service and gave Macandrew his cue to pad through to the bathroom, take off his towelling robe and sink down into the deep, warm bath he had just filled. He propped the glass up on the side and savoured the moment of immersion with a deep sigh of satisfaction. The stiffness from the long drive was just beginning to fade from his limbs when the telephone rang.

'Go away,' murmured Macandrew, still keeping his eyes closed. It couldn't be anything important. Probably someone on the front desk asking what time he wanted to eat. Why should telephones always get priority anyway? People stopped in the middle of doing all sorts of important things just to answer the damned phone. Why?... 'Because it gets on your damned nerves if you don't!' he said out loud, getting to his feet and dripping water over the carpet as he tiptoed over the floor, pulling his robe around him. 'Yes?' he snapped.

'John Macandrew?' asked the voice. It was male; it sounded afraid; its owner was speaking in a whisper.

'Who is this?'

'John Burnett. I need your help. They're holding me prisoner.'

'Burnett?' exclaimed Macandrew. 'A prisoner? Where? Who's holding you?'

'Listen!' urged Burnett. 'He's mad and he's dangerous. You've got to warn Simone.'

'Who is? Where are you? You're not making any sense.'

'I managed to steal a mobile phone from one of them. I've only got a minute.'

'Tell me where you are,' urged Macandrew, beginning to establish priority in his questions.

'I'm being held at a seminary in East Lothian. It's called St Bede's. You've got to warn Simone. I haven't told them anything yet but she has all my research notes. They'll stop at nothing.'

'Who are "they"? What should I warn Simone about?' asked Macandrew. He heard a sharp intake of breath at the other end of the line and suddenly felt afraid. 'Burnett?' he asked anxiously. 'Are you still there?'

There were muffled sounds of a scuffle.

Macandrew heard Burnett gasp and then the line went dead.

With trembling fingers, he dialled 999 and asked for the police. Explaining this wasn't going to be easy.

'Police.'

'I've just had a call from a Doctor John Burnett. He's in serious trouble. I think his life may be in danger.'

'Whereabout is this, sir?'

'He's being held at the seminary of St Bede in East Lothian.'

'Saint...? How do you spell that?'

'I've no idea. Look, the man's in danger...'

'And you are...?'

Macandrew gave his particulars and said where he was calling from.

'Any idea where in East Lothian, sir?'

'None. In fact, I don't even know where East Lothian is. I'm all American.'

'Oh well, I'm sure we'll find it. Don't go out sir, will you. We'll be sending someone round to take a statement.'

'I wasn't going anywhere,' said Macandrew wearily.

The police arrived at the hotel within ten minutes.

'Mr Macandrew?' asked the first policeman as Macandrew approached the desk.

'*Doctor* Macandrew,' corrected the girl on duty.

The policeman acknowledged her contribution with a blank stare then turned back to Macandrew. 'Well, at least it wasn't a hoax call.' The policeman flipped open his warrant card. 'DI Clements. This is Sergeant Malcolm. The fact of the matter is, sir, that we have no record of a seminary called St Bede's in East Lothian, or in Mid or West Lothian for that matter. We've checked.'

'I see,' said Macandrew with a sinking feeling. No one was on the way to help Burnett. 'But there must be! That's what he said, I'm sure of it.'

'Have you any idea why this man should consider himself to be in danger, sir?' asked Clements.

Macandrew shook his head and confessed, 'I hardly knew him.'

The policemen exchanged glances then Clements said, 'Have you any idea why he should call you instead of say ... us, for instance?'

Macandrew shook his head again and said, 'No. I haven't. He's a monk.'

'A monk?'

'Sorry, a postulant. Benedictine.'

'Good God, do they still have such things? And he telephoned you?'

'Yes.'

'From St Bede's?'

'On a mobile phone.'

'A monk with a mobile phone,' said Clements slowly. His sergeant covered his mouth to hide a smile. 'They do say everyone's got one these days.'

'He said he had stolen it from whoever was holding him against his will. This is serious, God damn it!' said Macandrew. 'A man's life is in danger.'

'Just trying to establish the facts, sir,' said Clements.

'Did you check the phone book?' asked Macandrew.

'And the local tax and rates registers. No St Bede's.'

'Maybe the Church authorities?' suggested Macandrew.

'We thought of that too. It's just a bit difficult to raise them at this time of night. Office hours, you know. Jesus apparently knocks off at five too.'

The sergeant's radio crackled into life and he half turned away to respond to the call. When he turned back again his face had taken on a new animation. 'It does exist, sir,' he said. 'The desk sergeant at Haddington remembered it. He says it's been closed for ten years or more but it was definitely called St Bede's and he's told us how to find it. It's off the road between Haddington and Longniddry. The local blokes are on their way.'

'Thank God,' said Macandrew.

'We'd best get down there,' said Clements.

'We'll keep you informed, sir.'

'I don't suppose you'd let me come with you?'

Clements indicated uncertainty with various facial contortions. 'I don't think that's a very good...'

'He's been ill and I'm a doctor,' said Macandrew.

'All right,' said Clement. 'Get your coat.'

CHAPTER TWELVE

'How did you come to know this man?' Clements asked as the police car sped south to join the city bypass. Sergeant Malcolm sat in front beside the uniformed driver. Clements and Macandrew sat in the back.

'He's a researcher in a field I'm interested in,' replied Macandrew. 'I thought that as I was in Scotland I would look him up. It was then I found out he was in the process of becoming a Benedictine monk.'

'That must have come as a bit of a shock,' said Clements.

'You can say that again.'

'What field would that be?'

'I'm a neurosurgeon. Burnett had carried out some interesting research on brain tumours and their after-effects. It seemed promising stuff.'

'But then it all went wrong and he killed someone?'

'Pardon?' said Macandrew, taken aback.

'Sorry, I thought I saw a guilt trip looming up,' said Clements. 'I had a Catholic up-bringing – spent a week in a monastery once. My mother – a devout woman all her days, God bless her – thought it would do me good to be exposed to truly good people who had denied themselves everything to follow God.' Clements snorted and turned to look out of the car window.

'I take it, it didn't work?'

'I don't think there was a single one of them – apart from maybe a little Irishman, who had never known anything else – who wasn't on some kind of guilt trip. They hadn't given up anything at all: they were running away from things; hiding; the lot of them; and mainly from their real selves. Show me a monk and I'll show you one screwed-up individual with a past.'

Macandrew didn't comment, but was forced to concede that guilt might well be playing a role in John Burnett's life. He had seemed a deeply troubled man.

'Shit!' exclaimed the driver suddenly and the car braked and swerved slightly as a slower car in front pulled out to overtake. The driver hit the siren and got the required response from the vehicle in front. Macandrew saw a very sheepish man cower behind his wheel and stare straight ahead as they passed.

'I don't know,' rasped the driver. 'We're lit up like a runaway Christmas tree and still the buggers don't see us!'

'Just drive,' said Clements. 'You all right?' he asked Macandrew.

'Sure.'

Macandrew sensed that they were slowing.

'Haddington,' said the driver.

'We're being met at the second round-about,' said Malcolm to the driver.

Almost on cue, the orange stripe on the side of a blue and white police patrol car was picked out in their headlights. It was parked on a grass verge to the left of the entrance to the roundabout, its blue roof light flashing silently up at the night sky.

'They haven't seen us,' said Malcolm.

A whoop of the siren and the silhouettes in the front seats of the panda sprang to life as if being attacked by a swarm of bees. Caps were replaced, the engine was started and the car bumped heavily on to the road to lead the way.

'Shit, I felt that...' murmured the driver.

It was less than two miles from the main road to the long stone building that had once been the seminary of St Bede's. The last four hundred metres took them up a rough, stony track that had the car bouncing on the limits of its suspension. When they finally came to the broad, ivy-covered entrance, there were two police cars already there and signs of intense activity.

'I think you'd better wait in the car,' said Clements to Macandrew. It made him nervous. He suspected that Clements knew what all the activity was about while he could only speculate. He watched Clements confer with a uniformed man with braid on his cap who seemed to be in charge. When they both glanced back at the car, he sensed that they were talking about him.

The two men were joined by Sergeant Malcolm and they disappeared inside the building. Macandrew was left alone with the driver. 'My sister's married to an American,' he said.

'He's dead, isn't he?' said Macandrew, ignoring the small talk.

'Looks like it,' agreed the driver quietly. 'They're setting up a mobile incident room.'

Macandrew let out his breath in a long weary sigh. He stared glumly at the comings and goings outside the building until Clements and the two others emerged and came towards the car. Clements got in the back and shut the door.

'You're going to tell me Burnett's dead,' said Macandrew.

'I'm sorry,' said Clements. 'At least you

two weren't close.'

'How did he die?'

Clements turned and looked at Macandrew with a look that suggested he might be editing his reply. 'He was murdered.'

'Shot? Stabbed? Strangled?'

'Stabbed ... in the end...'

'Jesus.'

'Do you feel up to identifying him?'

Macandrew nodded. He felt numb.

The building had clearly not been used for a long time. It harboured the kind of damp, clinging coldness that only stone buildings in the depth of winter can manage and there was a strong smell of mouldy plaster. There was no electricity so police torches and flashlights sufficed while they waited for a generator to arrive.

'He's in here,' said Clements as they came to a solid wooden door. He led the way and Macandrew followed. Sergeant Malcolm brought up the rear, doing his best to provide illumination of the floor ahead to complement Clements' horizontal torch beam.

There were two parallel rows of wooden benches facing a raised stone altar – currently without adornment – behind which, a tall, arched stained-glass window rose. Macandrew felt puzzled. There was no sign of Burnett's body. 'Where is he?' he asked.

'Behind you,' said Clements

Macandrew turned round to see John

Burnett, wearing the habit of a Benedictine monk. He had been crucified to the back of the chapel door.

'Sweet Jesus Christ,' he whispered, starting to feel vaguely unwell. His throat had tightened: he found he couldn't swallow.

'Are you all right?' asked Clements.

Macandrew nodded, putting his hand over his mouth until he felt composed enough to continue.

'Is it John Burnett?'

Macandrew approached and looked up into the monk's cowl. Sergeant Malcolm directed his torch beam up into the agonised face of the dead man.

'Yes, this is John Burnett,' murmured Macandrew. 'For God's sake, why do that to him?'

'Somebody wanted to know something,' said Clements. 'They tortured him by banging nails into him until he told them what they wanted to know or until they were satisfied that he really didn't know. At some point they broke his left kneecap too. They finished him off with a knife under the ribs to the heart.'

Macandrew noted the large bloodstain on the front of Burnett's habit. 'Sweet Jesus Christ,' he whispered.

'*Sic transit gloria mundae,*' said Clements dryly.

'Whatever happened to Brigadoon?' murmured Macandrew.

'Walter Scott and Disney both have a lot to answer for,' replied Clements.

Macandrew saw that the forensic team was anxious to be about its business. He turned and headed for the door. The fresh air smelt good. He took several deep breaths and relished the cutting cold of it. It seemed clean, antiseptically clean.

'I'm going to be here for some time,' said Clements, joining him outside. 'I'll have someone drive you back but we'll need to talk to you later.'

Macandrew didn't protest. He now regretted having come in the first place. He was pleased when the same driver who had brought them down was detailed to take him back to Edinburgh. He wanted to hear all about his sister and her American husband.

Macandrew threw back a second whisky and reflected on how his vacation had turned into a living nightmare. He couldn't understand how Burnett had ended up where he had. Why had he been 'called to Edinburgh' in the first place? Once again he was forced to conclude with a sinking feeling that the Abbot of Cauldstane would know the answers to these questions. But would he tell? And more importantly, did he really want to know any more?

The manner of Burnett's death had shaken

him to the core and the agonised expression on the dead man's face would live with him for a long time to come. Right now, he wanted to walk away from everything but it wasn't that easy. He felt an obligation to comply with Burnett's (last?) request that he warn Simone Robin even though common sense was telling him that the minute he set out on that course, he too would become involved and therefore be at risk. Jane Francini's plight was also playing a part in his thinking. Simone Robin knew something about Hartman's tumours that no one else did.

The whisky dulled his unease although he still felt far from relaxed about what he was getting into. He decided that he would go to Paris, but first – and much against his will for he had very little heart for it – he would confront the Abbot of Cauldstane yet again in an attempt to get more information out of him. He needed to know as much as possible up front if he were to cross swords with the sort of people who'd done what they had to John Burnett. He would drive up to the abbey in the morning after trying to contact Simone Robin by telephone. If everything went to plan, he would fly to Paris the following day.

Macandrew got the number for the Seventh University of Paris from International Directory Enquiries and tried calling at eight a.m. when it would be nine in France. There was no reply from Simone Robin's extension. He tried at fifteen minute intervals until, at a quarter to ten, a woman's voice answered, *'Oui?'*

'Dr Robin?'

'Oui.'

'You don't know me but my name is Dr John Macandrew. I'm calling from Edinburgh, in Scotland. I'm afraid I have some bad news for you.' He told her of John Burnett's death and heard the sharp intake of breath.

'But how?'

'There's no easy way to say this, I'm afraid. He was murdered.'

'Murdered?' exclaimed Simone. 'But that's ridiculous. John was the kindest, most gentle man. Who would want to murder *him?*... Who are you? How do you know me?'

'John telephoned me before he died: he asked me to pass on a warning to you that you were in danger too.'

'Who are you?'

'I'm a neurosurgeon at Kansas University Medical Center; I'm here in Scotland on vacation. I went to see John to ask about his – your – work on brain tumours. The university told me about his change of ... direction, so I went to see him at the monastery. He suggested I should come to Paris to speak to you.'

'John said you should speak to me?'

'Yes.'

'I don't believe you.'

'It's true,' insisted Macandrew. 'I admit it wasn't easy. He didn't want to tell me anything at all but I bullied or shamed or embarrassed him, whatever you want to call it, into helping me.'

'How can I help you exactly?'

'I have a patient back home. I carried out an operation on her to remove a Hartman's brain tumour. She's now confined to a mental institution.'

'I see.'

'John gave me the impression that you might be able to help. He gave me a token to give you,' Macandrew added. 'A silver St Christopher medallion.'

'I gave it to John when he decided to give up science,' said Simone distantly. 'You said you had a warning for me?'

'John seemed to think that you were in danger. Something to do with having his research notes?'

'What do you know about the people who killed him?'

'Absolutely nothing. I sort of stumbled into this whole damned thing and, believe me, I wish I hadn't.'

'You must know something?'

'I suspect that there's some kind of Israeli connection.'

'Israeli?' exclaimed Simone.

Macandrew told her about the Israeli news story and how Burnett had reacted. Simone went quiet. 'Mean anything?' he asked.

'Someone used it,' said Simone.

'That's what *he* said. What's going on?'

Simone ignored the question. 'Do you still intend coming to Paris?' she asked.

'You tell me,' said Macandrew. 'Will I hear something that might help my patient? If so, I'll come.'

'I can only tell you what I know,' said Simone.

'Can't ask for more than that,' said Macandrew. 'But it might be safer if you kept a low profile for the time being,' he added.

'We must arrange a meeting place,' said Simone.

'Just say where,' said Macandrew.

'Somewhere public,' said Simone.

Macandrew admired her caution.

'The square in front of Notre Dame. Tuesday afternoon at three.'

'How will I know you?'

'I'd prefer it if I were to recognise you,' said Simone.

'I'm thirty-six, six foot two, dark hair. I'll be wearing ... a grey suit over a dark blue roll-neck sweater.'

'If for any reason you can't make it, you can get a message to me at the number you've called today. Ask for Aline D'Abo;

she's my research assistant. She'll pass it on.'

'Understood,' said Macandrew, noting down the name.

'More sightseeing, Doctor?' asked the girl on the front desk when Macandrew passed on his way out the hotel in the morning.

'Such a lot to see,' replied Macandrew with a weak attempt at a smile. The prospect of the long drive north again had done little for his spirits but four hours later he was walking up the drive to the abbey and asking to see the abbot.

The monk he'd asked put his hands together as if in prayer and shrugged apologetically. He beckoned him to the door and Macandrew followed him into the abbey where they stopped outside a small, gloomy side chapel. The monk pointed to a figure kneeling in front of the altar. It was the abbot. Macandrew gestured that he would wait. The monk looked uncertain but Macandrew ushered him away with a series of reassuring nods and hand gestures.

Macandrew stood immobile at the entrance to the chapel, staring at the back of the kneeling abbot as if trying to engage him through telepathy. It was absolutely silent here but the sound of Latin chant came from somewhere else in the building. Snowflakes started to drift past the high windows.

'Father Abbot,' said Macandrew softly but firmly.

A slight raise of the head told Macandrew that he had heard but he continued to pray.

'Father Abbot, I need to speak to you.'

The kneeling man seemed to stiffen then got up slowly and with some difficulty to his feet. He genuflected to the altar and turned round, his eyes betraying annoyance.

'You've heard about John Burnett?'

'I was praying for his soul.'

Macandrew ignored the implied rebuke. 'You know more about this business than you told me yesterday.'

The abbot remained impassive.

'Lives are in danger. You must tell me what's going on.'

'I've already told the police all I know.'

'Will you tell me?'

The abbot, after appearing to consider for a moment, said, 'Would you care for some tea, Doctor?'

'Thank you,' replied Macandrew. He felt both surprised and relieved as he followed him out of the chapel. He had been expecting a bigger mountain to climb.

The abbot filled two earthenware mugs that looked as if they had seen better days but Macandrew was glad of the hot tea and cupped both his hands round his to warm his fingers.

'There are things that I cannot and will

not tell you because of the confessional but I can say that John Burnett did uncover something in his research that upset him greatly. His faith was important to him and he came here to seek reassurance and find help in saving it. In the course of my duties I submitted a report to Rome – as I'm obliged to do on any man who wishes to join our order. It appears now that the reasons given in the report for John wanting to join us may have fallen into the wrong hands.'

'I don't understand.'

'After I sent the papers, I received a request from Rome. A bible scholar named Dom Ignatius, working in the Vatican, asked if he could come here to speak to John about his research work. John was reluctant so I didn't grant the request at first but then Ignatius called me personally and sought my help in persuading John to speak to him. He was very persuasive and I finally agreed. Ignatius came here to the abbey and interviewed John at some length.'

'This man's a priest?'

'Yes, but he's an academic, a biblical scholar who had been working in the Holy Land for many years, engaged in the study of Holy relics and their validation.'

'Like the Shroud of Turin, you mean?'

'There are many lesser-known relics in the Church's possession. Ignatius has given his life to establishing their authenticity through the interpretation of ancient scrolls and manuscripts, or not. Many of these documents have still not seen the light of day ... for one reason or another.'

'I suppose translation must be very slow and difficult,' said Macandrew.

'That's just one of the problems. There was an unhappy time in our history when Holy relics appeared to ... multiply.'

'A piece of the genuine Cross for five ducats and no questions asked,' said Macandrew.

'Quite,' said the abbot coldly. 'This tended to fog the issue greatly. What I didn't know about Ignatius when he came here was that he had recently been recalled to Rome from Israel in disgrace after being caught misappropriating certain parchments originating from the Essene community at Qumran. He'd kept them for his own exclusive use and had failed to share the information with his colleagues.'

'Sounds serious.'

'The Vatican thought so too. The commission in Jerusalem had to be appeased so they reprimanded Ignatius, recalled him and put him to work on routine administrative duties in Rome – quite a comedown for an academic with an international reputation – even for one taught to fight against the sin of pride. In the course of these duties he must have come across my report on John.'

'Why should such a scholar be interested in John Burnett's research?' asked Macandrew.

'I don't know,' replied the abbot, 'but when you pointed out the Israeli story to John, he was extremely upset. He wouldn't say why exactly but insisted that he had to speak to Ignatius as soon as possible. He asked that I contact the Vatican to arrange it.'

'And did you?'

'I called Rome and was told that my request had been noted and would be passed on but that Dom Ignatius was currently unavailable; no one would tell me why. John became very upset, so much so that I couldn't make much sense out of what he was saying – something about Ignatius probably wanting more of the stuff.'

'Why did John go to Edinburgh?'

'We had a call, requesting John's presence in Edinburgh. We were told that the bishop wanted to see him before his vows were finalised. We saw him on to the train and wished him well but he never got there.'

'And that call?'

'It turned out that none of the bishop's staff knew anything about it. I had sent John to his death.'

'You weren't to know,' said Macandrew. 'Have you told all this to the police?'

'I said nothing about Ignatius. I called Rome this morning after the police had left and refused to be fobbed off with "unavail-able". It appears that Dom Ignatius had recently made an unauthorised return to the Holy Land and was the priest involved in the convent scandal in Jerusalem. Apparently he has formed some kind of an association with a doctor he met out there; a shadowy charac-ter named Stroud. They've both now dis-appeared.'

'John was tortured before he was killed.'

The abbot swallowed hard. 'How awful.'

CHAPTER THIRTEEN

The small aircraft operated by Air France on the Edinburgh to Paris service landed with an uncomfortable bump at Roissy Charles de Gaulle airport but Macandrew didn't notice; he was preoccupied with other things. It had been a while since he'd last been in Paris but it was one of his favourite cities and one which he always associated with fun and laughter – an enduring legacy of his first visit when he had been a nine-teen-year-old college kid, travelling on a shoestring budget.

This time it was different: the city seemed austere, less welcoming, suspicious of him, as if it knew it had a role to play as a link in a chain of intrigue and death. Macandrew took in the sights on the journey from the airport without any stirring of emotion. The overcast sky didn't help the uneasy feeling he had in his stomach.

As the bus drew into the Air France terminal at Porte Maillot, he checked his watch and saw that he had plenty of time. The arrangement with Simone Robin had included a two-hour margin for possible delays but the flight had landed ten minutes early.

He walked up to the head of the Boul'Mich and bought a copy of *International Herald Tribune* from a street vendor before finding a café where he could sit and read it over coffee. Choosing to sit outside – it was dull but not cold – he thumbed through the pages and caught up on the news from home until, bored with that, he watched the world go by until it was time to make a move. With the slightest suggestion of drizzle in the air, he started to make his way to Notre Dame, crossing the Seine at Pont Royal and pausing briefly to watch a barge glide under the bridge. The huge twin towers of the cathedral loomed up in front of him, reminding him of the timelessness of stone when compared with human life.

Even this late in the year, the forecourt in front of the great west doors of the cathedral was crowded with tourists, many of them in formal groups being lectured to in a variety of languages by their guides. There was no likely woman standing on her own near the doors so he walked down the narrow street on the north side of the building and looked in the windows of the souvenir shops until it was time to check again.

He found a place where he could command a good view of the comings and goings at the west doors and had only been there a few minutes when he caught sight of a slim, dark-haired woman hurrying across the forecourt, carrying a briefcase under her arm. Feeling reasonably confident that this might be Simone Robin, he started out on a path to intercept her but stopped suddenly in his tracks when something about the body language of three people off to his right caught his attention. Two men, one tall and well built, the other short and fat and wearing dark glasses appeared to be holding on to a young woman between them. Although there wasn't much movement, Macandrew got the distinct impression that the girl was being held against her will. As he watched, one of the men shook the girl by the shoulder and she responded by pointing at the woman he was walking towards. The tall man detached himself and started walking towards her too while the fat man remained, holding firmly on to the girl.

Macandrew, sensing danger, ran towards

the woman. He took her firmly by the arm and steered her in through the doors of the cathedral before she had any real time to protest.

'Doctor Robin?'

'What on earth do you think you're doing?' asked the woman, struggling to free herself from his grip.

'You were followed.'

'Don't be ridiculous!'

Macandrew pulled her behind one of the pillars in a corner to the left of the door. 'Please, just watch the doors.'

Macandrew was conscious of the sound of his own breathing as the seconds ticked by without sign of the man.

'This is ridiculous!' hissed the French-woman angrily.

Macandrew was beginning to have doubts himself. 'There were two men,' he said. 'They had a young woman with them. She pointed you out.'

Simone Robin's response was stifled when three people came in through the doors. It was the two men, holding a girl between them. Macandrew heard her gasp, 'Aline!'

'Your assistant?'

Simone Robin nodded mutely.

'You told her you were coming here?'

'I saw no reason not to.'

'It's you they're after. They must have gone to your lab and forced her to tell them where you were and then forced her to come here and point you out.'

'This is...'

'Sssh!' whispered Macandrew as he saw the tall man look about him and then leave the other two. He seemed to be heading almost straight towards the corner where they were hiding. There was a screened alcove behind them. Macandrew manoeuvred Simone behind the curtain and put his finger to his lips. He took up stance behind an adjacent pillar and listened for approaching footsteps.

There was no sound at all save for the muted chatter of tourists in the main aisles and an occasional echoing cough. This unnerved him. If he couldn't hear footsteps the man must be deliberately moving quietly. Did he know they were there?

Macandrew's nerves were being stretched to breaking point. His blood ran cold at the sound of a single metallic click. He knew instinctively that it was a switchblade knife being opened and had a flashback to Burnett's body and his bloodstained robe.

He couldn't hear the man and he couldn't smell him but he knew he was there; he could *feel* his presence. A mistake now could be fatal. He stopped breathing and listened. The slightest scuff of a shoe told him the man was on the other side of the pillar and slightly to his left. He riveted his eyes on the ground and tensed himself to act at the first sign of movement. The toe of a black shoe appeared and Macandrew edged round the pillar in the opposite direction. He was trying to keep directly opposite his opponent.

Fear had heightened Macandrew's senses. He found the smell of the cathedral – a cocktail of dust, old books and wood polish – almost overpowering. Although tourists were only a matter of twenty yards or so away from them, the sheer size of the dark, cavernous building absorbed the noise to such an extent that he heard Simone Robin make a tiny sound from behind the curtain. In that instant, he knew that the game of cat and mouse was over. He heard her gasp as the man snatched back the curtain to expose her hiding place.

Macandrew moved swiftly round the pillar and saw the knife being held at her throat. Simone let out a scream that echoed to the roof just as Macandrew, bunching his fist and using it like a hammer to avoid testing the suspect bones in his hand, brought it down on the back of the man neck. The man fell to the floor and lay perfectly still.

'Jesus!' exclaimed an American voice somewhere off to their right, 'What in tarnation was that?' The level of general hubbub rose appreciably. Macandrew held Simone close to him behind the pillar. He could feel her whole body tremble. 'It's all right,' he whispered. 'You're safe now.'

'He had a knife...'

'Ssh. It's all right.'

'It came from over there!' said a voice.

Macandrew knew that they must move quickly but suddenly there was another loud scream and attention was mercifully diverted from their corner. This scream was followed by several more and general pandemonium broke out. It gave Macandrew and Simone the opportunity to slip away from the alcove without attracting attention to themselves.

'He was going to kill me,' said Simone.

'I don't think so,' said Macandrew. 'You have something they want.'

In the gloom they could see that a crowd had gathered on the other side of the cathedral; officials were trying to get through. Among the many foreign voices, Macandrew picked up an occasional English one. 'She's dead, Frances. I'm telling you; the woman's dead.'

'Nonsense. She's probably just fainted.'

Simone Robin's hands flew to her face and Macandrew heard her gasp, 'It's Aline. I know it is.'

Macandrew told Simone to wait while he drifted off to mingle with the crowd. A young woman was being lifted up from the floor where she had fallen between rows of seats. Her arms hung limply as she was laid out gently along three chairs which had been pushed together. He looked down at the pale face of the young French girl the two men had been holding. The flickering candles, the musty smell and a faint hint of incense all contrived to make the scene seem surreal. As if ordained by some unseen film director, a thin trickle of blood escaped from the girl's mouth and rolled down her jaw to drip on to the floor.

'She's dead!' whispered a voice.

Macandrew was about to agree when, to his enormous relief, the unconscious girl groaned and put her hand to her jaw, feeling for injury. She started asking questions of those around her. Macandrew backed away to rejoin Simone.

'It was her, wasn't it?' she said. 'It was Aline?'

'One of them must have hit her and knocked her out but she's coming round: she'll be OK.'

'Thank God! I must go to her. This is all my fault.'

Macandrew put a restraining hand on Simone shoulder. 'I heard someone say an ambulance was on its way. She'll be in good hands but there's still a chance that they're waiting for you outside.'

Simone looked to the doors. 'Oh God,' she said slowly. She put her hands to her face and stared ahead unseeingly for a few moments.

229

Macandrew could see that Simone was approaching the end of her tether. He didn't feel so well himself. He watched her take a deep breath, as if to steady herself, then ask with an air of resignation, 'So what do we do now?'

'Let's attach ourselves to one of the tourist groups when they leave,' said Macandrew. It was a hastily improvised plan but he wanted to get outside before the cathedral attendants got round to thinking it would be a good idea to stop people leaving before the police arrived. He took Simone by the hand and they walked towards the doors. 'There!' he said as he saw a party of Germans start to leave; their guide had just completed a head count. 'Let's mingle.'

As they emerged into the light Macandrew put his arm round Simone's shoulder and they sidled up to a young German couple as if they were old friends. *'Das war Wunderbar!'* he said in his best schoolboy German.

The German woman looked puzzled. Had they missed all the excitement? she wanted to know. A woman had been assaulted in the cathedral in the middle of the day. It could have been any of them. This city wasn't safe.

Macandrew, picking up the sense if not the meaning of every word, adopted what he hoped were suitable changes of expression. *'Gott im Himmel,'* he exclaimed, hoping it might be the right thing to say but knowing it didn't really matter. All that mattered was that, if anyone was watching, they would see four people engaged in animated conversation. He didn't think either of the two men had got a good look at Simone or himself because it had been so dark inside. Nevertheless, he was still apprehensive as they turned into the lane that led to the coach park.

He became aware that the German woman had asked him something and both she and her husband were looking expectantly at him. He saw the first seeds of suspicion grow in the Germans' eyes. *'Himmel!'* he exclaimed, stopping in his tracks and putting his hand to his mouth as if he had just remembered something important. He turned to Simone and said, *'Helga! Komm!'* With that, he took Simone's hand and pulled her across the road into one of the tourist shops. There was sweat on his brow as he half turned to see the Germans moving on. The woman kept glancing back and saying something to her husband but the immediate crisis was over.

They spent the next ten minutes pretending to browse through tourist trash before Macandrew risked a look outside the shop and thought it safe to move on. They hurried across the Archeveche to the left bank of the Seine and half walked, half ran along the footpath to the head of the Boulevard San Michel.

'The university is just over there,' said Simone, pointing to the other side of the street.

'We can't risk going there,' said Macandrew, looking across to the sprawling concrete campus of the Seventh University of Paris, its tower blocks rising like urban weeds. 'They know where you work. That's how they got to your assistant.'

Simone put her hand to her head and said, 'Sorry, I'm just not thinking straight.'

Macandrew put an arm round her. 'Let's find a café,' he said. 'Somewhere to sit down. I don't know about you but I could use a drink.'

They turned away from the university and continued walking until they found a small café where they took a table as far back from the door as they could. Simone sat staring at the table surface, unaware that a waiter had joined them and was hovering at her elbow. Macandrew ordered coffee and brandy for both of them.

'I shouldn't be sitting here,' said Simone. 'I should go to the police... I'll have to inform the director... I need to find out how Aline is.'

'If you were to tell me what all this is all about, then maybe we could both go to the police,' said Macandrew. 'It's got something to do with the research that you and Burnett

232

were working on, hasn't it?'

Simone looked down at the table for fully thirty seconds before finally saying, 'Maybe.' She paused while the waiter put down their order and then took a sip of brandy before beginning, 'John Burnett did not start researching Hartman's tumours by accident. His wife lost her mind after the surgery to have one removed: she had to be committed to an institution. John took it very badly. He spent hours with her, trying to make sense of her condition. Over a period of time he became convinced that she was not raving incoherently as everyone seemed to imagine, but that she had assumed the personality of someone else – several other people in fact – but they were all mixed up inside her head.'

Macandrew nodded. 'I guess that's pretty much what I've seen in my patient.'

'The medical staff at the hospital listened to what John had to say and between them, they tried out a series of techniques involving stimulation and sedation to see if they could stabilise Anne – John's wife – to a single personality. To some extent they were successful. She would become one person for as long as a few hours under controlled conditions but she was never herself: she was never John's wife: she was always someone else. John was heartbroken but he never gave up hope. He decided to work full time on Hartman's tumours and their after-effects.'

'Could he just do that?' asked Macandrew.

'Luckily he could,' said Simone. 'He had already established an international reputation as a biochemist so his department at the university agreed to a change of research direction. They knew that if they turned down his request he would have left and gone elsewhere and they didn't want to lose him.'

'Makes sense,' agreed Macandrew.

'He made good progress, not least because he worked night and day on his new project. The thought of being able to do something to help Anne was such a strong driving force.'

Macandrew found himself regretting having lectured Burnett about the duty of a researcher.

'John discovered that Hartman's tumours secrete a protease that affects an area of the brain immediately behind the pineal gland. He managed to identify the specific brain cells involved and then obtained post-mortem samples of them from a number of people who had died of natural causes. He wanted to find out just what the normal function of these cells was – it's amazing how little we know about the human brain. He found that these cells produced a previously unidentified enzyme, which he called Theta 1.'

'So it's the lack of this enzyme that causes

the personality change?'

'That's right,' said Simone. 'John managed to get a grant from one of the cancer charities to expand the work and he employed a post-doctoral assistant to help with the research. He took on Ashok Mukherjee, an Indian biochemist with first-class credentials and Mukherjee succeeded in purifying the enzyme. It was a very exciting time for them and this was where I came in. I'm a molecular biologist. John took me on to clone Theta 1 so that we could produce unlimited supplies of it.'

'And you could start replacing it in brain-damaged patients?'

'That was the idea. We carried out some animal tests to see if there were any ill-effects associated with the enzyme but there didn't appear to be so...'

'John Burnett treated his wife with it?'

'It was highly unethical, I know, but ... yes, he did.'

'And?' asked Macandrew expectantly.

'Anne developed total memory loss. Her mind became a complete blank. She started each day without knowing anything at all. She didn't recognise anything or anybody.'

Macandrew grimaced.

'John still didn't give up hope. The fact that Theta 1 had affected memory suggested that he was on the right track. He started working on the protease that the tumours

235

produced. He hoped he could synthesise a chemical equivalent in the lab that would mimic the effects of a tumour.'

'Why?'

'He suspected that the problem with Theta 1 treatment might be something to do with dosage or potency. He thought the purified stuff we made in the lab might be too strong so his idea was to counteract it with a bit of synthetic protease. That way, he might be able to strike the right balance.'

'Clever,' said Macandrew.

'It was much easier to say than to do,' said Simone. 'Synthesising such a protease proved to be very difficult.'

'But he succeeded?'

'After six months' hard work.'

'What about his wife?' asked Macandrew. 'Did she ever get her memory back?'

'In a way,' said Simone uncomfortably.

'What way?'

'After more treatment she stabilised as a fourteen-year-old girl living in London. John's wife had, in fact, been born and brought up in London.'

'Are you saying that she had regressed to being a child?' asked Macandrew.

'Not exactly...' said Simone, pausing as if uneasy about what she was going to say next. 'She told us that her home had been destroyed in a fire that had swept through the city and that her mother had died of a great illness the year before. She was terrified of everything around her and recognised nothing.'

'Are you saying what I think you're saying...?' said Macandrew.

'The Great Fire of London was in sixteen sixty-six,' said Simone. 'A year after the Great Plague had ravaged the city. Anne could tell us about both these events in great detail.'

'My God.'

'Anne remained in character. John was left married to a fourteen-year-old child from the seventeenth century.'

Macandrew was left speechless.

'There was worse to come,' said Simone. 'Anne took her own life. She threw herself from a window at the institution.'

CHAPTER FOURTEEN

'John was never really the same after that,' said Simone. 'He seemed to lose all confidence and started to question everything he'd done with his life. He'd always been a deeply religious man in spite of the contradictions that his career threw up along the way but now, suddenly, he found himself hopelessly confused and uncertain. His own research had undermined the very foundations of his faith. What happened next really pushed him over the edge.'

Simone paused to sip her brandy. 'After Anne's death, none of us had much heart for the project so we decided that we would take a break. We agreed to meet again after one month to discuss what we were going to do – continue or abandon the whole project. John chose to go on retreat to a monastery; I came home to Paris; Ashok returned to India to see his family ... or so he said.'

'You mean he didn't?'

'Oh yes, he went back to India but he had something other than his family in mind. Ashok had been wondering what the lack of Theta 1 did to patients to cause such major changes in personality – admittedly it was scientifically intriguing. Unknown to John and me, he took a vial of the synthetic protease with him to India and started experimenting – Third World countries are a Mecca for unscrupulous researchers. They're like giant laboratories with unlimited human resources and very little paperwork to get in the way. In a land where people are willing to sell their kidneys for a few rupees, it was easy for Mukherjee to get "volunteers" to undergo tests with the protease.'

'How did you find out about this?'

'Mukherjee confessed everything to John when he came back. He was feeling so guilty.'

Macandrew waited while Simone took another sip of brandy.

'After giving them the protease, Mukherjee started to panic when his volunteers started behaving like the Hartman's tumour patients: they underwent severe personality change and started to assume new personalities. He tried to redress the balance by giving them some cloned Theta 1 but he had to use crude estimates and this wasn't very successful.'

'What happened?' asked Macandrew.

'He managed to stabilise a few of them but never as themselves. Like John's wife and your patient back in the States, their old selves seemed to have been wiped out for ever.'

'None of them recovered?'

'At first Ashok lied and told us that they had all made a full recovery, but after close questioning from John he admitted this wasn't so. None recovered. Four died and two were left deranged.'

Macandrew grimaced. 'What happened to Mukherjee?'

'There was no point in reporting what he'd done to the British police because the crime had taken place in India and the people who had suffered were Indian nationals. John fired him and told him that if he had anything to do with it he would never work in science again. Ashok went back to India. The last I heard he was working among the poor in Calcutta.'

'You don't have to be a psychologist to work that one out,' said Macandrew.

'I suppose not.'

'That still leaves the question about what Theta I does in the normal brain,' said Macandrew.

'It does,' replied Simone. When she looked up at Macandrew he saw that she looked very vulnerable.

'Will you say it or shall I?' he asked.

'Perhaps you?' said Simone, as if somehow hoping that some secret she was harbouring might still be safe.

'From what you've said,' began Macandrew hesitantly and painfully conscious of the enormity of the conclusion he was about to draw, 'it would appear that Theta 1 wipes out memories of ... lives we've lived before ... past lives?'

Simone conceded with a sigh. She closed her eyes for a few silent moments before saying, 'I think that's really why John had a breakdown. He just couldn't cope with the idea.'

'So he ran away from it.'

'He was full of doubts and questions about his faith: it had always been so important to him.'

For a few more moments, the only sound was a gentle hubbub of conversation from the other tables and the clink of coffee cups in the background.

'It seems to be the only explanation that fits with everything we've seen,' said Macandrew. 'On a bigger scale it would explain multiple personality disorder and changes of personality after brain surgery and why some people can undergo memory regression under hypnosis. If these cells behind the pineal gland get damaged and stop making Theta 1, the natural memory block breaks down and the patient remembers – and assumes – previous personalities. Only it's not just patients, it's all of us. Jesus, this could have enormous implications for society all over the world.'

'That's why we didn't publish anything about it,' said Simone.

'I can see how a lot of people might find it difficult to come to terms with,' said Macandrew. 'I take it you're not religious yourself?'

Simone shook her head. 'I'm a scientist. I need proof before I accept anything and I've long since stopped apologising for that or feeling guilty about it.'

'So the idea of a past life doesn't upset you?' said Macandrew.

'If anything, I find it reassuring that the end of this life might not actually be the final curtain I had assumed it to be.'

'You know,' said Macandrew, still considering the implications, 'it might be the same enzyme that helps us get over grief. People are always saying that time is a great healer and we all know how we recover from grief and pick up the pieces. After a while you tend to remember only the good things.'

Simone smiled. 'And you're left with summer days that went on for ever.'

'So John Burnett and Mukherjee gave up scientific research entirely and you changed fields?'

'I did ... but I continued to work on the tumour project part time. It had to be that way because we agreed that the work could never be published because of the possible repercussions.'

'So what have you been doing?'

'The original aim for all three of us was to find a way of helping people who had been left brain damaged, so I've continued to do as much as I could along these lines. One of the things that struck me was the fact that the Theta 1-producing cells were not actually destroyed by the tumours; they just stopped producing the enzyme. I've been trying to find a way of turning production back on again.'

'Sounds like a reasonable approach,' agreed Macandrew.

'I've managed to set up a cell culture system in the lab where I can turn off Theta 1 in cells using John's synthetic protease and then I try to turn it back on again using various chemical compounds.'

'Any luck?'

'I've come up with something that works in the lab. Whether it will work in patients or not is quite another matter.'

'But that's absolutely wonderful,' said Macandrew. 'You haven't tried it out yet?'

'Not possible,' replied Simone. 'There's no way I could get permission to set up any kind of trial without explaining the rationale behind it. I think this may be why John suggested you come here. You're a neurosurgeon with access to brain-damaged patients and you were already on the right track.'

Macandrew nodded, quickly diverting his eyes in case Simone would see the uncertainty there.

'Now it's your turn to answer questions,' said Simone. 'Who were these people at Notre Dame today? What did they want from me?'

'The man behind it all seems to be a discredited Roman Catholic priest named Dom Ignatius.'

'A priest?' exclaimed Simone.

'He's a disgraced academic, a scripture scholar and a specialist in the history and recovery of holy scripts and relics. He'd been working in the Holy Land for many years on old manuscripts and scrolls but apparently he did something dishonest and was found out. The Vatican recalled him to Rome and gave him a menial office job but it was through this that he came across a reference to John Burnett. He learnt what Burnett had been doing and became very interested. He travelled to the abbey in Scotland and persuaded him to tell him all about his work. According to the abbot, Burnett told him everything – maybe hoping to gain some kind of absolution. From what you've told me however, it sounds as if Ignatius managed to get his hands on some of John's synthetic protease and used it to carry out his own experiments, just like Mukherjee.'

'John took what was left of the protease with him when he cleared out his lab for the last time,' said Simone. 'He didn't want to leave it lying around.'

'So that makes sense,' said Macandrew. 'He must have given it to Ignatius. Everything points to Ignatius having used the stuff on a group of men in Israel.'

'But why?' said Simone. 'What did he hope to gain?'

'Ignatius has formed an association with a doctor named Stroud. Reading between the lines, they must have seen using the protease as a way of gaining more knowledge about the past. If they could regress native Israelis using the protease, they just might come up with some really interesting eyewitness accounts of times past in the Holy Land.'

'But this man Ignatius must have known that he would damage the people it was used on,' said Simone. 'John would have told him that.'

'From what I've learnt about them, I don't think that he or Stroud would see that as a problem,' said Macandrew.

Simone shivered. 'They must have used up the small quantity of protease that John gave them. They must need more. That's what this must be about.'

'I think, if I was them,' said Macandrew, 'I would want to know how to make the stuff. I suspect they're really after Burnett's lab notes but he didn't keep them, did he? He gave them to you. John must have told them that.'

'John wouldn't...'

'They tortured him.'

'Tortured?' exclaimed Simone, looking horrified.

'I'm sorry, but he would have told them everything.'

'Oh, poor John,' said Simone. 'He was such a nice man.'

'Well, he's at peace now,' said Macandrew, but he had to look away as the words conflicted with the image that sprang to mind of Burnett's body, nailed to the back of the door in the seminary. 'More coffee?'

Simone shook her head.

'You know, what I don't understand is why

Ignatius still wants the stuff,' said Macandrew. 'He's wanted by the police in Israel
– probably for murder by now if some of his
volunteers suffered the same fate as Mukherjee's. He can hardly go back and do it all
again so why does he want it so badly?'

Simone shrugged.

'The missing patient!' exclaimed Macandrew, answering his own question.

'What missing patient?'

'One of the Israeli volunteers Ignatius was
experimenting on; he and Stroud took him
with them when they made a run for it.
There must have been something special
about him.'

'You mean he already *has* his eyewitness?'
said Simone.

'I can't think of any other reason for ab-
ducting someone when you're trying to flee
the country,' said Macandrew. 'Can you?'

'No,' agreed Simone.

'It's about time we made contact with the
police and got you some proper protection.
Do you actually have any of the protease?'

'I have a little in the lab. I also have all
John's notes.'

Simone and Macandrew took a cab to police
headquarters where they were shown to a
second-floor office. A handsome man in his
early thirties, wearing a well-cut charcoal
suit, blue shirt and red silk tie and holding a

246

cigarette loosely between his fingers, introduced himself as Inspector Paul Chirac.

'So, *madame,* you say you know something about the assault in Notre Dame today and you think your life is in danger, is that right?'

'*I* say her life is in danger,' interrupted Macandrew.

'Why?'

Macandrew took a deep breath and began. 'It's a long and complicated story but I suspect that recently you and the other European police forces have probably received a request from the Israeli authorities to keep a lookout for a priest named Dom Ignatius...'

When Macandrew had finished, the policeman lifted the phone in front of him and asked for something to be checked. There was a long pause before he uttered several grunts and a final, *'Merci.'* He dropped the phone down in its cradle and said, 'We have had such an alert. Perhaps you would care to tell me how this concerns you?'

Macandrew wanted to give away as little as possible but had to say something and make it sound plausible.

'What exactly does this chemical do?' asked Chirac.

'It's a hallucinogen,' replied Macandrew.

Chirac looked at him. 'A synthetic hallucinogen? A designer drug?'

'If you like.'

'Why should a priest be interested in such a thing?' asked Chirac.

'I don't think he's a priest any more,' replied Macandrew.

A uniformed man came into the room, saluted and put down a sheet of paper on Chirac's desk. Macandrew could see it was a computer printout. Chirac read it while Macandrew and Simone exchanged reassuring glances.

'This drug,' began Chirac. 'Is it responsible for the condition of the men found by the Israeli police?'

'We think so.'

'And you, *madame*, are responsible for making it?'

'I was involved in the original research,' agreed Simone. 'Unfortunately, some of it fell into the wrong hands.'

'Why design such a thing in the first place?' exclaimed Chirac with a Gallic spread of the hands.

'It was a side product of our research into brain tumours.'

Chirac nodded in a way that suggested that he really didn't understand but didn't want to waste time pursuing it. 'And now your life is in danger because this man, Ignatius, wants to know the formula for this drug. Is that right?'

'Yes.'

248

Chirac looked back over the notes he had been making then asked Macandrew, 'Was Ignatius one of the men at the cathedral today?'

'I wouldn't know. I've never seen him.'

Chirac looked at the paper in front of him again and read out, 'One metre ninety, slim build, sallow complexion, prominent nose, black hair swept back, brown eyes, a small scar on the left cheek – this is from the Israeli police.'

'Doesn't sound like either of the men in the cathedral,' said Macandrew.

'Probably travelling in the company of an Austrian psychiatrist named Stroud,' continued Chirac. 'Stroud is wanted by the Egyptian police after attempting to smuggle illegal artefacts out of the country.' He read out a description.

Macandrew shook his head.

'Can you describe the men in the cathedral?'

Macandrew told him what he could about height and build and the fact that they had both been wearing dark suits. One had been wearing dark glasses.

'And you, *madame?*'

'I saw the face of the man with the knife but it was quite dark in the corner and I was terrified at the time. But there was one thing...'

'*Oui?*'

'I think he had a prosthetic eye.'

'You're sure?'

'I was scared, but...' Simone paused for a moment before continuing, 'his left, yes it was his left eye, didn't move with his right. I'm pretty sure it was prosthetic.'

'That's certainly something we can ask the computer about,' said Chirac. He wrote quickly on a pad in front of him and pressed a button on the telephone. Someone came in and took away the note. 'In the meantime, *madame,* we will provide you with protection until we arrest these men.'

'I'm grateful, monsieur.'

'We would, of course, like you to make full statements about what happened in Notre Dame today before you leave.'

'Of course,' said Macandrew.

'When you have done that we will arrange transport for you *madame.* And you, *monsieur,* what are your plans?'

Macandrew shrugged and said, 'I don't have any firm plans. I was hoping Dr Robin and I might talk further before I left Paris.' He looked at Simone who nodded. 'Then I'll return to Scotland and probably leave for the States at the weekend, unless there are any objections?'

Chirac shrugged once more in true French fashion and said, 'Not for my part, *monsieur,* although we would like a contact address. Do you know where you will be staying in

Paris tonight?'

'Not yet,' confessed Macandrew.

'You can stay at my place,' said Simone. 'There's plenty of room and I think I'd rather not be alone this evening.'

'Thank you,' said Macandrew.

As Simone and Macandrew were later escorted to the door of the building a uniformed man caught up with them and handed something to Chirac. Chirac showed it to Simone. It was a photograph.

Simone caught her breath.

'Is this the man, *madame?*'

Simone nodded.

'You were right about the left eye,' said Chirac. 'He lost it in a knife fight in Naples in 1984. He's Vito Parvelli. The computer knew him. Ignatius and Stroud are not associating with choirboys.'

CHAPTER FIFTEEN

The police car took them to the Montrouge district of Paris where Simone had an apartment on the second floor of a three-storey building. She was assured that a gendarme would be on duty outside at all times and that, if she wanted to go out, she should inform the man on duty. She thanked the officers but her eyes reflected the unease she felt at being in such a situation. She entered the code for the entry system and the latch clicked open, admitting them to a half-tiled entry hall that smelt vaguely of antiseptic.

There was a central elevator of the open-cage type that spoke of a nineteen-thirties origin but Simone headed for the stairs which spiralled round the elevator shaft and Macandrew followed. He noticed on the way up that a dentist had his surgery on the first floor – the source of the antiseptic smell.

Simone's apartment was light and airy and furnished with elegant simplicity. A Rene Magritte print of *The Black Flag* hung in the middle of a long white wall above a cream leather sofa. The floors were polished wood and the curtains oatmeal with orange tie-backs, which provided the only splash of colour.

'When did you last eat?' asked Simone.

Macandrew realised that he hadn't thought about food in a long time. 'On the plane this morning, I guess.'

'I don't suppose either of us is much interested in food,' said Simone. 'But it's best that we eat something. An omelette?'

'Great.'

'Help yourself to a drink.' Simone pointed to a tray with three or four bottles of spirits and half a dozen glasses sitting on it. 'Campari and soda for me.'

Macandrew watched Simone disappear into the kitchen. He poured the drinks, whisky for himself, and took Simone's through to her. 'Can I do anything?' he asked.

'This kitchen is too small for two people,' said Simone, tensing her shoulders at the voice behind her and keeping her back to him. 'Please just go and make yourself comfortable.'

Macandrew returned to the other room where he stood at the window looking out at the early evening traffic but his thoughts were of Simone and the fact that she was so much on edge. He was just thinking that her nerves had been strung so tight that something had to give soon when he heard a crash come from the kitchen.

'*Merde!*'

'Are you all right?' Macandrew found Simone standing with her hands held up to her face. She was looking down at a plate that lay broken on the floor but she wasn't seeing it. He could see that her fingers were trembling.

'Hey,' he said softly. 'It's over. You're safe now.' He wrapped his arms round her and shushed her gently as the tears came.

'I keep seeing the man with the knife...' murmured Simone, her cheek warm and wet against Macandrew's chest. 'And yet you were so calm.'

'I think paralysed with fear might be a better description,' confessed Macandrew, 'but I'm glad you thought it was calmness ... a man thing, you understand,' he added tongue in cheek.

Simone managed a smile through her tears. 'And I suppose you regard bursting into tears as a woman thing,' she said.

'*Vive la difference*,' said Macandrew.

Simone pulled away and brushed away her tears with both hands. 'God, I feel so stupid,' she said. 'I'm behaving like a silly schoolgirl. I must look a sight.'

'Obsession with appearance ... another woman thing,' said Macandrew.

Simone smiled and pretended to thump her fists on Macandrew's chest.

Macandrew caught her wrists gently and said, 'The main thing is that we're both still alive ... and it's all over. It really is.'

There was a long pause when Simone looked at him questioningly and he hoped that she couldn't tell what he was thinking because care and concern were now secondary to another emotion he felt well up inside him. He let go of Simone's wrists and looked away to seek diversion but she reached up and turned his chin towards her, her eyes asking the question. Her lips parted and Macandrew kissed her, gently at first but then hungrily as he felt her move in close to him. He pulled her even closer and felt her tongue probe his mouth.

He broke away a little to murmur, 'You're sure about this?'

'I need to *feel* alive, John,' said Simone. 'I have to know it... I don't need flowers... I don't need dinner... I don't need romance... I need to be fucked.'

The word had an electric effect on Macandrew, who, despite now wanting Simone so badly, still had reservations about the situation – mainly the fear that he was taking advantage of it. He felt the last of them wash away as she uttered the word. He pinned her to the wall and freed himself before reaching under her skirt to push her panties to one side and enter her hard and long. He cupped his hands round her backside and pulled her on to him, matching the thrust of his hips and being exhorted to ever greater efforts by Simone's moans in his ear. 'Christ, I want you,' he gasped.

'Then have me...'

The all too brief outcome of such passion left Macandrew holding Simone to him and resting his forehead on the wall as his breathing subsided.

Simone broke the silence. 'Tell me how you feel,' she murmured.

After a moment's thought, Macandrew said, 'Embarrassed. Dare I ask about you?'

'Fucked,' replied Simone.

Macandrew smiled, feeling such a surge of relief when he saw that Simone was smiling too. She ran the tips of her fingers softly down his cheek. 'Let's go shower,' she said.

Showering together was as gentle an experience as their lovemaking had been passionate. They took lingering pleasure in tracing the contours of each other with soap and sponge and found it deliciously sensual. 'Do you know what I'm going to do now?' murmured Simone.

'Tell me,' said Macandrew drowsily as he closed his eyes and put his head back on the shower wall.

Simone reached up and yanked the regulator over to COLD, causing Macandrew to let out a yelp of surprise. 'Make an omelette,' she said.

'Will you come with me to the lab tomorrow?' Simone asked from the kitchen.

'If you like.'

'I'd like you to see my results with the *in vitro* cell system. I haven't been able to show them to anyone and you would be the perfect collaborator. It's no good having a cure that only works in the lab...'

Macandrew was slow to respond to this and Simone noticed. 'There's something wrong with that idea?' she asked.

'It might take time to set up,' said Macandrew. 'Getting permission to perform any

256

kind of surgical research in the Midwest of the USA isn't easy.'

'I see,' said Simone, in a tone that suggested that she didn't. 'Is that all that's worrying you?'

Macandrew had no heart for verbal chess. 'I'm not operating at the moment. I'm not sure if I ever will again.'

Simone stopped what she was doing and came through to stand in the doorway. Macandrew had his back to her but knew she was there. He told her what had happened while continuing to gaze unseeingly out of the window.

'But that is absolutely awful!' Simone came over and joined him. She took his hands gently in hers. 'When will you know?'

'The pain has all but gone and I seem to have freedom of movement but whether it's going to be good enough for surgery ... well, that's something I still have to find out. I'll spend some time in the autopsy room when I get back and see how I get on with a knife in my hand. *Practice on the dead makes perfect on the living,* as an old professor at med school used to say.'

'What an absolutely awful thing to happen,' said Simone. 'So this is how you came to be in Scotland in November?'

Macandrew nodded. 'I had to get away. I needed something to take my mind off things so I thought I'd do what we Americans tend to do and come to Europe to trace my roots.'

Simone said, 'And you got more than you bargained for.'

'And then some.'

They ate and spent the rest of the evening getting to know each other, telling each other about their backgrounds and how they came to enter medicine. A second bottle of wine came into play and the conversation moved on from talk of the academic systems in their respective countries to memories of student days and finally to childhood confessions as they became perfectly comfortable with each other.

Macandrew learnt how Simone had once stolen her sister's clothes while she was bathing naked in a pool near the family's summer home in Provence. He owned up to once emptying large amounts of liquid soap into the fountain in the grounds of his school in Boston on prize-giving day.

As it grew late, the wine and the events of the day started to take its toll on both of them. Macandrew noticed Simone's eyelids coming together. He said gently, 'It's been a long day: you're tired.'

Simone smiled and said sleepily, 'Thank you for saving my life today.'

'Don't mention it,' replied Macandrew. 'It's a man thing.'

The morning was cold and damp and a fine drizzle settled on Simone's hair as they waited at the front door for the police car that was to take them up to the Seventh University of Paris. When it finally did arrive, they got in and sat in silence as they made painfully slow progress through the early morning traffic.

'Not very lovely, I'm afraid,' said Simone as they pulled up outside a concrete campus which was still scarred by graffiti from student protests of many years before. 'Nineteen sixty-eight,' said Simone in answer to Macandrew's unspoken question.

'Of course,' said Macandrew after a moment's thought. 'The famous Paris student riots – the folks who were going to change the world. Wonder what became of them,' he said as he tried to decipher the messages living on in the fading spray-paint.

'They became doctors and lawyers and accountants like every other generation, I suppose,' smiled Simone.

'And now, with something to lose,' said Macandrew, 'they're a bit more reticent with their demands for social justice.'

'Do I detect a certain cynicism there?' smiled Simone.

'People are people. Don't expect too much and you won't be disappointed. That's my motto.'

'Definitely cynical.'

'I prefer realistic.'

They arrived at a tower-block building with the number 43 on it. 'This is where I work,' said Simone. The police driver who had been walking a few paces behind them took up station at the entrance while Simone and Macandrew went inside. Macandrew carried his travel bag over his shoulder. It was his intention to catch a flight back to Edinburgh in the afternoon.

'If you do find that your hands are all right for surgery...' began Simone cautiously.

'Then I'd like nothing better than to collaborate with you,' interrupted Macandrew.

Simone relaxed. 'Good; maybe I should give you some brain sections to examine,' she said. 'You can study them along with the topographical sketches I can also give you. You might like to carry out some feasibility studies while you're down in Pathology. You could pinpoint the relevant area of the brain in cadavers and maybe think about the best surgical approach.'

'I think I already have an idea how I might approach it but a lot depends on what has to be done to the cells to stimulate them.'

'I'm hoping that simply bathing them directly in the activator will be enough to trigger them back into production,' said Simone. 'That's what happens in the test tube.'

'Then that should be possible with a minimum of invasive surgery – perhaps through the introduction of a flexible needle via the nasal route.'

'I'd like you to see my data,' said Simone. She brought out a thick file of papers from her desk and thumbed through them before picking out a graph and sliding it over to Macandrew. She came and stood behind him to emphasise various points.

Macandrew was aware of her nearness and her perfume.

'This is where the protease was applied,' said Simone. 'You can see that production of Theta 1 stops almost immediately.'

Macandrew saw the flattening of the curve until it became a plateau. 'Certainly does.'

'And here is where I added back the activator.' Simone pointed with the tip of her pen. 'Production of the enzyme starts again after a delay of only a few minutes.'

Macandrew followed the line which took a steep rise. 'No doubt about that and it's back to normal in ... four, five, six ... less than seven minutes. That's really impressive.'

'Do you think so?' said Simone, suddenly seeming vulnerable again and looking directly at him. 'It would be so good to be able to do something for these people.'

'If this works as well *in vivo*, then you've done it,' said Macandrew. 'You've found a cure.'

'It's still a big if,' said Simone, turning away.

She brought out a flat wooden box from a cupboard behind her desk and flicked open the lid. It contained rows of microscope slides. She ran her finger down the index on the lid and removed three, which she installed in a smaller cardboard box fitted with plastic guides to keep the slides apart. She sealed the box with tape. 'These are the brain sections I mentioned,' she said.

Macandrew slipped the box into his bag, checked his watch and got to his feet slowly. 'Well, I guess I should be going,' he said.

Simone sensed his awkwardness. 'Maybe we should shake hands?' she suggested mischievously.

'No,' replied Macandrew.

Simone came towards him. 'No, I don't think so either.'

They kissed but were interrupted by the telephone. When Simone had finished taking the call the moment had passed. 'Maybe I should give you a copy of John's research notes?' she said. 'Just in case anything should happen...'

'Nothing's going to happen, Simone,' said Macandrew, taking her in his arms again. 'The police will catch these men and the guard will remain with you until they do.' Macandrew kissed her again and they hugged for a moment. 'I'll call you as soon as I get back.'

'And the secret, Mac?'

'It's safe with me.'

Macandrew told the gendarme on the door that Simone was still in her lab but that he would now be leaving. He walked up to the Seine to take a last look, very much aware that his European adventure was coming to an end. He would make arrangements for a flight back to the States as soon as he got back to Scotland. It was time to find out if he still had a career. The thought made him look down at his hands as he gripped the top rail near the approach to Pont Neuf. He flexed his fingers in unison as a Bateau Mouche passed underneath with its recorded commentary for the tourists drifting across the water. They felt fine.

There was a queue at the check-in desk for the Edinburgh flight and it didn't seem to be moving. Macandrew could see that the fault lay with a couple at the front who had a problem with paperwork and were arguing loudly with the girl behind the desk. He adopted his grin-and-bear-it philosophy – which he always brought with him to airports – but occasionally glanced back at the queue starting to stretch out behind him as the minutes ticked by.

He was aware of two men some four places back in the line where one kept asking the other if he was feeling all right. He didn't give it much thought – lots of people were nervous at the thought of flying – but, as he was moving off after getting his boarding card, a commotion broke out. He turned to see that one of the men had collapsed on the floor and was being assisted by two members of ground staff. The man was helped to his feet and supported as he was led to a small room behind the check-in desks.

Macandrew hesitated, wondering if he should offer his services, but argued himself out of it. The airport must have its own medical people and the man had probably just fainted. A few seconds later, however, the door of the room opened and an agitated young woman made an urgent appeal for a doctor.

'Can I help?' said Macandrew, returning to the desk.

An overweight man was lying on the floor holding his chest; his companion was bent anxiously over him. 'I think he's had another heart attack.'

The word 'another' prompted Macandrew to ask the ground staff to call an ambulance immediately. Heart attacks tended to have a finite number; a bit like cats' lives, though seldom stretching to nine: more a case of three strikes and you're out. 'Make sure that they have clear access when they arrive. Every second counts.'

'*Oui, monsieur.*'

Macandrew was left alone with the two men. He knelt down beside the prostrate figure and immediately realised that all was not as it seemed. The patient's eyes reflected no pain or distress at all. They were cold, alert and calculating.

'What the...'

Before he could say or do anything more, he felt a sharp needle jab in his thigh and a wave of dizziness sweep over him. He had a vague notion of being made to change places with the man on the floor before passing out.

Macandrew woke with a splitting headache and a burning sensation in his throat. Despite having been unconscious, he knew exactly what had happened. He had been drugged and abducted. The question was, by whom? And why? He tried getting up from the rickety bed he was lying on but found that his hands were tied behind his back. The creaking noises from the bed however, attracted attention from next door. The room door was unlocked and the fat 'patient' stood there, saying nothing but perspiring profusely. He had thick, moist lips and wore small round glasses that magnified his eyes out of all proportion to his face. Macandrew felt like a lab specimen being examined by an overweight schoolboy. The eyes blinked slowly and regularly like those of a frog on a rock but he still didn't say anything when Macandrew asked him where he was. A taller man – the other of the pair at the airport – joined him and Macandrew recognised him immediately as the man with the knife in the cathedral, the man later identified by the police as Vito Parvelli.

'What the hell's going on?' croaked Macandrew. 'What do you want with me?'

'I think you know that,' said Parvelli. 'The woman has something we want and you are going to help us get it.'

'You've made some mistake,' said Macandrew, stalling for time. He felt groggy from the effects of the drug and his head was pounding.

'No mistake,' said Parvelli. 'You got in our way last time. Now you're going to help us.'

Macandrew felt a shiver run down his spine as he realised that these two were probably the men who had tortured and murdered John Burnett. 'No way.'

The words sounded brave but only because he was trying the hide the fear he felt inside. He was thinking about the two hoods in Kansas and it was turning his insides to water. These two were even more frightening.

Parvelli dropped the telephone into Macandrew's lap and said with an air of finality, 'Phone Dr Robin.'

'She hardly knows me,' said Macandrew.

'Just do it.'

As if driven to pick away at some awful secret, Macandrew asked, 'And if I refuse?'

The fat man turned and said something to someone who was still in the outer room. A thin, gaunt man with sloping shoulders appeared in the doorway carrying what appeared to be a small toolbox. He looked at Macandrew dispassionately and made a lazy gesture with his right arm. Parvelli and the fat man pulled Macandrew upright and sat him down on a chair. They tied him to it tightly but secured only one of his legs, leaving the other to be stretched out in front of him while his shoe and sock was removed. His bare foot was placed on a small stool.

Sweat broke out on Macandrew's brow as he watched the man he thought might be Ignatius's accomplice, Stroud, open the toolbox and bring out a soldering iron. Every muscle in his body tensed as Stroud knelt down beside his foot, untangling the cable and handing the plug to the fat man to plug into a wall socket. The smell of burning dust filled the air as the iron started to heat up.

'Call Dr Robin,' said Parvelli.

Macandrew took the phone. Any added threat was entirely unnecessary. He couldn't be any more afraid. Parvelli told him what to say.

The fat man took a firm hold of his lower leg and pressed his heel down on the stool so that it was impossible to move his foot. Stroud licked his forefinger and held it briefly to the tip of the soldering iron. It hissed.

Macandrew dialled Simone's number and placed the receiver to his ear.

'*Oui?*'

'Simone? It's Mac.'

'Mac, you can't be back in Scotland already. Where are you?'

'I was intercepted at the airport. I'm being held somewhere in the city. I don't know where exactly.'

'Being held? Oh my God ... who?'

Macandrew's eyes never left the tip of the soldering iron. 'The men from the cathedral,' he croaked because his throat was so tight. 'They want you to hand over Burnett's lab notes and any of the protease you might have.'

'Have they hurt you, Mac?' asked Simone anxiously.

'No,' Macandrew croaked. '...Not yet.'

Parvelli took the receiver and said, 'Listen carefully, *madame*. You will tell your police guard that you have decided to go down to the south for a few days. Get on the eight o'clock TGV from Gare du Nord to Marseilles on Friday morning. Bring the stuff and the notes with you. Tell the police that you won't need any further protection once you are on the train.'

'What if they insist on coming with me?'

'Make a point of going to the bathroom just before the train enters the station in Lyon.'

'And if I don't do this?'

Parvelli handed the phone back to Steven and nodded to Stroud who pressed the tip of the soldering iron into the sole of Macandrew's foot and kept on pressing. Macandrew's scream of pain tore through the room as the iron sank into his flesh.

Parvelli took the phone from him and clicked it off.

The shock of what had happened, followed by a tsunami of pain, forced Macandrew to spiral down into merciful unconsciousness.

When he came round, he didn't feel much pain at all but then his head felt fuzzy so he knew that he had been drugged. Gingerly, he used his left foot to feel if his right had been bandaged: it had but it didn't feel like a proper bandage. He had just started to wonder how bad the damage to his foot was before he found himself drifting back into semi-consciousness again. He was to remain in this drug-induced twilight state for many hours to come, reacting only to major stimuli.

At one point, he was aware of being carried from the apartment and knew that it was night because of the darkness of the sky and the fact the street lights were on. He realised later that he was travelling through city streets because of the motion of the vehicle and vague traffic sounds. At intervals, Stroud loomed up out of the mists that surrounded him and his curiously expressionless face came close to his as he was given yet more medication to keep him in a drug-induced limbo.

Macandrew had absolutely no conception of the passing of time over what was in reality an interval of some thirty-six hours. When he finally did come round, the agonising pain in his foot told him that medication had stopped. On top of this, he was thirsty – very thirsty. His mouth felt like the floor of a sun-scorched desert. He tried sitting up but found that his right wrist was handcuffed to the head of the bed. It felt warm in the room and he could see the sun shining outside. The fact that the window was open suggested that he was no longer in Paris. He remembered the instructions given to Simone and deduced that he must now be somewhere in the south of France.

As full consciousness returned, pain and thirst made him call out. The fat man responded. He came into the room and surveyed Macandrew with his slow-blinking stare for a few moments before leaving again. Stroud appeared and Macandrew asked for water and something for the pain.

He was given a plastic cup, half full of tepid water, which he steeled himself to sip rather than gulp down. He held out the cup for more and the fat man complied mutely.

As Macandrew worked the water round his gums he became conscious of the fact that he hadn't had a wash since leaving Simone's apartment and God knows how long ago that was. The stubble on his face rasped against his shirt collar and he saw the sweat stains on it. Then, as he looked down at his bandaged foot, a vaguely sweet smell in the air registered with him. It was unpleasant and somehow disturbingly familiar. An alarm went off in his head as he realised what it was. It was the smell of a bacterium, *Staphylococcus aureus!* – a constant bugbear in all surgical units. The wound site must be turning septic! The appearance of the bandage confirmed his fears. It was filthy.

Macandrew started to panic. 'Christ, man, my foot's infected!'

'There's nothing I can do,' said Stroud.

'I have to clean the wound.'

'Later,' said Stroud.

'At least give me something for the pain?'

Stroud left the room and came back a few moments later with two capsules which he tossed on the table. Macandrew threw them into his mouth and washed them down with the last of the water in the cup. He held it out for more and the fat man complied.

The capsules dulled the pain but the nightmare of infection was adding to Macandrew's anguish. If the wound was left to fester, blood poisoning would almost certainly ensue and he might well die. His head fell back on the pillow as he faced up to another unpleasant fact: he was worrying about a long-term problem when he might not actually have a long-term to worry about. As soon as Simone handed over the notes, both he and she would become expendable. The thought had no sooner entered his head than he heard Simone's voice next door. Voices were raised and she was demanding, 'Where is Dr Macandrew?'

Simone's eyes filled with horror when she saw the state of him. She sank to her knees beside him, putting her arm round his shoulders and pushing his matted hair back from his forehead. 'Oh Mac,' she said. 'What have they done to you?'

'I'm sorry,' said Macandrew hoarsely. 'I couldn't refuse to make the phone call.'

Simone put her finger to her lips. 'You couldn't do anything else.' She looked down at his foot. 'My God, what did they do to you?'

Macandrew told her and Simone gasped. 'The bastards!'

'Enough! Have you brought what we told you to bring?' interrupted Stroud who was standing behind her. Parvelli, who had brought Simone to the apartment, stood threateningly beside him.

When Simone didn't respond Stroud snapped angrily, 'Come! You wanted to be sure he was alive and you can see that he is.'

'Only until you hand the notes over,' said Macandrew. 'Then we both become surplus to requirements.'

'I haven't got them on me,' said Simone.

'What?' said Parvelli.

'I'm not entirely stupid. I wasn't going to take the risk of you just taking them and then killing us.'

Parvelli took a menacing step towards her but Stroud stopped him. 'Where are they?' he demanded.

'I have a proposition,' said Simone.

Parvelli made to move closer but Stroud again put a restraining hand on his arm. 'Go on.'

'You want the notes very badly. You think that once you have them, you will be able to make as much of the protease as you want. Am I right?'

'What's your point?' asked Stroud.

'The chances of you being able to synthesise the chemical would be about the same as me flying to the moon on a broomstick.'

'You're lying.'

'No, it was difficult even for a top-flight biochemist like John Burnett to synthesise it. Amateurs would have no chance. You need us alive. Dr Macandrew and I are both trained scientists. I suspect that you are not.'

Macandrew closed his eyes and wished Simone well with her gamble. He personally had trouble reconstituting TV dinners let alone carrying out complicated biochemical syntheses.

'What have you done with the notes?'

'I mailed them along with the protease.'

'To whom?'

'To myself ... at the post office ... here in Marseilles.'

CHAPTER SIXTEEN

Simone was left alone with Macandrew while Stroud and the others left the room to consider the situation. 'You are in a lot of pain,' she said.

'I think the wound's infected: the dressing was dirty and hasn't been changed.'

'Animals!' said Slinone.

'Were the police on the train?'

Simone nodded. 'They were but they had to keep their distance in case I was being watched. I was snatched when we stopped outside the station at Lyon. I don't think the police were expecting that.'

'You don't think they were able to follow?'

'I'd like to think so but it all happened so quickly. The train stopped at a signal outside the station. They obviously knew about that – maybe even arranged it – and that's when they grabbed me. They had a four-wheel-drive vehicle waiting in a field by the track. It was over in seconds. I really don't think the police were prepared for it. They were expecting to follow from Lyon station because they thought that's where I'd be met. I hate to say it but we may be on our own.'

'So we concentrate on staying alive and look for a chance to escape,' said Macandrew. 'You were brilliant through there.'

'Do you think they'll go along with it?'

'It's my guess they're trying to contact Ignatius right now,' said Macandrew.

'But maybe two vials of protease are all he needs,' said Simone. 'If he only has the one subject...'

'I don't think he can afford to take that chance,' said Macandrew. 'With half the police forces of Europe looking for him, he can hardly go around recruiting biochemists if he hits a snag. He'll want you to make some more; I'm sure of it.'

'Let's hope you're right.'

'Where exactly did you send the stuff to?' asked Macandrew.

'The main post office, here in Marseilles. I

sent it *post restante*. I have to pick it up in person.'

'If you get a chance to escape,' said Macandrew. 'You must take it.'

'We are in this together.'

Macandrew squeezed her hand and insisted, 'We must be practical. If you get the opportunity you have to make the most of it. It makes much more sense to tell the police what's happened.'

Simone nodded.

Several hours elapsed before Stroud returned. The effects of Macandrew's earlier painkillers had worn off and he was starting to run a fever. There was a persistent thin film of sweat on his face. The pain had largely put a stop to conversation with Simone and he was staring up at the ceiling, trying not to think about it when Stroud came into the room.

'My colleague has agreed to your coming with us,' said Stroud.

'Where?' asked Simone.

'That needn't concern you. You will pick up the package and then we can be on our way. When you've synthesised the chemical, both of you will be released. Let's get started.'

Macandrew and Simone knew that any talk of release was nonsense but they had achieved their immediate objective. They were to be kept alive for the time being. For the moment they were satisfied with that.

'Come,' said Stroud, holding the door for Simone.

Simone did not move. 'I will do nothing until my friend has had his dressing changed. He also needs antibiotics and something for the pain.' She said it with her back to Stroud so that he couldn't see that she was biting her lip with nerves.

'You are in no position to...'

'That's the deal,' said Simone. She sounded calm but Macandrew could see that her hands were trembling.

'I don't have any dressings,' said Stroud.

Simone turned to face him. 'There must be something,' she insisted. 'Clean sheets, a pillowslip?'

'If you are so concerned, you can do it,' said Stroud. 'And I don't have any antibiotics.'

'Then get some!'

There was silence as Stroud and Simone stared each other out.

'We'll call in at a pharmacy after we have picked up your package,' said Stroud.

Simone felt a flood of relief. It threatened to make her a little unsteady on her feet but her gamble had paid off. Macandrew squeezed her hand in acknowledgement.

'He needs painkillers now,' said Simone as Stroud turned away.

Without looking round Stroud said simply,

'I'll get him something.'

Macandrew looked at Simone and nodded his thanks. The pain was too bad to permit a smile.

'Try to take it easy, Mac,' whispered Simone. 'You're going to be all right.'

The fat man brought through a clean cotton pillowslip and a bottle of green disinfectant solution.

'I'll need hot water and soap too,' said Simone. The man left and came back with a bowl of warm water, a towel and a bar of carbolic soap. He put them down on the floor. Stroud followed, holding a syringe up in front of him as he expelled residual air. Without saying anything, he pushed up the sleeve on Macandrew's right arm and injected the contents of the syringe.

Macandrew felt an immediate warm glow spread throughout his body, releasing him from the pain that had been building up an ever-tightening web around him. He felt as if the sun had come out from behind a dark cloud on a cold day to bathe him in warm sunshine. 'Christ!' he murmured softly as his tensed-up muscles started to relax in unison.

Simone smoothed his damp hair back from his forehead and smiled as she saw his drawn expression relax. Stroud left the room and she started to unwind the dirty bandage. 'This may still hurt,' she said.

'I didn't ask. Are you a medical doctor?'

murmured Macandrew.

'PhD in molecular biology. You'll have to help me.'

'It's not going to be a pretty sight.'

'Mmm, it could well be a question of which one of us passes out first,' said Simone as she removed the final layer of the old dressing – slowly because it had stuck to the wound. She stopped in the middle and said to the fat man, who was watching the proceedings with a look of revulsion on his face, 'Get me a sponge, will you.' He did and then left the room, looking pale.

Simone started cleaning the wound gently. Macandrew put back his head and looked up at the ceiling. He had to grit his teeth against the pain when the antiseptic was applied but Simone kept her cool throughout. She continued until the site had been thoroughly cleaned and then applied strips of bandage torn from the pillowslip.

'All done,' she announced.

'Well done,' said Macandrew. 'You were great.'

Simone pressed his hand and said, 'It's a woman thing.'

Macandrew managed a smile.

'Now we'll see about getting you these antibiotics.'

Simone left with Stroud for the post office, leaving Macandrew to enjoy what respite he could from the pain before the effects of the injection wore off. He didn't know when he might get another one. He closed his eyes but couldn't manage anything more than a light doze. He was aware of distant traffic noise as Marseilles went about its business. A police siren wailed every so often and there was the constant murmur of conversation from the two men in the room next door. He could smell French cigarettes and somewhere in the distance a child was crying – not in pain, but in frustration at not getting its own way. Although recovering from the infection was a priority he recognised that being unable to walk was going to be a distinct drawback in any escape bid. This was not a happy thought.

Macandrew continued to doze fitfully until the sound of Simone's voice broke though his jumbled thoughts and restored him to full alertness. She came into the room and announced, 'Got them.' She handed over a small package.

Macandrew read the label. Tetracycline hydrochloride. He opened the plastic bottle and threw two capsules into his mouth. 'Thanks.'

'I hope they work, Mac.'

'You and me both.'

'I think we are leaving tonight,' said Simone quietly. 'I overheard Stroud say something to the other two about the boat being ready.'

'Boat?'

'That's all I heard. Nothing about where we are going.'

Macandrew rested his head back on the pillow and thought about the implications of a boat trip. Being cut off from land was not such a wonderful prospect from the point of view of escape but on the other hand, any kind of sea voyage might afford them a bit more time – time to let his foot recover.

Stroud and the fat man were out for most of the remainder of the day, leaving Macandrew and Simone in the sole custody of Parvelli. Macandrew hoped that this might give Simone the chance to escape at some point but Parvelli was no fool. He kept them locked up in the room and acted with caution at all times. They were only allowed out of the room one at a time and only once during the course of the afternoon, to visit the lavatory. Any other requests, for food, drinks, washing facilities, et cetera, were denied with a curt, 'Later.'

The sun was going down when the fat man brought in a meal of pasta, bread, and water and put it down. 'Eat quickly,' he said. 'You don't have much time.'

Macandrew and Simone did as they were told, if for no other reason than the fact that they were very hungry. Shortly afterwards, they were escorted out of the building and put into the back of an unlettered van waiting outside. The familiar smell of it told

Macandrew that it was the van that he had been brought down from Paris in. It came as no surprise to either of them when, twenty minutes later, the van doors opened and they were ushered out on to the quayside at Marseilles harbour.

The night was still and warm and, although they were some way away from the cafés at the water's edge, Macandrew could smell the coffee and cigarette smoke on the night air. He looked at the lights wistfully before having to turn all his attention to the business of climbing down a harbour wall ladder on to the motor yacht that lay waiting there. Parvelli ushered him slowly across the cobbles and saw him on to the first rung.

Simone – her arms held by Stroud – watched from above as Macandrew held his injured foot clear of the rungs and used arm strength to lower himself – a rung at a time – on his good foot. Thankfully, there was very little swell on the water so he was able to time his fall from the bottom rung of the ladder into the waiting arms of the fat man and one other whom he took to be a member of the crew. He was taken below and locked up in a small cabin.

He hadn't learnt much on the way down, just that the vessel was named *Astrud G* and that she had been registered in Marseilles. According to a plate above the cabin entrance, she was owned by Aristo Charters.

He heard the door of the cabin next to his being opened and hoped that this was where Simone was being put. When the footsteps died away, he opened the one small porthole in his cabin and softly called out her name.

'I'm here,' she replied. 'Maybe if we were both to cry out for help...'

'We won't be heard,' said Macandrew. 'We're too far away and they could get nasty. Let's bide our time.'

The cabins occupied by Simone and Macandrew were on the seaward side of the boat so they couldn't see what was happening on the quayside. The first indication that they were about to get under way came when a shudder ran through the boat as the main engine was started: it drowned out the sound of the small pump which had been slurping bilge water out into the harbour.

The vibration increased and Macandrew was aware of heightened activity on deck culminating in the sound of a mooring rope being thrown onto the ceiling of his cabin. He watched the harbour lights disappear behind them as the yacht turned to clear the outer basin before heading off out into the Mediterranean.

The engine note picked up as they cleared the harbour proper and then settled down to a constant throb. Macandrew checked his watch before taking two more tetracycline capsules. It was vital not to let the antibiotic level in his bloodstream fall. It was too early to say if the infection was responding to treatment, but there had certainly been no noticeable improvement. If anything, the pain had got worse. He tried telling himself that his foot had taken quite a few knocks on the journey to the boat and that might be the reason, but it would be another day or so before he could be sure.

He turned off the cabin light and lay down on his bunk until his eyes became accustomed to the dark and he could see the stars through the porthole. He concentrated on the brightest of them until his eyelids became heavy and he fell into a troubled asleep.

Macandrew and Simone were kept below deck throughout the entire first day at sea, although Simone was allowed to visit Macandrew's cabin during the late afternoon. He had continued to feel ill and was now almost certain that this must be down to the spread of infection rather than anything more innocent. The antibiotic wasn't working. He'd give the drug one more day before opting for more drastic measures but, if he left it any longer, there was a strong chance that he would not be in any fit condition to do anything at all. He said as much to Simone.

'What will you have to do?' she asked.

'Cut it open and drain it,' replied Macandrew.

Simone grimaced. 'But you don't have any instruments or anaesthetic,' she said as if the words were freezing on her lips.

Macandrew stayed silent.

'Maybe the boat carries medical supplies. I could ask.'

'It's worth a try,' said Macandrew. Stroud had earlier given him some painkillers in tablet form. He took two as his level of discomfort rose.

'You should try to get some sleep,' said Simone.

She saw to it that he was comfortable before asking to see Stroud. She was taken up on deck.

'The infection in Dr Macandrew's foot is spreading,' she told Stroud who responded with a shrug.

'He needs proper medical care. A hospital.'

'Don't be ridiculous.'

Simone had not expected anything else. 'You must help him. You're a doctor.'

'I'm a psychiatrist,' countered Stroud. 'I've given him antibiotics and painkillers. I can do no more.'

Simone stared at him angrily. 'If anything happens to him, hell will freeze over before I'll synthesise anything for you!'

Stroud looked at her dispassionately before replying, 'We'll cross that bridge when we come to it, *madame*.'

'I mean it...'

Simone saw uncertainty appear on Stroud's face and felt encouraged. She said, 'A boat this size must carry medical supplies, local anaesthetic, minor surgical equipment. Give me access.'

Stroud looked to the skipper who had been professionally pretending not to hear what was going on. The man nodded.

'Don't you know what these men are doing to us?' Simone demanded in French.

The man, middle-aged and deeply tanned, said, *'madame,* I have been contracted to carry five people from A to B. I have been paid well. That is the end of the matter. I have no interest in who any of you are or what any of you are doing. That way, I keep up the payments on my boat.'

'You don't understand...' protested Simone.

'Enough!' said Stroud. 'Take her below.'

'What about the medical kit?' said Simone, pulling against the arm that had started to guide her off the deck.

'Tomorrow.'

Simone returned to her cabin feeling mentally exhausted but relatively satisfied with the way things had gone up on deck. Apart from having got Stroud to agree to give them access to the boat's medical supplies, she had managed to sneak a look at the chart and ruler in the wheelhouse. She now knew that they were heading south-east. It wasn't much but it was something.

Any last remaining doubts about the spread of infection faded when Macandrew woke in the early hours of the following morning with sweat pouring down his face and feeling that his veins had filled with fire. He struggled to get himself upright and then wished he hadn't when consciousness threatened to leave him. He had miscalculated the spread of the infection. He had been hoping against hope that the antibiotics might win through in the end but now there was a real chance he had left it too late. He would have to fight to remain conscious at all costs. If he didn't operate on his foot he would die.

Fever was the biggest threat. He had to cool himself down. He opened the porthole to let the breeze in then he dragged himself across the floor to the wash basin where he splashed cold water up into his face before soaking a towel and crawling back to his bunk where he lay with it across his forehead, eyes closed, taking slow, deliberate breaths and trying to use logic and reason to combat the toxins that were invading his bloodstream.

In the landscape of his dreams, a village fell from a cliff and sank beneath the waves. A tombstone rose up from the ground to reveal an old man wearing a Stetson. Doors opened to reveal bodies nailed to the backs of them and a set of shears snapped towards his body guided by disembodied hands with broken fingers.

'Mac! Can you hear me? Mac! Wake up! You've got to come round!'

Simone's voice reached Macandrew though his nightmare and he opened his eyes. His head felt as if an iron band was being tightened around it. 'Simone,' he murmured.

'Mac, I've got the medical kit. You're in no fit state to do anything. You'll have to tell me what to do.'

Macandrew groaned as Simone replaced the towel across his head. It was cool again. Slowly things came into focus. 'Help me up,' he said.

Simone propped him up on the bunk and helped him bring his foot up on his other knee so that he could see the wound site but it wasn't ideal and his vision was blurred.

'Is there any anaesthetic?'

'Novocaine?' said Simone.

'Hypodermic?'

Simone held up a syringe in its plastic wrapper and then a needle, also encased in plastic.

'Scalpel?'

Simone put down the syringe and held up a scalpel and a pack of sterile blades.

'Swabs, dressings, antiseptic...' said Mac-andrew sleepily as delirium threatened again.

Mac! I've got all these things. Just tell me what to do.'

'First ... the anaesthetic.'

'Where?' asked Simone. 'Here? Here?' She pointed to different spots near the wound until Macandrew nodded in favour of two sites. 'Two injections ... wait five minutes.'

'What now?' asked Simone after she'd waited for the local anaesthetic to take effect.

'Cut. Cut deeply. Don't just break the surface.'

Simone nodded. Her eyes were wide and unblinking with apprehension.

'Get rid of as much of the crap as possible then clean up the site with disinfectant.'

Simone nodded again, her eyes like saucers. She was too anxious to say anything.

'Soak a clean swab in disinfectant and – this is most important – push it inside the wound ... right inside. Understand?'

Simone's eyes rebelled at the thought but she croaked her assent. 'And leave it in there?'

'Yes.' Macandrew gasped as a wave of nausea swept over him.

'Easy, Mac,' whispered Simone. She eased his head back on the pillow and reposi-tioned the towel on his forehead.

Simone removed the syringe from its sterile

wrapper and fitted the needle. She filled the syringe with the anaesthetic and expelled residual air before gathering up her courage to push the needle through Macandrew's skin. She heard him gasp but his foot remained immobile. Gently she applied pressure with her thumb to the plunger and saw the contents of the syringe disappear into Macandrew's foot. She felt better but her pulse was still racing. She refilled the syringe and did the other side.

'Was that all right?' she asked.

Simone repeated the question but there was no reply. Macandrew had passed out. She was on her own. She looked at her watch and used the intervening time to clean up the outside of the wound with an alcohol-soaked swab. When she felt sure that she had done a thorough job and five minutes had passed, she removed one of the sterile surgical blades from its foil wrapper and slotted it into the scalpel handle. She pricked the wound site with the tip of the blade and looked for a reaction from Macandrew's sleeping form. There was none. She tried again, harder this time. Again, nothing. It was time to begin.

She placed a wad of gauze beneath Macandrew's foot and made the first incision. She underestimated the amount of pressure required and the cut only resulted in a thin, crescent-shaped line of blood appearing.

She swallowed hard. She was starting to feel lightheaded.

She made a second, deeper incision and this time a wave of foul-smelling exudate welled up from the wound. Almost immediately, the swelling in Macandrew's foot started to subside and Simone felt the tension in her slack off in harmony. She wiped away the mess and encouraged more drainage by applying gentle pressure to the sides of the incision. She kept this up until the wound had been completely drained then set about disinfecting it thoroughly.

She thought the worst was over until she came to comply with Macandrew's final instruction that she insert a swab inside the wound itself and leave it there. A wave of revulsion threatened her as she prised open the incision with one pair of forceps and tried to push the swab inside with another. She couldn't make the swab lie flat inside the wound; it kept scrunching up. She suspected that it would be agonising if she left it that way. It was going to be painful enough as it was.

She fought against the frustration of successive failures until she finally succeeded in making the swab lie flat. Pausing briefly to regain her composure and wipe the sweat off her brow, she closed the incision site and secured the swab with fresh tape and bandaging. Her hands started to shake as she thought about what she'd done and then she felt herself go icy cold. She had to put her head between her knees for a moment to avoid passing out then she slumped down in a chair like a rag doll and let her arms dangle over the sides. It was over.

An hour passed and Macandrew was still out cold but Simone thought that he appeared calm and untroubled and took comfort from this. It might be a different story when he came round and the effects of the anaesthetic wore off, but for the moment all seemed well. He was sleeping peacefully.

CHAPTER SEVENTEEN

Simone was allowed to stay with Macandrew until he came round – another concession won in her psychological battle with Stroud. She had noticed in her dealings with him that he was distinctly uncomfortable in the presence of women – something she intended to exploit ruthlessly, suspecting now that he would give in just to see the back of her. It turned out to be a long vigil: Macandrew was out cold for nearly five hours but the fever had gone and she could see that he was just making up for lost sleep: the rest would do him good. For her part, she passed the time reading old magazines or simply sitting by the porthole, looking out at the sea. She still felt close to mental exhaustion. Every hour that passed without incident would help.

In the last hour, the sea state had changed and the boat took on a roll as it started to ride a heavy swell. Simone started to feel uncomfortable at not having a stable horizon to concentrate on. She was about to turn away from the porthole when she thought she glimpsed land. She looked again but they were now down in a trough and, at that moment, Macandrew let out a low groan. She hurried over to him.

Macandrew blinked against the light. 'God, what happened?' he asked in a hoarse whisper. His throat was dry.

'You passed out,' said Simone, giving him a glass water. 'You've been out for several hours.'

'My foot ... did you do it?'

'Just like you told me,' said Simone.

'God, you are bloody wonderful,' said Macandrew, flopping back on the pillow.

'You seem a lot better,' smiled Simone. 'Your fever's gone.'

'God, I feel better,' said Macandrew, 'definitely better.' He squeezed her hand.

'I think the voyage is almost over. I'm sure I caught sight of land a few minutes ago.'

'I wonder where.'

'We've been heading south-east ever since we left Marseilles,' said Simone. 'I caught a glimpse of a chart in the wheelhouse. Corsica? Sardinia maybe. I don't think there's been enough time for us to reach Sicily.'

'I've lost all track of time,' said Macandrew.

Simone went back to the porthole and said as they rose on the swell, 'We're getting quite close. Another fifteen minutes perhaps.'

'And then what?' muttered Macandrew under his breath.

Simone reported what she could see until they reached harbour and clattering feet in the gangway outside the cabin suggested that they hadn't been forgotten. Parvelli secured Simone's hands behind her back without speaking and tied her to the chair beside Macandrew's bunk. In spite of her protests, he fixed a length of adhesive tape over her mouth before turning his attention to Macandrew.

'I promise not to run away,' said Macandrew sourly but Parvelli didn't smile. He tied and taped him too. As he left the cabin, the engine note dropped to an uneven burble and they could hear voices. Parvelli had drawn a curtain across the porthole so Simone and Macandrew could only listen to what was going on.

The snatches of conversation they picked

up from the quayside were in French so Simone's guess at Corsica was probably right, thought Macandrew. On the other hand it soon became apparent that their current location was largely irrelevant. The smell of diesel in the air and the sound of boxes being slid across the deck above them suggested that they had just stopped to take on fuel and supplies.

In a little under an hour the engine note rose again and once more they were under way. Shortly after that, they were released from their bonds. Simone rushed back to the porthole to see what she could see. 'It's my guess that we're in the channel that runs between Corsica and Sardinia,' she said. 'We're still heading east.'

'To somewhere on the west coast of Italy?' suggested Macandrew.

'Or down to Sicily,' said Simone.

'Or even North Africa,' said Macandrew.

'Or anywhere,' sighed Simone.

'As far as I'm concerned, the longer we're at sea the better,' said Macandrew. 'It'll give me time to get better. Then maybe I'll be a bit more help round here. I've been about as much use as a paperweight.'

Simone was pleased to see the improvement in Macandrew's spirits. It was good to see him clear-eyed and alert again. She gave him a hug.

They were at sea for two more days, by which time Macandrew knew that he had beaten the infection and was gaining strength by the hour. He had replaced the packing in the wound twice but now he thought that he would let the wound start to heal naturally.

On the afternoon of the second day, he and Simone were allowed on deck to get some fresh air. Macandrew sat with his back to the mast with his legs stretched out in front of him. Simone sat beside him at ninety degrees. The sky was blue and the sea state calm. Their eyes were closed and they were enjoying the sunshine.

'A pity we're not doing this under different circumstances,' said Macandrew.

Simone just smiled.

'Maybe, if we come out of this?' suggested Macandrew.

'Maybe,' answered Simone, giving his arm a little squeeze.

'I think I'll just throw Stroud and his cronies over the side right now and take over the boat.'

Simone looked at Macandrew's foot and said, 'Isn't there a saying in English about walking before you can run?'

'Touché,' replied Macandrew.

'Besides,' added Simone. 'We are approaching land.'

Macandrew could see that she was right. There was something solid on the horizon.

They stood up to get a better look.

'An island,' said Simone.

They watched in silence as it seemed to take an eternity for the *Astrud G* to near the island. When they had closed to about half a mile, Simone whispered, 'I think I know where we are; I've been here before. It's Malta.'

'Well done,' murmured Macandrew.

'I came here many years ago when I was a student with a group of friends on a scuba diving trip.'

'Does that mean you know the island well?' asked Macandrew.

Simone shrugged. 'It was a long time ago but it's not that big really.' Almost as an afterthought she added, 'Strongly Catholic.'

Their conversation was interrupted by Stroud directing that they be taken below.

This time, they were not tied up or blindfolded. They watched from the porthole as the *Astrud G* was brought close to a rocky outcrop and her anchors were dropped.

'We're not going into harbour,' said Simone.

'I guess they'd have to explain us to the authorities,' said Macandrew. 'It's my bet we'll be transferred to a smaller boat for landing somewhere quiet along the coast.'

When darkness fell and nothing happened, Macandrew grew tense. He and Simone had both been feeling the strain of the wait and their conversation had fallen away to nothing. Eventually Macandrew said what they had both been thinking. 'Maybe this isn't our destination after all. Maybe we're just stopping here overnight.'

No sooner had this been said when they heard the distant sound of a powerful outboard motor. It grew louder and they could hear activity above them on deck.

'Well, well...' said Macandrew, feeling adrenalin start to course through his veins.

Simone started plundering items she thought would come in handy from the boat's medical kit. She passed them to Macandrew who stuffed them into his pockets.

'They're coming,' warned Macandrew as he heard footsteps on the deck ladder.

Simone hastily shut the lid of the wooden box. The cabin door opened and they were herded up on deck by Parvelli. The night was clear and an almost full moon shone down on a calm sea. A large, rigid, inflatable boat was tied up alongside the *Astrud G*, her powerful twin Yamaha outboards murmuring as they idled impatiently. Simone was helped over the side first and made to sit at the back of the boat while Macandrew – who had hopped across the deck to reach the rope ladder – took the weight on his arms and lowered himself to stand on the sidewall of the inflatable. Although the sea was calm, there was still a bit of swell and he couldn't find enough balance on one foot to allow him to hop down on to the floor of the boat. He took an ungainly dive forwards and clattered down hard on his elbows.

'Are you all right?' exclaimed Simone.

'Apart from lost marks for artistic merit.'

The crew freed the inflatable from the *Astrud G* and pushed her away from the side. The Yamahas responded to the throttle like eager greyhounds and the inflatable creamed over the water towards the dark shoreline. No one spoke. There was no point; the engine noise was deafening. Macandrew sat with his arm round Simone, both holding their free hands to their faces against the intermittent spray thrown up from the bow. In other circumstances it might have been fun.

The engines died and they drifted in the last few metres on their momentum. Macandrew braced himself for what he though might be a sudden grounding but the operation was carried out with such skill that the boat came smoothly to a halt on the gritty bottom.

There was a van waiting on the shore. It looked very old – even by the light of the moon. Macandrew and Simone were ushered into the back and the doors slammed shut. It was pitch black inside and there was a smell of rotting vegetables. It didn't mix well with the smell of the sea from their clothes and hair. After several attempts the van's engine was coaxed into life and they fought to steady themselves as it lurched forward over a patch of rough ground to join the road. A final jolt as the back wheels scrabbled up on to the tarmac, sent the pair in the back reeling against the sides.

They were now travelling along a smooth highway and, as the minutes passed, Macandrew became aware that he could see periodic flashes of light through the crack where the back doors joined. He crabbed across the floor and found that he could see out though it. He said to Simone, 'Maybe you should be doing this. You might be able to figure out where they're taking us.'

Simone slid across to take Macandrew's place. He kept her steady with his arm around her waist. After ten minutes she said, 'We're entering a small town.'

'Recognise it?'

'I was only here once, on holiday,' protested Simone.

'Sorry,' said Macandrew. 'Keep trying.'

'Of course.' Simone sounded irritated but was secretly pleased at Macandrew's restored positive attitude.

Macandrew could hear traffic noises outside as they started to slow. 'Sounds like quite a big town, he said.

'I don't think it's the capital,' said Simone. 'So if it's not Valletta … it might be…Yes, it's

Mosta. I've just seen the cathedral.'

'Good on you,' said Macandrew.

'We anchored off the north coast,' said Simone, 'so we must have travelled south-east to reach Mosta... That would suggest that we are probably not going to Valletta at all.'

'And we are not stopping here by the sound of it,' said Macandrew as they started to pick up speed again.

'No,' agreed Simone, taking up position at the back door again. 'We're leaving Mosta behind.'

Neither spoke for the next few minutes. Simone relaxed her vigil, saying that there was nothing to see. It was dark and they were on country roads.

'The more I think about it, the more I'm convinced that Ignatius must have had a good reason for coming here,' said Macandrew.

'Why d'you say that?'

'It's a long way across the Mediterranean from Israel to Malta. There were lots of other islands a whole lot nearer if he was just looking for somewhere to hide out for a while.'

'I see what you mean,' agreed Simone. 'Why pick a small island in the middle of the Med when it would have been much easier to disappear in Cyprus or Crete or even in the mountains of Sicily?'

The van shuddered as the engine started to labour. The gearbox protested loudly at being asked to engage a lower gear and then a lower one still. 'A steep hill,' said Macandrew.

'That's interesting,' said Simone. 'The island is pretty flat except for a high plateau where the old medieval capital stands.'

Simone started to keep watch again as they continued to labour uphill. 'That must be it,' she said. 'There's nothing else this high on the island. We're going to the old capital. We're going to Mdina!'

'Now we just have to work out why?' said Macandrew.

'Very few people actually live in Mdina,' said Simone thoughtfully. 'It's maintained as a sort of tourist attraction, but I do remember one particular building that *was* inhabited... It was a convent, a large enclosed convent, a nunnery.'

'Brilliant,' said Macandrew. 'That must be it! If Ignatius has managed to con them into helping him like he did the convent in Israel, it would be the ideal cover for him and Stroud.'

'But wouldn't they have been warned?'

'Not necessarily,' said Macandrew. 'It's not in the nature of the Catholic Church to circulate bad news or encourage adverse publicity,' he continued. He recalled the Abbot of Cauldstane complaining of how hard he'd found it to get information out of Rome about Ignatius.

The van stopped climbing and was now moving quite slowly. Simone peered out. 'We're here. We're crossing the stone bridge over the old moat outside the city. I remember it. I think the convent is quite near here.'

The streets outside were eerily quiet as the van drew to a halt and the doors opened. Macandrew and Simone were ushered inside a large stone building with poor lighting to be led down seemingly endless steps. Macandrew noticed the smell of incense in the air and, when he was put into a small stone cell with a crucifix on the wall, a religious painting above the bed and a Bible beside the lamp, he knew for sure that they were in the convent. He called out Simone's name but there was no reply. It wasn't surprising; the walls looked as if they had been carved out of solid rock.

Macandrew lay down on the small, hard bed and stared at the featureless wall in front of him. Things were not looking good if this was where they were to be held. Escape from here would be well nigh impossible. Even if they hadn't been brought down to the cellars, the glimpse he'd managed of the outside of the building suggested a thick-walled Arab fortress; very few windows and all of them high up. He emptied his pockets of the supplies that Simone had thought of raiding from the *Astrud G*'s medical box and gave thanks for her foresight. Not for the first time, he reminded himself that if it hadn't been for Simone he'd be dead. Such a thought made him feel guilty about his own lack of usefulness so far. Simone had been a tower of strength while he had been little more than a passenger. He owed it to her to get her out of this.

He was awakened by the door being unlocked and the fat man bringing in a tray. He didn't say anything; he just put down the tray and left. Macandrew got up and found a large mug of black coffee and a lump of bread. The smell of the coffee was good; at that moment it seemed to symbolise the normal everyday things that had been missing from his life and which he desperately missed, not for their own sake but for what they represented. He had been living in a nightmare world for so long that stress had been building up inside him like a cancer. A mug of steaming coffee afforded him a much-needed remission.

Fifteen minutes later the fat man returned and indicated that he should follow him. He did so at his own pace until they stopped outside a door some thirty yards along the corridor where Simone, escorted by Parvelli, was already waiting. Macandrew asked with his eyes if she was all right and she nodded.

They entered what appeared to be the convent sick bay and were then shown into a small office where they came face to face with a tall, slim man wearing the black cassock of a Roman Catholic priest. He fitted the French Police description of Ignatius. He eyed them with a cold dispassion that Macandrew found chilling.

'I'm Dom Ignatius,' said the man evenly. 'This is where you will fulfil your part of the bargain.'

Macandrew exchanged glances with Simone and saw that she was afraid.

'I have obtained the chemicals listed in the protocol for the synthesis of the protease and the laboratory has been equipped with the necessary apparatus. Let me know if you need anything else but don't waste my time. I'm not a stupid man. I'll know if you are stalling. I suggest you start work immediately. There are two rooms. You will work in one and sleep in the other until your work is done.'

Macandrew felt anger at the man before him, calmly issuing instructions like a schoolmaster. The religious garb only made it worse. This man was responsible for torture and murder. 'What's this all about?' he asked.

The fat man tightened his grip on him.

Ignatius regarded Macandrew with a baleful stare before saying, 'Knowledge, Doctor, that most precious of commodities. I suspect you know by now what the chemical can do. A five-minute conversation with an eyewitness to human history is worth more than all the arguing and conjecturing of an institute full of posturing academics for over a decade.'

'And the Israeli you kidnapped is your eyewitness? What do you hope to discover in your five minutes with him?'

'That needn't concern you.'

'The protease will kill him.'

Ignatius fixed Macandrew with a stare and Macandrew stared him out as he felt the tension rise in the room. 'This isn't really about knowledge, is it? There's something else.'

Ignatius replied with icy calm. 'They thought they would end my career. They took me away from my life's work and destroyed my reputation. They put me to work as a clerk like some peasant priest when I had the finest brain of the lot of them. They claimed to be teaching me … humility,' Ignatius lingered over the word, wrapping it in sarcasm, 'while they themselves played out the traditional Vatican games of back-stabbing, manipulation and double-dealing. Well, I will show them a thing or two before I'm through. Now, I suggest you get to work.'

'Don't you care anything about the people you damage?' asked Simone. 'They'll never recover.'

'Progress has always been painful,' said Ignatius.

Macandrew shot Simone a warning look about pursuing the argument. She changed tack. 'How do you expect to explain away our presence here in the convent?' she asked.

Ignatius said, 'You are Christian volunteers being trained in basic medical techniques before being sent out to our missions abroad. There is no call for you to fraternise with the sisters of the convent; they are an enclosed and contemplative order. Apart from that, one of you is a man. This clinic and your living quarters have been isolated from the rest of the building.'

Macandrew and Simone were ushered into an adjoining room with white and blue ceramic tiles on the walls. There was a single window with vertical iron bars on it; it looked out on a narrow lane some twenty metres below and across to the wall of a neighbouring building less than three metres away. Lighting came from a fluorescent fitting bolted to the ceiling. There was a long laboratory bench with various pieces of equipment on it and two Bunsen burners, their umbilical tubes attached to the same 'Y' fitting gas tap.

There were two boxes containing bottles of chemicals listed in Burnett's notes and there were several wall-mounted cupboards containing glassware and general lab apparatus. A small adjoining room held two camp beds and a toilet and shower cubicle; it had no window.

'What do you think?' asked Macandrew, when the door was locked behind them.

'He's raving mad,' whispered Simone.

'Right, and he's only going to keep us alive as long as he thinks we're going to make him more protease.'

Simone looked about her and shrugged. 'I'm betting neither Ignatius nor Stroud know very much at all about biochemistry. We can fake problems until we think of a way out of here.'

'What do you want me to do?'

'Think of a way out of here.'

CHAPTER EIGHTEEN

Stroud prepared to inject Benny Zur. This time he would use a more sophisticated metering device than the simple hypodermic he'd employed first time. This would give him more control over dosage. When he appeared to delay for too long, Ignatius asked why.

'I'm having second thoughts,' said Stroud. 'I'm not sure he's strong enough.'

Ignatius looked at the heavily sedated figure of Benny Zur. His skin looked pale – almost translucent – and his breathing was shallow. It had been some time since he'd last seen daylight and he'd lost weight through being kept under heavy sedation.

'Haven't the sisters been looking after him?' asked Ignatius.

'It's not that,' said Stroud. 'His cardio-vascular system hasn't been exercised in a long time; muscles waste very quickly when they're not used. I'm not sure he's going to stand up to the stress of regression.'

'We'll just have to take the chance,' insisted Ignatius. 'We've wasted too much time already. It could take us years to find someone else like him. We might never do it. He has to tell us all he knows.'

'If he dies we'll end up with nothing,' said Stroud. 'It would be safer to wait. We could ease off the sedation so that he remains conscious for longer periods: we could exercise him, improve his physical condition.'

Ignatius waved away Stroud's suggestions. 'No more waiting, we do it now,' he insisted. 'Get on with it.'

Stroud shrugged and connected the tube leading from the reservoir to the shunt needle he had taped into place in Zur's arm. He opened up the small, plastic micro-valve in the line and the contents started to drip-feed slowly into the man's arm. He kept his eye on the gauge as the level dropped then closed the valve and said, 'You can begin.'

Benny Zur's head started to move on the pillow as if stirring from a deep sleep.

Ignatius had a notebook open in front of him. It was the record of Benny's earlier regression. 'What is your name?' he asked.

Benny did not reply. Ignatius kept repeating the question until he did. Benny became distraught. Sweat started to flow freely down his face and a rasping sound came from his throat. Stroud looked worried but Ignatius watched dispassionately. 'Who are you?' he asked. 'Tell me your name.'

'James ... James of Caesarea.'

Ignatius leant forward. 'How old are you?'

'Forty-four.'

Ignatius exchanged an excited look with Stroud. 'Do you remember being in jail in Caesarea?'

'Years ago.'

'You met Paul of Tarsus there. Tell me about it. I want to know everything you can remember.'

'Paul was a good man. He persuaded me that I should become a Christian.'

'That must have been a dangerous thing to do in a Roman prison.'

'There was a risk but I saw how things were going and decided to take the chance. It came off. When they let Paul go, they let me go with him.'

Ignatius looked puzzled. 'But you were a convicted thief, why should the Romans let you go?'

'When they arrested Paul, the authorities didn't realise that he was a Roman citizen: they beat him up pretty badly. Of course, when they discovered their mistake, they knew they were in deep trouble. It was the right of every Roman citizen to put their case before the emperor in Rome if they felt an injustice had been done to them and that's exactly what Paul insisted on doing.'

'But you weren't a Roman citizen, why should this affect you?'

'When Paul said what he intended to do he started to get better treatment and so did his friends – I think the governor hoped Paul would change his mind about taking his case to Rome.'

'But he didn't?'

'No, and eventually he was released into the custody of the centurion Marcus Aurelius for the journey to Rome. Paul requested that I and two others be allowed to accompany him on the journey.'

'Why you?'

'I was still in the process of becoming a Christian and Paul thought I needed support: he didn't want me backsliding while he was away. Luckily, the governor was still anxious to please Paul. He was worried about what he might say in Rome so, in the end, I was allowed to go.'

'What happened then?' said Ignatius.

'We were put on board ship.'

'Bound for Rome?'

'Not straight away. There was an important Greek on board and we had to take him to Thessalonica – but first, we stopped at Sidon to take on supplies. Paul was allowed to visit old friends in the port after he'd given his word to Marcus that he wouldn't try to escape. He took me with him.'

'Why?'

'He wanted me to meet his friends. They were followers of Jesus before even Paul himself. Paul hadn't always been a Christian. There had been a time when he'd actually fought against the movement so I think he still felt guilty. Maybe that's why he worked so hard to make amends. He never seemed to rest.'

'What about these friends?' asked Ignatius.

'They'd heard all about Paul's success in converting people to the cause of our Lord. They were very pleased to see him and gave him something to take with him to Rome. They said it would protect him and help him in his mission.'

'What was it that they gave him?'

'A sword.'

'A sword,' repeated Ignatius.

'It was the one used to pierce the side of our Lord on the cross.'

'A sword, not a spear?'

'A sword,' replied Benny.

Ignatius seemed spellbound. His eyes didn't blink for a full thirty seconds. The sword, if it still existed, would be a relic to rival even the Holy Grail itself. He was almost afraid to look at Stroud whom he sensed was positively shaking with excitement.

'What was this mission?' he asked, trying to keep his voice calm.

'Paul's real reason for wanting to go to Rome was not to complain about his earlier treatment; he really wanted to try and convert the Emperor Augustus to the way of our Lord. If anyone could do it, Paul could. He burnt with an inner fire that people found impossible to ignore. They listened when he spoke. They wanted to believe.'

'So Paul left Sidon with the sword. What happened next?'

'We had to sail south of Cyprus because the winds were in the wrong direction. We should have taken that as an omen. Things didn't go well at sea. We seemed always to be either becalmed or struggling to make progress against headwinds. It was never easy.'

'But you did make progress?'

'We eventually reached Myra where Marcus had us transferred to a larger vessel sailing out of Alexandria to Rome.'

313

'Did conditions improve?' asked Ignatius.

'No, we were becalmed again for many days and then, when we did get going, we lost two of the crew overboard. Finally we got caught in a storm and ran aground off Melita.'

Ignatius looked at Stroud and mouthed the word 'Malta.' He turned his attention back to Zur. 'What happened then?'

'The ship broke up on the rocks and we were thrown into the sea but we all managed to make it to land, some swimming, some hanging on to bits of wood, others being kept afloat by their friends. The God of Israel was with us that day.'

'What about Paul?'

'He was always a tower of strength. As soon as we reached the shore he organised us into working parties. Some were detailed to build shelters, others to collect wood for the fire. I had to forage for food. As it turned out, there was no need. The local people were very friendly. They lit fires, gave us food and provided us with shelter until we got organised.'

'And Paul? What did he do?' asked Ignatius.

'Paul was taken to see the governor of the island, a man named Publius and they became friends. As I said, Paul was good with people. Publius invited him to stay in his house and arranged living quarters for the rest of us until a ship could be found.'

'Where was the sword all this time?' asked Ignatius.

'Paul kept it with him.'

'Did he have it when he left the island?'

Benny appeared to hesitate. 'I suppose,' he said.

'You suppose?' repeated Ignatius slowly. He said it in almost threatening fashion. 'Think!'

'I ... can't remember.'

'I think you can,' said Ignatius. 'Tell me!'

'There were lots of problems over the sword. Important people on the island got to know about it. Some of them wanted to buy it.'

'Buy it?' exclaimed Ignatius.

'They offered Paul as much gold as he could carry if he would leave the sword behind on the island but he said no. Selling it was unthinkable.'

'So if he didn't sell it ... what happened to it?'

'Two men broke into Publius's house one night and tried to steal it. They were caught and punished. They had their hands cut off. Both of them bled to death.'

'Who ordered that? Publius?'

'No, they were servants of a rich merchant, Salicus of Mdina. Salicus himself ordered it. He even carried out the sentence himself.'

'What would servants want with such a thing?'

'Everyone knew that Salicus himself had ordered them to steal it but no one dared say it. He was such a powerful man, second only to Publius on the island.'

'So the sword was safe.' Ignatius suddenly changed tack. 'How long did you all stay on the island?'

'About three months.'

'And then you set sail once more for Rome?'

'There was a ship that had been wintering in the harbour. When it left for Syracuse, it took Paul and the others with it.'

'But not you?'

'I had to stay behind ... I was sick.'

'And the sword?'

'Paul must have taken it with him.'

'I think not,' hissed Ignatius as if he was pronouncing a death sentence.

Benny started to sweat profusely.

'That sword never left this island or history would have said so.'

'I don't know what you mean...'

'I think that the sword was stolen from Paul by one of his own people. You!'

'No! No!'

'No mention of that sword was ever made again in Christian annals. It never reached Rome. It must have stayed in Melita ... just like you did. Salicus bribed you to steal the sword after his own men failed, didn't he? He knew you were the weak link in the chain just like I do. It's written through everything you've told me. You weren't converted to Christianity in jail. You just saw a way out of prison and, like the opportunist you are, you took your chance. Now, I'll ask you again. What happened to the sword?'

Zur's breathing became laboured and irregular as he tried to fend off Ignatius's barrage of questions and accusations. Stroud was becoming anxious but Ignatius was not to be swayed.

'You weren't left behind because you were sick,' snarled Ignatius. 'You were a prisoner of the Romans! They wouldn't leave a prisoner behind because he didn't feel well! They would have put you to the sword and thrown your body to the fishes without a second thought! You stole the sword and made a run for it. You went into hiding and, if I'm not mistaken, you hid in the house of Salicus, something you arranged beforehand. Admit it! Salicus bribed you to steal the sword didn't he?'

'Who are you? How do you know these things?' Benny cried out.

'I'm from the future. Call me part of your eternal damnation if you like,' rasped Ignatius.

Benny let out a cry that made Stroud warn Ignatius. Ignatius held up a palm and continued with his questions. 'What happened to the sword?'

'I don't know.'

Ignatius picked up one of Stroud's shunt needles from the tray and took off its plastic shield. With a sharp downward movement, he pushed the needle in up to the hilt in the upper aspect of Benny's thigh.

Benny's eyes opened wide like a fish lying on a slab and he let out a scream of pain. Ignatius remained as emotionless as ever. 'Now then,' he said, 'are you going to answer truthfully or am I going to investigate your capacity for pain?' He moved the base of the needle with a circular, grinding movement as if to illustrate his point. Zur cried out again and said, 'All right, I'll tell you ... no more ... no more.'

'Go on.'

'I did steal the sword for Salicus. He said that he would hide me in his cellars and give me my freedom when Paul and the others had left the island. I didn't want to let Paul down but being a prisoner of the Romans was no life for any man.'

'And the sword?'

'It brought nothing but misfortune to Salicus and his family.'

'How so?'

'Salicus's wealth came from his ships. He had a fleet of five, which sailed the Mediterranean, bringing spices from the east. Two were lost in storms before three months had passed. His wife died of a terrible disease that made her waste away and their only son was found dead in his bed one morning. No one knew why.'

'And Salicus blamed the sword for this?' said Ignatius.

'He was convinced of it,' said Zur. 'He said he could feel its malevolence whenever he held it in his hand.'

'Probably guilt,' said Ignatius. 'Did *you* feel anything when you held it?' he asked.

'No,' replied Zur.

'So what did Salicus do about it?' asked Ignatius.

'He went to Publius and owned up. He handed the sword over and begged for forgiveness. Publius was furious because of the shame Salicus had brought upon him and the island but decided that he had suffered enough. He'd lost just about everything that mattered to him. He decided that the whole affair should be kept quiet and that he would take care of the sword until it could be returned to Paul.'

'But it was never returned to Paul,' said Ignatius.

'Publius hid it in a secret place so no one else would be tempted to steal it. There was a well in the courtyard of his house. It had a chamber hollowed out of the stonework about two thirds of the way down.'

'How do you know this?'

'Because I put the sword there.'

'You? A convicted thief and a cheat?'

'Salicus was pardoned by Publius but I wasn't. I was to be executed for my part in stealing the sword. The execution was to be carried out immediately after I had hidden it so that I could never tell anyone.'

'But?'

'Publius relented at the last moment and let me live.'

'That was a very dangerous thing to do. You were dishonest and knew too much.'

'Publius was a good man. He didn't want my blood on his hands. He had me put on board a Roman vessel bound for the east.'

'As a passenger?'

'As a galley slave. In many ways that was worse than being executed.'

'So you never returned to Melita?'

'Yes, I did.'

It wasn't the answer Ignatius had expected. He looked to Stroud with renewed excitement. 'When? How?'

'After two years of living hell in the galleys, I escaped. We got caught in a sudden squall coming into Syracuse. It threw our vessel against the harbour wall and damaged the hull. I and three others were freed from our chains to repair it. That was when I got away. I swam under the ship when our guard's back was turned and made it to the shore. I had no money and no possessions and only the slave's rags I stood up in but I was free. I stole food and clothing from local houses to survive then I got work on a ship bound for Africa. It stopped in Melita to take on water and it was then that I had the idea.'

'You would return to Publius's house and steal the sword?' said Ignatius, his eyes wide with excitement.

Benny snorted. 'I didn't want the sword. What good was a sword to me? It was the gold I was after. When they sent me down the well to hide the sword, I saw the big box that was sitting there. I had a look inside. It was full of gold.'

'So you returned to Publius's house?' said Ignatius, his voice dropping to a whisper. 'What happened then?'

'I came to the house after dark... I climbed over the wall and lowered myself into the well...'

Benny stopped and closed his eyes as if trying to remember something. He didn't respond when Ignatius shook him. 'What's wrong with him?'

Stroud pushed up Zur's eyelids and turned pale. He looked at Ignatius. 'He's dead.'

'He can't be!' fumed Ignatius. 'What happened?'

'I don't know,' said Stroud with a shrug. 'But surely he's told us enough. If that sword is still there, it must be worth...'

'You don't know what you are talking about,' said Ignatius.

'But we just have to excavate the site of the well in the grounds of Publius's house...'

'Don't be ridiculous. The governor's house was destroyed centuries ago.'

'But there must be some record of where it stood,' said Stroud.

'Oh, yes,' said Ignatius bitterly. 'There is and now something else stands in its place.'

'What?'

'Mdina Cathedral,' replied Ignatius.

'The cathedral!' exclaimed Stroud, 'But we...'

'Exactly,' interrupted Ignatius. 'We cannot excavate the entire floor of a cathedral looking for a two-thousand-year-old well. Not only that, Mdina Cathedral is the *second* cathedral to have stood on that site since Roman times. The first was destroyed in an earthquake hundreds of years ago.'

'But there must be old documents in the island's records house,' suggested Stroud. 'There must be some information there about the original positioning of the house.'

'Then I suggest you start looking,' said Ignatius coldly. 'In the meantime I'll make sure that we get a new supply of protease. We're going to need it when we start all over again.'

CHAPTER NINETEEN

'Is it ready?' asked Ignatius.

Macandrew said not.

'What's the hold-up?'

'It's not pure,' said Simone. 'We've hit a problem with a contaminating substance: we can't seem to get rid of it.' She held up a chromatogram that she'd faked up, using filter paper and black ink, and pointed to one of the blots on it.

'This means nothing to me,' said Ignatius, waving it away. Stroud just shrugged. Ignatius looked at Macandrew and Simone in turn as if trying to decide whether or not to believe them. 'What difference would this substance make?'

'If it's toxic,' said Simone, 'it might kill anyone injected with it.'

'You said, "if".' Ignatius turned to Stroud. 'Well, Doctor, does that mean there's an equal chance it might not be?'

Stroud stalled, uncomfortable with his lack of knowledge. 'If the identity of the substance is not known, there's no way of telling without trying it.'

'I thought I'd try passing it though an acid cleaning column to see if we can get rid of it,' said Simone.

'How long would that take?'

'Two, maybe three days.'

'What do you think, Doctor?'

'It might work,' said Stroud. 'I really don't have a feel for this sort of thing. It's outside my area.'

'Ah yes,' murmured Ignatius, 'the age of the specialist.' After a few moments of silent consideration he said to Simone, 'You can have until tomorrow. You can work through the night. After that, we will test the compound, pure or not.'

Simone tried protesting but to no avail.

'Tomorrow,' said Ignatius.

When they were alone again, Macandrew sighed and rested his forehead on the back of the door. 'So now we know. Tomorrow they'll find out we've been conning them. The protease is nothing more than salt water.'

'We were deluding ourselves to ever think that we were going to escape before they got a chance to test the stuff,' said Simone. 'It just isn't going to happen.'

'At least we'll have a clear conscience,' said Macandrew. 'No one is going to die because of anything we did.'

'I don't think I'm big enough to take comfort from that,' said Simone. 'Sorry but I'm scared. I am so scared.'

Macandrew wrapped his, arms around her. 'It's not over yet,' he whispered. 'Let's do something positive. What d'you say we dispense the saline into vials and get rid of absolutely everything else; pour all the chemicals away and make it as difficult as possible for them to try on their own?'

Simone considered for a moment and then picked up a reagent bottle to empty its contents down the sink with symbolic slowness. 'Agreed,' she said.

The desperate nature of their position was eclipsed for the next few minutes by their gesture of defiance as they started flushing all the chemicals down the lab sink. Macandrew was just about to start disposing of a bottle of hydrochloric acid when he stopped. He turned and looked at the barred window, as if trying to work out something.

'What is it?' asked Simone.

'The acid,' said Macandrew. 'We could use it on the window bars.'

Simone looked dubious. 'I don't think there's enough time left for it to eat through the metal – even if there were, we couldn't climb down the wall. It's a sheer drop and we're at least ten metres above the ground.'

'I wasn't thinking about climbing down,' said Macandrew. 'The lane can't be more than ten feet wide. I think I could make a jump for the building across the way.'

Simone looked out and then down. She shuddered and said, 'It would be a standing jump; no run-up.' She made a rocking gesture with her hand to signify things could go either way. 'It would be a terrible risk.'

'I think we've just moved into terrible risk territory,' said Macandrew. 'I'm going to try the acid anyway. We've got twelve hours at least. Let's see how far that gets us.'

Simone smiled and gave him a brief hug.

Macandrew fitted a rubber suction bulb to a pipette and gently withdrew the stopper from the acid bottle. A gentle curl of smoke rose from the neck and made him recoil slightly as the acrid fumes reached his nostrils. He filled the pipette slowly and gently discharged it round the base of each of the four window bars in turn.

'They'll smell the acid,' warned Simone.

'You told them we were going to use an acid cleaning column,' countered Macandrew. 'We can set up a dummy column and keep the acid bottle beside it.'

Simone smiled at Macandrew's resourcefulness and then said, 'I think you're crazy but I suppose you're right. It's best to be doing something and right now anything's worth a try. You carry on with the bars; I'll see to the column.'

'Good girl.'

When he had seen to it that each bar had a little puddle of acid round its base, Macandrew set about obscuring this by lining up bottles and lab equipment on the bench in front of them. He stepped back in order to appraise his work before making some minor adjustments to make things look more natural. His efforts were put to the test an hour later when food was brought in. The fat man wrinkled his nose at the fumes but Simone put on a show of pipetting acid into the separating column on the bench and he left without comment.

They set about systematically disposing of all remaining chemical stocks while retaining the bottles and refilling them with varying amounts of water to suggest outwardly that nothing was amiss.

Simone held up the Burnett protocol they had been using for the synthesis of the protease and said, 'I suppose it's too much to hope that this is the only copy?'

'Let's destroy it anyway,' said Macandrew.

Simone set it alight and held it over the sink until the last charred remnants were flushed away.

At intervals throughout the night Macandrew checked on the progress of the acid on the bars and refilled the puddles around their base. At one in the morning he started to see a definite grooved tapering where black iron had changed to bright shiny metal. He took encouragement from this, although when he looked out of the window, the gap between the convent and the dark building opposite seemed to widen with each passing hour. Maybe it was a crazy idea, but it was the only one he'd had. Half an hour later, Simone, who had drifted off into a light sleep, awoke and came through to ask how things were going.

'Getting there,' replied Macandrew.

She sat down on the floor with her back to the wall and after a few moments Macandrew joined her. They looked up at the moon through the window bars. It was so bright that the thin clouds drifting across its face did little to dim its light.

'It's not exactly the time or place to say it but I'm glad I met you,' she said.

'For what it's worth, I'm glad too,' said Macandrew. He kissed her gently and put his arm round her shoulders.

'I'm so frightened, Mac.'

'I don't feel so brave myself.'

'It's not so much dying; it's more what they might do to us before that happens.'

'Then we shouldn't leave that up to them,' said Macandrew. 'Let's go down fighting?'

'You're serious? Do you think we'll get a chance?'

'Of course we will.'

'When?'

'I think they'll want us to be present when they try out the new "protease",' said Macandrew. 'That's when we might get an opportunity. We could pick a moment when they're all concentrating on something else and then make our move. Parvelli's the main threat, him and the fat man. I don't see Ignatius being a problem...'

'You've already given this some thought,' said Simone. 'What do you want me to do?'

'When I give the signal, I'll go for Parvelli. You attack the fat man with everything you've got: try to disable him in any way you can. Kick, bite, scratch, and hit him with anything that comes to hand; do anything to keep him fully occupied while I take on Parvelli. I don't want fatso helping him out.'

'All right,' said Simone in a very small voice.

'But all that won't be necessary,' said Macandrew.

Simone looked up at him.

'The acid will be through the bars by morning. I'll make the leap, call the police and it will all be over by lunchtime.'

'The full moon is said to affect the human brain...' said Simone but she still managed a smile.

When morning came the acid had eaten less than halfway through the bars and there was no discernible weakness when Macandrew tried pulling at them with all the strength he could muster.

'I should have started this sooner,' he grunted.

'The alley is too wide anyway, Mac. Forget it.'

Macandrew put more acid round the bars. 'There might still be time.'

Simone smiled without conviction.

The strain on their nerves grew with each passing hour and both were close to breaking point when the door was finally unlocked in mid-afternoon and Ignatius stood there flanked by Parvelli and the fat man. 'Is it ready?' he asked.

'Yes,' lied Simone.

Macandrew stood beside her, his hand resting lightly and protectively on her shoulder.

'Bring it with you.'

Simone picked up the rack containing the vials and moved towards the door. Macandrew made to follow but Ignatius held up his hand. 'Just the woman.'

Macandrew started to protest but Parvelli moved threateningly towards him and a knife appeared in his hand.

Simone looked round and Macandrew saw the anguish in her face. They hadn't considered that they might be separated. Their plan was in ruins. He gave her a thin smile of encouragement but at that moment he was really thinking that he might not see her again. God knows what would happen when Ignatius discovered the vials contained nothing but saline. He considered taking on Parvelli and the fat man there and then but knew it would be little more than a hollow gesture; Parvelli already had a knife in his hand and he'd be no use at all to Simone dead. While he stayed alive, there was always a chance.

Simone was led away and Macandrew was left in suffocating silence with only his imagination for unwelcome company. He went over to the window and started pulling at the bars again in sheer frustration. He wrenched at them until his palms bled and sweat poured down his face but they still didn't budge.

Simone was taken downstairs to a small room in the basement, where she and Macandrew had been held when they'd first arrived. To her surprise she found a young nun standing there. She was wearing the kind of open, honest smile that tended to make others feel guilty.

Simone made to hand over the vials to Ignatius but he said, 'No, Dr Stroud is otherwise occupied at the moment: you will carry out the test, Dr Robin. Sister Noni has kindly volunteered to help us with our work. I'm sure she will feel more comfortable in the hands of a woman.'

Simone gave Ignatius a look that didn't mask her loathing for the man but she remained silent.

'Actually, I didn't volunteer; Mother Superior chose me,' said the nun with disarming honesty.

Simone smiled at the girl, suddenly very glad that she would be giving her nothing more harmful than salt water. It was impossible not to like her.

'What would you like me to do?'

'I need to examine you first,' said Simone. 'Perhaps Dom Ignatius would leave us alone?' She desperately needed a few minutes alone with the girl.

Ignatius looked as if he was about to refuse.

'I have to assess muscle to fat ratio on her body in order to determine dosage,' lied Simone.

'Two minutes.'

As soon as the door clicked shut, Simone gripped the girl by the shoulders and said, 'Listen to me! We are both in grave danger. That man is not really a priest; he's a criminal wanted by the police all over Europe. Is there any way we can get out of here without him knowing?'

The nun's eyes opened like saucers. 'I don't understand...'

'There's no time to explain. Is there a way out?'

'I don't think so, *madame*. There is only one door and it was locked behind me.'

Simone wrung her hands in frustration. She gripped the girl again and said, 'Then you must do exactly as I say if either of us is

332

to leave here alive. Do you understand?'

The girl looked terrified

'I will have to give you an injection but it's harmless and will have no effect on you at all. Dom Ignatius will not know that. You must pretend to be sleepy and answer any questions you are asked in a sleepy voice. Do you understand?'

The girl said, 'I think so...'

Simone wondered if she was taking in anything at all. 'You must pretend to be someone else, a girl who lived in the past. Make up a name, any name. Do it now! Tell me!'

The girl looked about her. 'Maria,' she said.

'Maria who?'

'Maria ... Portelli.'

'Good. Keep your eyes closed and make up the answers. If things get difficult, talk rubbish. If at any time I should pinch your arm like this...' Simone demonstrated. 'Pretend to pass out. Do you understand?'

'No,' answered the nun truthfully, 'But I trust you, *madame*. I'll do as you ask.'

'Good girl. As soon as you're back with the sisters you must call the police. Understood?'

Simone heard Ignatius return and pretended to be helping the nun rearrange her habit when the door opened.

'It's time. Let's get started.'

'Would you lie down here, please, Sister,' said Simone in a pleasant but deliberately formal way. Her eyes sought Noni's as she swung her legs up on the table. All she saw there was innocence and bemusement but at least she wasn't saying anything to Ignatius.

Simone set up the delivery apparatus and inserted a needle in Noni's arm, apologising for the discomfort and seeking eye contact again to see whether or not she was going to play along. She noticed the girl's skin was parchment white and unblemished. She could not have been more than eighteen years old.

Simone opened the delivery valve. 'Just relax,' she said quietly, 'Let your mind go blank. Relax completely.'

To Simone's relief the girl closed her eyes. She pretended to be making adjustments to the flow for the next minute or so before saying to Ignatius, 'I think she's ready.'

Ignatius, his eyes full of anticipation, stepped forward. 'Who are you, girl?' he asked.

'Maria...' replied the nun sleepily.

Simone offered up silent thanks.

'Maria who?'

'Maria Portelli.'

'Where do you live, Maria?'

'...Marsaxlokk.'

'What do you do there, Maria?'

'Help my mother.'

334

'What year is it?'

Silence.

'What year is it?' Ignatius repeated.

'Nineteen ninety-seven...'

Ignatius looked cold and hard at Simone and then stood back from the table. Simone pinched Noni and she let her head fall to the side. 'She's passed out completely,' said Simone. 'I don't think we got rid of all the contaminating substance. She's going to need proper medical help. Perhaps the sisters could call...'

Ignatius ignored her. The nun's answer had made him suspicious. He snapped open one of the vials, wet his finger and put it to his lips. Without saying anything he approached the table and slapped Noni hard across the face. The nun let out a scream and scrambled off the table to take refuge in Simone's arms.

'Are all the vials like this?' snapped Ignatius.

'Yes,' said Simone defiantly but inside she was so afraid that she felt nauseous.

Ignatius brought up the back of his hand in a sweeping arc and caught Simone on the left cheek bone. The force of the blow was sufficient to throw both her and Noni across the room where they ended up in a heap on the floor. Noni was sobbing, Simone holding the side of her face and trying to clear her head.

Ignatius stood over the pair of them, his right hand nervously fingering his cheek, lips twitching. Simone could sense the anger in him. She could feel it in the air; smell it; almost touch it. She had difficulty breathing as she waited for the explosion of violence she knew must come. Noni sensed it too. She closed her eyes and started praying out loud, clinging ever more tightly to Simone.

The awful moment was interrupted when the door opened and Stroud stood there, looking absurdly pleased with himself. 'I have the information we need,' he announced.

A look of disbelief appeared on Ignatius's face. 'You found a plan of the governor's house?' he said, sounding incredulous.

'No, but I came across something just as good. As you rightly said, the old cathedral was destroyed by an earthquake so there wasn't much information about that and there was none at all about the governor's house but, when the builders were preparing the foundations for the new cathedral, they came across an old well shaft...'

Scepticism seemed to evaporate from Ignatius. The anger that had shone in his eyes was replaced with excitement. 'Go on,' he said.

'And it caused big problems,' said Stroud. 'The workers found a skeleton lodged in the shaft and saw it as some kind of omen. They downed tools and refused to go anywhere near it. All building work came to a halt.'

'So what happened?'

'The architect, a man named Lorenzo Gafa, called in the Church in the shape of Bishop Palmieri to break the impasse. Palmieri declared the well to be a hallowed grave and read the burial service over it. After that, they just closed up the opening and built on top of it. The site of the shaft is marked here on Gafa's plan of the new cathedral.' Stroud showed Ignatius the photocopy of the plan he had made at the records office.

'Brilliant,' said Ignatius, who seemed to have forgotten all about the women for the moment. 'Absolutely brilliant. And do you know what? I can tell you who the skeleton belonged to.'

Stroud looked at him in disbelief.

'Think, man,' whispered Ignatius. 'James of Caesarea.'

'My God,' murmured Stroud. 'That's why he couldn't tell us any more about his return to the house of Publius. He died there. You took him right up to the point of his death!

'What's been going on here?' asked Stroud, acknowledging for the first time that Simone and Noni were in the room. They were still huddling together.

Ignatius didn't reply at first: he was pre-occupied with the cathedral plan, using a ruler to take measurements and making notes on a small pad. After a long pause, the question finally registered and he said, 'They've been making fools of us – making salt water. The sister knows too much. Give them something to keep them quiet and lock them up in the cellars. We'll take care of them all later.'

Night was falling and Macandrew was almost out of his mind with worry. Simone had not returned and he was being forced to consider the worst. Apart from that, the whole routine of the place seemed to have changed. Neither the fat man nor Parvelli had come to check up on him. He had listened frequently at the door for any clue as to what was going on but the place seemed as silent as the grave.

Once more he stopped pacing up and down to bang on the door and shout for attention, but to no avail. He tried pulling at the window bars yet again. If only he had a lever, he thought, and not for the first time. Although the acid had eaten a fair way into the metal, direct pulling clearly wasn't going to work just yet. He looked around yet again for something to press into use but there was nothing obvious. Then his gaze settled on a chest of drawers below the bench.

The drawers were each about four feet wide and six inches deep. If he could remove a drawer front... He pulled the top drawer out and dropped it on the floor to smash away its flimsy bottom and sides until all he was left with was the solid drawer front. He was left holding a perfectly serviceable four-foot lever.

He slipped it between the first and second bars on the window and applied pressure. He was almost at the limit of his strength when the window bar snapped at its acid-weakened base and he felt a surge of euphoria. He grabbed at the free end of the bar and worked it loose from its top mounting. The first bar was out. He dropped it on the floor and started with renewed vigour on the second.

The second bar yielded just as quickly but the third refused to budge for the best part of fifteen minutes. Macandrew was close to exhaustion by the time it finally succumbed and joined the other two on the floor. He cursed the humidity that was making him sweat so freely and had to rest for a few minutes just to recover his breath but he could see that the window space was now big enough for him to squeeze out through.

He steeled himself for what was to come. It was not going to be easy but there was no other option if he was to be of any help at all to Simone – assuming that he wasn't too late already. This was something he pushed to the back of his mind as he climbed out on to the broad window ledge and looked down at the lane some thirty-five feet below, a move that caused his stomach to turn somersaults. He steadied himself and raised his eyes to concentrate on the building across the lane. The jump seemed a lot more improbable than it had when he'd first considered it. It was still possible ... but only just and that was because the window ledge opposite was slightly lower than the one he was jumping from.

He focused on it before closing his eyes for a moment and going through the leap in his mind. One powerful spring and his hands would grasp the arched stone relief above the window opposite while his feet landed safely on the ledge. He would then open the window and climb inside to raise the alarm. The police would be there within minutes...

He inched forward on the window ledge until his toes – and most importantly the wound site – were clear of the edge and the balls of his feet were in the best position to provide thrust. He took a deep breath and prepared to jump. He had bent his knees and was on the very point of take-off when a wave of doubt seized him and he seemed to sense instinctively that something was wrong. He aborted the jump at the very last moment, almost overbalancing in the process but managing to rescue the situation while teetering on the very edge of disaster. There was something about the glass in the window opposite... He felt himself go weak as he saw what the problem was. The window across the way was barred, only the bars were on the *inside* and not immediately obvious behind the dirty glass. He could just about make them out when the light hit the window at a certain angle – the angle he achieved when he bent his knees. If he had made the jump, he would have been stranded on a ledge, high above the ground, with no way into the building and no way back.

Macandrew crawled slowly inside and felt the bitter taste of failure sap his remaining energy. 'Jesus Christ...' he murmured. 'What an idiot.'

When he'd stopped reliving the near disaster, he came to realise one important thing. He had made an awful lot of noise in the last hour or so but still no one had come to see what all the fuss was about. Could he be alone in this wing of the building? He looked first at the door and then at the iron window bars lying on the floor. He now had the tools he needed to break out … and he could make as much noise as he pleased.

The door was solid so there was no chance of smashing straight through it. Instead, he attacked the lock. It took some time to gouge out the area surrounding it but once he got the bar behind the mechanism it broke away without much resistance. He could hardly believe it when he found himself standing outside in an empty corridor.

Still with an iron bar in his hand, he made his way along the passage, looking into each and every room as he went. The clinic, for whatever reason, seemed deserted. All the rooms were empty. The main connecting door to the convent proper was still locked but the door to the back stairs was open. He made his way down to the basement and started looking in the cells along the bottom corridor. There was still no sign of life. He got the impression that Ignatius and the others had had to leave suddenly ... but what had they done with Simone?

At last he found evidence of recent occupation in one of the rooms. An architectural plan, a ruler and two pens lay on a table but no people. He stood there, feeling almost ill with apprehension, when he noticed a trap-door cover in the floor of this room. It had caught his attention because it was slightly raised as if it had been opened and not replaced properly.

He pulled at the iron ring and looked down into darkness. He couldn't find a light switch but could see that there was a rough wooden ladder leading down into the blackness. There were candles back in the cells. He fetched one, lit it and sat down on the floor to swing his legs round into the opening. He descended awkwardly, feeling relieved when his feet finally made contact with the solid stone floor.

He held up the candle to illuminate what appeared to be a long, Roman-style bath-house. Rows of sunken, square stone chambers stretched out as far as he could see along one side of the cellar, each about ten feet square and five feet deep. Each had a stone chute leading up to and disappearing into the outside wall.

His blood ran cold as he looked down into the first one and saw Simone lying there. Beside her was a young nun. Both lay perfectly still. He hurriedly propped up the candle by the side of the bath and lowered himself into it, cursing the fact that there were no steps and briefly wondering why not. He squatted down beside Simone and felt for a pulse, thanking God out loud when he found one. She was unconscious but she was alive. The nun was breathing too.

He made to lift Simone up into his arms only to discover that she and the nun were chained to a ring in the wall and a padlock was fitted to the end. There would be no way of freeing them without a key. He started back up the ladder to begin a frantic search of the room above. The lack of furn-ishings made searching easy but he didn't find any key. He had to conclude that Ignatius or Stroud must have taken it with them. But where had they gone?

The only clue he had was the architectural plan on the table. It was a photocopy of a much older document. After a few moments' anxious examination, he recognised it as the floor plan of a large church. Mdina Cathedral? he wondered. Could that be where they'd gone? It didn't seem to make sense but he had nothing else to go on. He saw that one area of the plan had been circled – the Chapel of the Cross. He made a mental note of this and its location before climbing back down the ladder to try and make Simone and the nun as comfortable as possible. He left them lying side by side on the floor of the stone bath, both still deeply unconscious.

CHAPTER TWENTY

Macandrew moved along the corridor as fast as he could, ignoring the pain that came from his injured foot. He ran up the stone steps leading to the side door where he and Simone had first been brought in to the convent, anticipating problems when he reached the door but his luck held. The door was secured on the inside by a Yale lock and two sliding bolts – the original iron locks, although still present, were no longer in use. He undid the bolts slowly to avoid attracting attention and put his weight against the door so that the Yale would turn more easily. He put it up on the snib and slid out into dark, deserted streets.

He could see from a ceramic plaque on the wall opposite that he was in Villegaignon Street but it didn't mean much. He knew hardly anything at all about Mdina save what Simone had told him – that it had once been the capital of the island but was now a piece of history, a daytime tourist attraction. He looked to his left and recognised what he thought must be the road they had come in on. Simone had mentioned the bridge spanning an old moat. He was pleased that he at least knew the way out of Mdina. Please God, he and Simone would be using it in the very near future. For the moment, he hurried off in the opposite direction to look for the cathedral. He paused when he reached a junction, which opened out into a large open square, and wiped the sweat from his brow: the air was oppressively humid.

The square appeared to be deserted but its openness made him uneasy. He couldn't bring himself to believe that he was entirely alone despite Simone's assertion that practically no one lived in Mdina. It didn't feel right. He felt sure that the towers and turrets must conceal a thousand watching eyes. A street sign told him it was St Paul's

Square. More importantly, he could see, standing before him on the opposite side of the square, the huge stone front of Mdina Cathedral.

Somewhere inside his head, the thin small voice of reason was telling him that he should be looking for a police station; raising the alarm and calling out the cavalry, but the thought of having to explain things to blank faces who would think him mad made him baulk at the idea. He took cover in an arched doorway to work out a plan of action.

The only thing he had in his favour right now was the element of surprise. Apart from that he was alone, unarmed and probably outnumbered four to one. He looked across to the main doors of the cathedral and decided on a look and learn policy. After that, he would play it by ear.

Although he had no notion of the significance of it, he was working on the assumption that Ignatius and the others would be in the area that had been circled on the plan – the Chapel of the Cross. He'd also learnt from the drawings that the cathedral was well endowed with pillars and alcoves. The chances were good that it would also be in darkness so cover should not be a problem once he got inside.

There was no question of entering by the huge front doors – he could imagine the echoing sound that would make. He would seek out a more modest entrance at the back or side of the building, preferably on the opposite side from the Chapel of the Cross. He crossed the open square as fast as he could and felt a sense of relief as he melted into the shadows of a narrow lane.

The first door he came to was locked but the handle on the second turned easily enough. He edged the door open slowly, an inch at a time and just until the opening was wide enough to let him squeeze through: the last thing he needed at this moment was a squeal of protest from a noisy hinge. He squeezed inside, taking great care not to let the heavy iron handle clatter back against the wood. Once there, he stood stock still in the darkness and just listened until his eyes became accustomed to the gloom. All was deathly quiet.

He started to make out shapes. The cathedral wasn't in complete darkness. He could see a dim yellow light but wondered about its rectangular pattern until he realised that he was looking through the trellis top of a screen placed just inside the door. He moved to the end of the screen and crouched down before moving out into the open.

The light was coming from candles positioned at various points in the cathedral. They did little to provide illumination but much to create atmosphere. The building was alive with flickering shadows and they felt hostile. There was, however, a more constant source of light on the other side of the building and a good way along to his left. By his reckoning, it was coming from just about where the Chapel of the Cross should be.

It was clear that restoration work was going on inside the building. Scaffolding had been erected at a number of places around the walls and tarpaulins had been spread on the floor. As he drew nearer, Macandrew could see that this also applied to the Chapel of the Cross where the stonework on the right-hand wall had been under repair. This had proved useful to Ignatius and his cronies because two large tarpaulins had been picked up from the floor and draped over the iron-railed gates that guarded the entrance to the chapel. They effectively kept in most of the light but they also prevented Macandrew from seeing what was going on inside. There were sounds coming from the chapel.

He was close enough to hear muffled voices but still couldn't see much, other than the reason for calling this place the Chapel of the Cross. A huge crucifix bearing the body of Christ was hanging on the back wall above the altar. It was over twenty feet high and suspended by a steel cable so that it leant out from the wall at the top while the bottom rested on a small ledge on the wall behind and above the altar. Macandrew thought it looked more like a predatory eagle than a symbol of hope. It was flanked by two smaller statues, one of the Virgin and another of a saint.

What he needed to find was some kind of vantage point so that he could see what was going on down on the floor of the chapel, but there was no obvious way to achieve this. The chapel itself comprised a stone-walled cul de sac, richly decorated and separated from the main church by the two wrought-iron gates, currently adorned with tarpaulins.

Something metal fell to the floor behind the screens and the sound echoed up to the ceiling. Macandrew heard muttered recriminations but shortly afterwards the sounds changed from anger to excitement. He heard Stroud's voice say, 'They're through! They've found it.'

The noise level dropped and leaping shadows on the walls above the tarpaulins told Macandrew that they were reposition-ing the light sources. He felt increasingly frustrated at not being able to see what was going on. He considered crawling right up to the tarpaulin screen, hoping to find a chink to look through but he could see from where he was that no light was escaping – therefore no chink. There was, however, a bank of scaffolding on the right-hand side that extended into the Chapel of the Cross and reached right up to the back wall.

This could give him the height he sought but there would be little or no cover for him once up there. If any of the four should happen to look up, he would be like a clay pipe in a shooting gallery. There was a slim chance that he might be able to see enough from the outside end of the scaffold, where he would still be protected by dark shadow: it all depended on where the men were working in relation to the tarpaulin screens. There was only one way to find out.

He put his foot on the bottom tube of the scaffolding and gripped the one above his head, testing both for firmness before committing his full weight to the framework – the last thing he wanted was for the structure to start shaking when he started climbing. He raised himself slowly up on to the first element and then repeated the manoeuvre to gain a height of about six feet. The next level seemed a good deal more unstable but he still managed to pull himself noiselessly up on to the wooden platform at a height now of just over ten feet. He paused before tackling the final two frames. Two more moves and he was twenty feet above the floor of the cathedral.

The last move set up a slight tremble in the framework when he was forced to take the weight off his injured foot a little too quickly, but it was not enough to attract attention from inside the chapel and happened to coincide with a distant roll of thunder. He crawled slowly forward until he could see Ignatius and the others. They were looking down into a large black hole in the chapel floor.

Parvelli's head appeared in the centre of the hole and he handed something up to Ignatius who turned round and held it up reverently in both hands. Macandrew could see it was a sword and the look on Ignatius's face suggested that it must have some very special significance for him. He appeared oblivious to anything else going on around him. Macandrew lost sight of him as he moved into the shadow of the tarpaulin screens, still holding the sword up in front of his face.

Stroud was helping with the removal of something heavy from the shaft. He was pulling on a rope while Parvelli pushed from below. At the fourth heave, a large iron box made it over the rim of the opening and was supported on the edge by Stroud until Parvelli had climbed out and helped pull it back.

The echoing voice of the fat man came from the depths of the shaft but he was told by Parvelli to be quiet. Stroud was trying to lever the clasp away from the lid of the box without much success. Parvelli took over and

351

used brute force of a higher order to greater effect. The lid swung back to reveal the gleam of gold, which brought gasps of excitement and an outburst of animated chatter. It died when Ignatius cautioned them to be quiet.

Parvelli was about to start emptying the contents of the chest out on to the marble floor but Stroud stopped him and pointed to his watch. Parvelli hesitated then nodded and started to winch the fat man up while Stroud closed the lid of the chest and started tidying up. When he finally emerged, the fat man was cradling a human skull in his hands. Ignatius, who had emerged from the shadow of the screens, walked over and took it from him. Macandrew felt a shiver at the sight of Ignatius standing there with a sword in one hand and a skull in the other.

'Meet our benefactor, gentlemen,' said Ignatius. 'James of Caesarea, the architect of our good fortune but alas ... of no further use to us.'

He held the skull out over the shaft in the floor before letting it fall from his grasp. 'Time we were going...'

The fat man leant over the edge to look down at the splintered skull but, as he did so, Parvelli suddenly pushed him hard in the back so that he toppled head-first into the opening and plunged to the bottom. His scream was cut short by a sickening thud. Almost in the same movement, Parvelli took out an automatic pistol and levelled it at the other two who were staring open-mouthed.

Ignatius and Stroud both started to back away, each trying to reason with Parvelli, whose intentions were now very clear. He was going to kill them and take everything for himself. He pulled out a silencer from his pocket and calmly started screwing it on to the end of the gun.

Macandrew held his breath as he watched Parvelli walk towards the two men. He was thinking pragmatically that twenty-five per cent of his problem had just disappeared down the shaft and another fifty per cent were in imminent danger. On the other hand, so was the key to the padlock. This would present him with a real problem should Parvelli choose to dispose of all the bodies down the shaft...

Ignatius and Stroud split up as they backed away. Parvelli moved towards Ignatius first. The priest raised the sword above his head but looked more ridiculous than threatening. Parvelli took aim and Ignatius panicked and stumbled over backwards. The sword flew from his grasp and sailed over the chapel gates to clatter down on the floor of the cathedral proper. He lay transfixed on the marble floor, as Parvelli moved in for the kill.

'I don't want the gold,' he stammered. 'I have no interest in it. I only want the sword.

353

Take the gold, all of it, it's yours. You're welcome to it!'

Macandrew noticed that, despite his apparent panic and pleading, Ignatius was crabbing sideways on the floor, a little at a time. He could now see why. He was making sure that Parvelli could not see what Stroud was up to. Ignatius moved again and Stroud was now completely out of Parvelli's line of sight ... and on the move.

Just as Parvelli prepared to fire, Stroud arrived silently behind him and plunged a long slender knife into his back. He knew exactly where to insert it for maximum effect. Parvelli died uttering nothing more than a single gasp. Stroud let the body slump to the floor and, for a moment, Macandrew wondered if Ignatius might be about to be awarded the same fate, but Stroud put away the knife and helped the priest to his feet.

Overhead, a crack of thunder – much nearer than the last – rang out and echoed off the walls. Macandrew took the opportunity to edge back along the gantry and begin his descent. He moved quickly across the tiled floor and into shadow, pausing only to pick up the sword. If Ignatius thought it so special, it might be worth holding on to. He took up position in a small alcove some twenty feet back from the chapel gates to wait his chance. With Parvelli and the fat man out of the way he felt that the odds had swung in his favour.

He looked down at the sword and wondered about it. It was a simple, short, two-edged Roman weapon but it obviously held some special significance if Ignatius cared more about it than the gold. It felt heavy and, although surprisingly free from corrosion, the metal was dull in colour and the cutting edges even duller. If he were forced to use it in anger, it would have to function more as a blunt instrument than anything else.

His plan was to ambush Ignatius and Stroud when they started to hunt for the sword. Ignatius would have a vague idea of where it had landed but his life had been in danger at the time so he wouldn't have been concentrating. It was odds-on that the two men would split up in their search. He would take them out one at a time. Please God, one of them had the key to the padlock.

Sheet lightning dispelled the shadows for a moment before yet another loud clap of thunder was followed by the sound of torrential rain outside.

As the noise of the thunder died away, Macandrew heard Ignatius say, 'I'll take that'. He suspected he was talking about Parvelli's gun. This was bad news. Next he heard the sound of something being dragged across the floor. This was followed by a distant thud. He guessed that Parvelli had joined the fat man at the foot of the shaft.

The main lights in the Chapel of the Cross were extinguished and Ignatius and Stroud started removing the tarpaulins, as yet unaware that anything was amiss. Their voices became clearer without the screens being in the way.

'I'll secure the box: you get the sword,' said Ignatius.

Stroud swung back one of the ornate iron gates and stepped out on to the floor of the cathedral where he stood still for a moment, and was silhouetted by another flash of lightning against the back wall of the chapel. He looked first to his right and then to the left before saying, 'I can't see it.'

'What do you mean?'

'It's not there.'

Stroud started to walk in Macandrew's direction; he was taking small steps, head bowed, looking to right and left. Macandrew willed him to come closer. His pulse rate was rising. This was the man who had cold-bloodedly mutilated him without the slightest compunction. The idea of using the sword on him was tempting and his fingers closed tightly on the hilt. There would be a strong sense of poetic justice about bringing down the blade on his neck, but he dismissed the idea: he was no cold-blooded killer – and apart from that the blade was too blunt.

When Stroud was about six feet away, Macandrew raised the sword. The lighting was at its poorest here and Stroud had had to stoop even more to see what was in front of him. He was practically kneeling when Macandrew stepped smartly out of the alcove and brought the base of the sword's hilt down on the back of his head. It was a short, sharp blow and the man collapsed in a crumpled heap and lay silent.

What Macandrew hadn't reckoned on was the sound of keys and money spilling out from Stroud's pockets. The noise of coins hitting the marble floor and rolling seemed to go on for ever as Macandrew appealed to the heavens for more thunder to cover the noise. It was not to be. He watched in horror as the last coin pirouetted to an agonisingly slow halt.

When he looked up, he saw Ignatius standing at the chapel gates with Parvelli's gun in his hand. A bullet whined off the floor in front of him and marble chips flew up in his face just before he dived back into shadow. As if to mock him, a clap of thunder now filled the cathedral, prompting him to curse fate out loud.

He knew that he didn't have a hope of making it across the floor to the exit and that there was a limited number of hiding places on this side of the building. He decided on the desperate gamble of not moving away at all from the area of the Chapel of the Cross. His impromptu plan was to get back up on the scaffolding and lie perfectly still until Ignatius concluded that he must have escaped after all. It was a long shot but he was facing a man with a gun. Anything he did now was going to be a long shot.

Above the sound of the rain, he heard a groan come from the direction of his previous hiding place and knew that Stroud was coming round. He should have hit him harder but hadn't wanted to risk killing him. Now – and too late – he was having second thoughts about that.

'Pull yourself together, man!' he heard Ignatius say. 'It was Macandrew who hit you! He has the sword! He mustn't get away!'

While Ignatius was occupied with Stroud, Macandrew saw his chance to crawl across the floor in front of the Chapel of the Cross and pull himself back up on to the scaffolding. There was no tarpaulin screen now to give him shadow, but the lights Ignatius and the others had been using had been extinguished so candles were now the only source of lighting apart from occasional flashes of lightning. Still keeping hold of the sword, he reached the uppermost level and stretched out along the planks, preparing for a long wait. When he thought about it, he cursed himself for not leaving the sword behind. It was this that Ignatius was after and he wasn't going to go anywhere without it.

As he lay, listening to the torrential rain on the cathedral roof, he wondered about Simone and whether or not he was going to survive to help her. He was picturing her lying unconscious in the stone bath beside the nun when a nightmare was born. He suddenly realised that it wasn't a bath at all that the two women were lying in; it was a water cistern! That was why there were no steps down into it and why there was a chute in the wall. These 'baths' were for collecting rainwater; Simone and the nun were going to drown if the storm continued.

Macandrew's pulse was racing but he held his breath as he heard Ignatius's voice again. 'He's still here, I tell you!'

'Come on,' said Stroud's groggy-sounding voice. 'We've looked everywhere.'

'He's here, I tell you. We're just not thinking.'

Macandrew's heart was thumping in his chest. He felt sure that Ignatius must hear it if he came any closer. He couldn't risk turning his head to look but he was sure that he was nearby, maybe even directly below.

The scaffolding moved a little as a hand was slapped against an upright. 'We haven't checked up *there*,' said Ignatius. His voice sounded confident and Macandrew feared that the game was up. He was hopelessly trapped. The only direction he could now move in was further into the Chapel of the Cross and that led to a dead end. He wished he hadn't thought of that expression.

He felt the scaffolding move again as if someone had started to climb up it. Then he heard something clunk against one of the bars below. When he thought that one of them must just be about to clear the top section, he made a lunge towards the end of the structure in order to hit whoever appeared first. There was no one there.

Macandrew saw that he had been duped. They had only been pretending to climb up. In reality, Stroud and Ignatius had been shaking the structure and hitting the bars in order to make him break cover. Now both were looking directly up at him and Ignatius was pointing the gun at his chest.

Ignatius's features relaxed into a condescending smirk and Macandrew threw himself flat as he saw him purse his lips as a precursor to pulling the trigger. The bullet hit a pillar behind his head and stone chips fell like hail below. Macandrew scrambled sideways along the gantry but he was just moving further into a cul de sac. He was now as far away from the gun as he was going to get but that was only into the far corner of the chapel. He was merely delaying the inevitable. He was trapped in a corner twenty feet above the altar with nowhere to go.

Stroud and Ignatius moved in for the kill.

They pushed open the gates of the chapel in unison and walked side by side towards the altar, keeping their eyes on him all the way.

Thoughts of Simone and her plight compelled Macandrew to make one last gesture of defiance. It wasn't something he could explain afterwards but, as the two men came to a halt, he stood up straight and swung the sword round his head like an avenging angel. He brought the blade scything round into the steel cable that supported the giant crucifix above the altar and cut clean through it.

The heavy cross, already leaning at an angle out from the wall, pitched forward and came down on to the two men below who could only watch in horror as it fell directly on top of them.

From where Macandrew stood up on the scaffolding, it looked as if the figure of Christ had struck them down with his outstretched arms; one man lay crushed under each horizontal element, eyes wide open in death. Macandrew surveyed the scene in utter disbelief. He was not going to die after all … but Simone was if he didn't get a move on!

He lowered himself to the floor and scrambled over to the bodies to begin a desperate search for the padlock key. Outside the rain seemed heavier than ever.

He found the key in Stroud's inside jacket

pocket – practically the last one he looked in – but thunder drowned out his expletive-filled diatribe about what fate had against him. He stumbled out into the storm, getting soaked to the skin before he'd managed to cross the square. A mixture of anguish and adrenalin drove him all the way back to the convent though streets that were more like rivers, thunder threatening his eardrums and raindrops peppering his face like steel rivets. There were moments when he wasn't sure if he was really awake or in the throes of some awful nightmare but he was still carrying the sword and it felt real enough.

The side door to the convent was unlocked – just as he had left it. He half ran, half stumbled down the steps and along the corridor to the room with the trap door, flinging himself to the floor and yelling Simone's name into the dark opening. There was no reply. All he could hear was the deafening sound of rushing water.

He grabbed at the candle he'd used earlier, cursing as the first match he scrabbled from the box refused to light, and then broke through his own clumsiness. He had a second failure when water dripped from his hair on to the candle flame but a third attempt saw him climbing down the wooden ladder, candle in hand.

Down here, the sound of water running into the cisterns was so loud it pained his ears. He held the candle out over the cistern and saw in one heart-stopping moment that two bodies were floating in the water. The nun was face-up, although water was lapping over her face but it was the back of Simone's head that he could see. With a cry of anguish, he jumped down into the water and tried to turn her over but it was difficult because of the chain securing her to the wall.

He couldn't tell if she was alive or dead, and the candle had been extinguished when he'd dropped it on the floor to jump in, but he could tell that the chain was the limiting factor. Practically all its free length had been used up and, if the water continued to rise, it would shortly cover both women completely.

Macandrew took a deep breath and sank beneath the surface of the cistern to start work on the padlock in complete darkness. The water, still rushing in from the rain chute in the wall, buffeted him as he worked by feel alone. His lungs were close to bursting when he felt the key finally turn and the padlock snap open to slip off the ring.

He surfaced and took in a great gulp of air before submerging again to free the women completely from the chain. He pushed them up, one at a time, onto the edge of the cistern, having to half roll their bodies over the lip as energy drained away from him. Simone was first and then the nun. He was perilously close to exhaustion as he started to pull himself out, his arms at one point reaching an uneasy equilibrium on the side of the cistern when it seemed that strength would desert him and he would slide back down into the water One final, desperate heave brought him out.

The nun was breathing but Simone wasn't. He had to get air into her lungs. He rolled her onto her back and started mouth to mouth respiration, willing her to start breathing with every fibre of his being. Thirty agonising seconds had passed before Simone coughed slightly and water welled up from her lungs. Macandrew thought it the most beautiful sound he'd ever heard as she continued to cough and retch. He rolled her over on to her front and helped her expel the remaining water.

'You're safe,' he murmured as he finally stopped to turn her again and cradle her in his arms. 'It's over.' Simone couldn't hear him. He'd said it as much for his own benefit.

He sat holding her, rocking back and forward, seeking refuge in a kind of mental limbo where he could escape all that had happened if only for a few moments. He had no idea how long he'd been sitting there when a change in the sound of the water pouring in brought him back to his senses. The storm had ended: it had stopped raining. It took less than five minutes for the sound of running water to stop completely, returning the cellar to an eerie silence where even the occasional drip sounded loud.

Macandrew felt Simone stir in his arms and did his best to reassure her as she came round.

'Mac?' groaned Simone. 'What happened? My head...'

'How much do you remember?'

'Stroud gave us something to knock us out while they went to the cathedral to get some sword Ignatius kept talking about.'

Macandrew filled in the blanks. He had just about brought her up to date when Noni started to come round too and Simone moved over to comfort her, holding her and reassuring her as Macandrew had done for her. When both women had recovered sufficiently, Macandrew helped them up the ladder. Noni was dispatched to tell Mother Superior to call the police.

'Dry clothes would be nice too!' added Simone.

As Noni left, Simone saw the sword lying on the floor. 'Is that what all the fuss was about?' she asked.

'It was in a shaft under the floor of the cathedral, along with a stack of gold bars and a skeleton. Ignatius seemed more interested in the sword than anything else.'

'It doesn't look much,' said Simone, picking it up and running her hand lightly along the flat of the blade. 'What do you think is so special about it?'

Macandrew shook his head. 'I guess Ignatius and Stroud have taken that secret to the grave with them.'

'What will you do with it?'

'Hand it over to the cathedral museum, I guess.'

'You don't think it has ... well, special *powers*, do you?'

Macandrew found himself strangely embarrassed by the question. There had to be some rational explanation as to why this blunt, two-thousand-year-old weapon had cut through a modern, one-inch steel cable and saved his life but ... at that precise moment, he just couldn't think of one.

CHAPTER TWENTY-ONE

'The wanderer returns!' exclaimed Saul Klinsman as Macandrew came into his office. 'I guess you were having such a good time over there that you didn't want to come back, huh?'

'Something like that,' smiled Macandrew.

'How are you feeling?'

'Just fine.'

Macandrew sensed that his reply was inadequate: Klinsman needed more. 'I'm itching to come back, Saul. I think I'm OK for surgery again.'

'That's what I wanted to hear,' said Klinsman, who looked as if he genuinely meant it. 'How do you want to play it?'

'I thought I'd ease myself in with some cadaver work down in Pathology.'

Klinsman nodded. 'Good idea. Talk to Carl Lessing. He'll know what the situation is with donated bodies. I'm sure the med school could spare a few in a good cause.'

Macandrew had coffee with Klinsman who wanted to know all about his trip to Scotland. Macandrew confined what he told him to his success in finding the graves of his ancestors. With contact re-established and pleasantries exchanged, he went down to Pathology where he went through the same again with Carl Lessing who welcomed him back and assured him that he would make cadavers available. He could start next morning if he had a mind to. 'You can have the small autopsy room all to yourself. You can probably do without an audience.'

Macandrew spent the rest of the morning saying hello to friends and colleagues and generally playing the role of the staff member just back from vacation. He thought he was doing well until he had lunch with Karen Bliss down on the Plaza and she saw through him.

'So you had a really good time, huh?'

'Sure did.'

'And you're real glad to be back?'

'Sure am.'

'Want to go for three in a row?'

Macandrew smiled and conceded the point. 'All right, I had a nightmare time. I've been through hell and nearly lost my life but I don't want to talk about it right now. I wouldn't know where to begin. The good bit is that I met a Frenchwoman and I've fallen in love with her. I'm already missing her like crazy. How's that to be going on with?'

'The falling in love bit doesn't sound so bad. Does she know you're in love with her?'

'I think so.'

'You think so! Didn't you tell her?' exclaimed Karen.

'Not exactly.'

'I may be a psychiatrist but sometimes I think I'll never understand men,' said Karen. 'What's her name?'

'Simone.'

'And you just walked away and left her?'

'It wasn't quite like that,' said Macandrew, growing uncomfortable with the cross examination. 'Simone's a research scientist with a career to think of ... and I'm not sure of anything just yet.'

'Oh,' said Karen. 'Sorry, that was insensitive of me, but you're going to be fine, Mac; I know it.' She took his hands in hers. 'Tell me all about her. What kind of research does your lady do?'

'Biomedical. It's a long story – one I'll get round to telling you soon – but the bottom line is that she's come up with a way of treating certain kinds of brain-damaged patients. If things work out the way we hope they will, we're going to collaborate in running a clinical trial on the new technique – but, of course, that all depends on me being able to operate again.'

'That sounds exciting,' said Karen.

'I'll need your help in coming up with a list of patients who might be suitable candidates.'

'What kind of brain damage are we talking about here?'

'Altered personality.'

Karen looked at him questioningly but didn't say anything, although her train of thought became evident when she said after a long pause, 'Mrs Francini won't be on the list. Her husband moved her out of Parley Ridge thee weeks ago. He'd heard about some new clinic up in Michigan where they turn water into wine.'

'You have to admire his devotion.'

'What about the paperwork?' asked Karen. 'Won't this all take time to set up?'

'I've checked. What we're planning won't come under experimental surgery,' said Macandrew. 'I just need the relatives' permission.'

'That'll certainly make life easier,' said

Karen. She looked down at Macandrew's hands. 'How do they feel?'

'I'll probably have to retire a bit early from surgery and I guess I can look forward to arthritis in old age and when the weather gets cold, but I think they're OK. Either way, I'm going to find out in the morning.'

'I'll be rooting for you, Mac, and I'll start checking out possible patients for your trial.'

Macandrew went through his normal pre-op ritual of scrubbing up and gowning and masking properly before entering the autopsy suite just because he needed the trappings of normality. He needed to embrace the routine. The cadaver of a forty-three-year-old man who had died from lung cancer had been laid out for him on the table by Lessing's staff in the small room usually reserved for performing autopsies on dangerous bodies – containment of bacteria and viruses was easier here. He picked up a scalpel from the steel instrument tray and immediately felt vulnerable, pausing before making the first incision, knowing that it was yet another milestone moment in his life. Finally, he brought the knife round in a smooth confident sweep and started to feel better.

He had set himself a series of ordered tasks, starting with large organ removal and proceeding to more demanding dissections where he would have to work for progressively longer periods within millimetre margins of neighbouring tissue that he had determined he mustn't damage. On a corpse, it didn't matter. On a living patient, a nicked artery could turn the whole world red and spell disaster for both surgeon and patient.

He was working on his third cadaver of the day, a thirty-seven-year-old woman who had been killed in a car crash up on the interstate, when Saul Klinsman came into the room and watched him work in silence for a few minutes. Finally he said, 'It's after seven, Mac.'

'I didn't realise it was that late.'

Klinsman moved in closer. 'Supposing I were to tell you, Doctor, that this patient has a tumour the size of a pea thee centimetres to the right of where you're working and lying at a depth of one and a half centimetres...'

Macandrew took a fresh scalpel and forceps and exposed the area swiftly and skilfully. He said, 'I'd say you were misinformed.'

Klinsman grunted and made to leave. He turned as he got to the door. 'Welcome back.'

Macandrew returned to scheduled surgery the following Monday after Klinsman had worked out a wind-down schedule with the locum who had been covering for him in his absence. It was agreed that Macandrew would return with a light workload, which would increase over the coming weeks until a complete handover had been effected. It had been a tough day for him but one that had gone well and now, at the end of it, he knew that he was back in business. He was still feeling good when he phoned Simone early in the evening to tell her the news.

'I'm so glad, Mac. I wish I was there to give you a big hug.'

'Me too,' said Macandrew with heartfelt feeling.

'Does this mean that we can go ahead with the trial?'

'I think it does,' replied Macandrew. 'I spoke to Karen Bliss, one of our staff psychiatrists: she's going to come up with a list of patients she thinks might be suitable. She'll get back to me soon.'

'I'll start preparing the activator.'

Two days later, Karen Bliss appeared in Macandrew's office with the case notes of seven patients suffering from altered personality that she thought he should consider. He stayed on in the evening to go through them.

He eliminated two almost immediately because their brain scans showed that they were damaged in areas outside the region behind the pineal gland. The other five, however, did show signs of damage in this area. He eliminated one more because of complicating factors in the patient's medical history, which made any kind of further surgery inadvisable, but that still left four good candidates.

It took a further week to secure the consent of the patients' relatives – although they didn't take much persuading. It was more difficult to convince Saul Klinsman that brain surgery for free was a good idea.

'Call it an investment in the future, Saul.'

'And if it should go wrong?'

'The relatives know the risks and have signed papers to that effect. They're prepared to take the chance because they feel they haven't got anything to lose. These patients do not have any kind of quality of life at all. They're kept sedated out in Farley Ridge because they'd end up committing suicide if they weren't. Being a semi-comatose vegetable isn't my idea of life. I suspect it isn't theirs either, if only they could tell us.'

'You're sure about the permission situation?'

'I've checked thoroughly and it's been agreed that the surgery is not experimental.'

'Then I wish you luck. Who's first?'

'George Elroy – been up in Farley Ridge for eight years after suffering severe head trauma in an accident on the farm he worked on.'

'Elroy?' said Klinsman thoughtfully. 'I think I remember him. I did the remedial surgery myself if I'm not mistaken.'

'You did,' agreed Macandrew. 'It's in his records. When he got sent home, his wife maintained that he'd become hell to live with and that he simply wasn't the George she had known and loved for more than twenty years. He got worse over a period of time and in the end was taken into Farley Ridge and kept under sedation after trying to cut his wrists a couple of times. His wife never divorced him though; she always hoped he'd get better one day. She was more than happy to give her permission when we approached her.

Klinsman nodded. 'I hope you didn't build her hopes too high.'

'I told her the truth – that I didn't know what the chances were.'

Macandrew operated on Elroy on the second Monday after his return to surgery. He used the least invasive route to reach the pineal gland, entering at the corner between nose and right eye and then introduced a length of plastic three-millimetre tubing to give access to the region of the brain immediately behind. When the scanner told him that the end of the tube was in exactly the right position, he injected a small quantity of activator into the space and let the fluid bathe the area for fully two minutes before draining it off into a steel bowl and closing up.

Macandrew left the patient in the charge of the nurses and went down to see Elroy's wife, Ethel, and her eldest son who'd accompanied her, in the waiting room on the ground floor. He assured her that the surgery had gone well. The only thing they could do now was wait and hope for the best. It was a ritual he'd gone through hundreds of times before but this was the first time that he had been more anxious than the waiting relatives. During the recovery period, he paced up and down his office, occasionally sitting down to try and work but always getting up again after only a few minutes to resume pacing. He snatched at the phone when it rang.

'Mr Elroy is coming round,' said the nurse.

Macandrew hurried down to the recovery room.

'Where...?' groaned Elroy.

'You're in Kansas University Med Center, George,' said Macandrew, kneeling down to be beside the patient's ear. 'You had an accident.'

'The baler ... it hit me. I was crossing the yard and I tripped over that damned fool dog. Duke – that mutt's got less brains than a fence post. Chuck didn't see me lying there when he came out the barn... Damned thing hit me... Jesus!'

Macandrew realised that Elroy was talking about the accident on the farm. 'It did, George, but you're OK now. Do you remember anything about what happened after that?'

Elroy looked blank. 'No ... not a thing. How long have I been out?'

Macandrew felt the correct answer might be around eight years but he settled for 'Quite some time, George.'

'Ethel ... can I see Ethel?'

'You certainly can.' Macandrew nodded to one of the nurses who went to fetch his wife. Ethel Elroy looked extremely nervous when she came into the room on the arm of her son. Macandrew stood back to let them come to the bedside.

'George, how are you?' she whispered.

'Just fine, honey,' replied Elroy. 'That was a real dumb thing to do, falling in front of the baler like that...'

Ethel turned and looked up at Macandrew before starting to sob quietly into her handkerchief. The look in her eyes brought a lump to his throat. Words failed her but the nod of her head was all the thanks that Macandrew needed.

He returned to his office: he needed to be alone for a few minutes. In recent times he'd plumbed the depths of despair but now he was riding a high and he liked the feeling. He didn't want the moment to end. The treatment worked! It really worked! He called Simone in Paris with the news and smiled when she broke into a torrent of excited French.

'I know; it's absolutely wonderful,' he said

when he managed to get a word in. 'Let's hope it works for the others.'

It worked just as well for the next two patients, prompting Saul Klinsman to suggest that Macandrew invite Simone over to the US for the final operation. The university would be happy to pay in view of the positive publicity the success of the new technique was going to generate. Simone arrived in Kansas City four days later – on the evening before Macandrew was due to operate. He picked her up at the airport where they had a happy reunion before he took her to her to the Best Western hotel near the Med Center on Rainbow Boulevard where Saul Klinsman's secretary had reserved accommodation for a 'distinguished guest of the university'.

'God, it's so nice to see you again,' said Macandrew as the porter left the room.

'And you too, Mac. God, you went through such a lot and they hurt you so badly.'

'No looking back. It's all over,' said Macandrew, wrapping his arms around her. 'My God, the nights I've spent thinking about you.'

'Really?' murmured Simone, trying hard to suppress a smile. 'Now why would that be?'

'You've no idea?'

'I just can't imagine what you're talking

about, Doctor...'

Macandrew kissed her hungrily.

'I thought neurosurgeons might have a strict rule about no sex before an operation,' said Simone.

'Only during one.'

'Idiot.'

The operation the next day was another success story and Saul Klinsman threw a party at the hospital to celebrate the breakthrough and to honour Simone's research achievement. Both she and Macandrew had to insist that the new treatment would not be applicable to all cases – in fact, only to those with damage in the pineal area – but even at that, it was still going to make a big difference to a number of otherwise hopeless cases. The world seemed full of people who wanted to congratulate them.

'When will you publish?' Klinsman asked Simone.

Simone was at first surprised and then annoyed at herself for not having seen the question coming. 'Soon,' she replied, moving away to avoid any further talk along these lines. She found Macandrew and linked arms with him to steer him to a quiet corner. 'Your boss just asked me about publication,' she said. 'He's right, you know. We will have to publish.'

'We just have to stick to the facts,' Macandrew assured her.

'Which are?'

'Some cases of multiple personality disorder are due to damaged cells located behind the pineal gland and in some instances, these damaged cells can be reactivated using a simple surgical procedure and a chemical that you will have to describe in some detail. As for the normal function of these cells in the human brain ... well, that's conjecture and, as such, has no place in a medical journal.'

'I love you,' whispered Simone. 'You're so devious.'

'It's a man thing.'

'Better not be.'

Simone gave a seminar to the medical and science faculties about the new technique and received a standing ovation from an academic audience that was clearly delighted that a Midwestern university was playing such a pivotal role in such an important medical advance. Macandrew struck while the iron was hot and persuaded Saul Klinsman that he should have some more time off in order to take Simone to Boston to meet his family and spend Christmas there before she returned to Europe.

'I guess the locum can cover again if he's agreeable. You two are pretty serious about each other, huh?'

379

'We are.'

'Does that mean we'll be losing you?'

'You were always straight with me, Saul: I don't know right now. You'll be the first to know if I do.'

'Maybe you could persuade Simone that Kansas City isn't that bad? I'm sure the faculty could be persuaded to offer her every facility to continue her research...'

'Maybe.'

Macandrew had just left Klinsman's office when he heard himself being paged with a request that he go to his own office. Feeling puzzled, he opened the door to find Tony Francini standing there. The nurse with him said before leaving, 'Sorry, Mac, he insisted.'

Macandrew's blood ran cold. Just looking at Francini brought back the nightmares. His hands started to ache just at the very thought of the car door: the happiness he had been feeling seemed to evaporate in an instant. 'You've got a nerve,' he said.

Francini swallowed and said, 'I know that. Christ, I don't even know what to say to you.' He put his hand to his head and let a sob escape.

Macandrew remained dispassionate.

'The word is you've been helping folks like Janey...'

'We've been conducting a clinical trial of a new treatment. It won't work on everyone.'

'But it would work on Janey?'

380

Macandrew swallowed before finally saying, 'It might.'

'Christ knows I've no right to ask you this, but I don't have an alternative. I love her so much. I'll pay anything. Will you...?'

Macandrew was looking into the eyes of a desperate man – the eyes of a man faced with a steel cable and nothing but a blunt sword to cut it with. He relaxed his face muscles. 'Have her here at the Med Center tomorrow afternoon.'

Francini was about to be effusive in his thanks but Macandrew stopped him. He had no wish to associate with the man any longer than absolutely necessary. He recoiled from contact.

Simone agreed that Macandrew should delay their departure to Boston to operate on Jane Francini, saying that this was exactly what he should do.

Jane Francini's operation proved to be just as successful as the others. She came out of the anaesthetic as the Jane Francini Macandrew had known before the first operation. Like the others, she remembered nothing of what had happened after going into surgery the first time. Macandrew left the recovery room before Tony Francini was allowed in, not wanting to see him again, but he did go back to visit Jane when her husband had left and she was being settled down for the night.

'I'm so grateful to you,' she smiled.

'It's good to see you looking well,' said Macandrew. 'I just thought I'd come and say goodbye to a fellow Scot.'

'You're going away? Tony will be so disappointed. He really wanted to thank you personally. Where are you off to?'

'Christmas in Boston. I'm taking the lady in my life to meet my folks.'

'I'm so happy for you.'

Macandrew could see that Jane was very tired but she was also very much at peace with herself and the world around her. He said, 'I have a little present for you.'

'For me?'

Macandrew opened his briefcase and took out the doll he'd brought back from Scotland. 'It's very old,' he said. 'You'll have to be careful.'

Jane reached out and took it from him, her eyes showing a mixture of surprise and bewilderment. 'You know,' she said. 'I've got the strangest feeling I've seen this before...'

This Large Print Book, for people
who cannot read normal print,
is published under the auspices of

THE ULVERSCROFT FOUNDATION